Advance Praise for
Vixen Investigations

"A fast, fun read. With her inquisitive mind and bold attitude, Paige is one investigator no cheating heart wants to cross."

–LIS WIEHL, *New York Times* Bestselling Author

"Ashley Papa's *Vixen Investigation* has all of the elements you want in a story. It's got intrigue, glamour, an admirable, charming star character, and a seductive and captivating plot line, to make the narrative even more enticing."

–DR. ROBI LUDWIG, Psychotherapist, Author, and TV Commentator

"...vivid relatable characters, Papa takes modern mystery writing to a fresh new level."

–COOPER LAWRENCE, Author of *The Yoga Club*

"In her debut novel, Ashley's heroine is not only funny, inquisitive, and a romantic herself, but one investigator no cheating heart will want to mess with."

–KEVIN MCCULLOUGH, Syndicated Radio Host

"The book will have you hooked from the minute you read the first page until you finish the last sentence."

–LYSS STERN, CEO Divamoms.com
and Founder of the uber-popular DivaMoms Book Club

"Smart, savvy and sexy, Paige Turner, the Vixen Investigator, is a force no vow-betraying lowlife wants to mess with."

–JENNA MCCARTHY, Relationship Writer, Author, and Speaker

VIXEN INVESTIGATIONS

THE MAYORAL AFFAIRS

VIXEN INVESTIGATIONS

ASHLEY PAPA

A POST HILL PRESS BOOK

Vixen Investigations:
The Mayoral Affairs
© 2017 by Ashley Papa
All Rights Reserved

ISBN: 978-1-68261-437-2
ISBN (eBook): 978-1-68261-438-9

Cover Design by Christian Bentulam
Interior Design and Composition: Greg Johnson/Textbook Perfect

Post Hill Press
New York • Nashville
posthillpress.com

Published in the United States of America

DEDICATION

To Mom and Dad. Because of you, I feel nothing can stop me from reaching new goals. From those morning figure skating practices to moving me out to Nebraska for my first job, you've been my partners in all my adventures. I love you both so much.

Ashley

If there is anything that makes a New Yorker feel like packing their bags and saying good riddance to the Big Apple, it's the dating scene. I've had my share of bad dates and failed relationships, like most girls and guys here. I've gone through phases where I figured, why even bother trying? I spent my twenties wrapped in my new broadcasting career and had made a name for myself as a local reporter. What did I need a significant other for anyway? After I came to realize that the bitterness wasn't helping anybody, I knew it was up to me to take that negative energy from the reoccurring heartache and use it for my benefit and be a hero of the lovelorn. By combining the bad blood and frustration I developed towards men and romance with my journalistic know-how, I built a business like none other. I go after heartbreakers, love fakers, and vow betrayers, for a price. And I am pretty damn good at it.

Only a few days into the new year and I am already neck deep in my current case, which involves 29-year-old Molly Carlson. Molly moved to New York City from Atlanta five years ago. She is the epitome of a sweet, Southern belle, with a Pollyanna attitude. She thinks everyone is big-hearted, just like her, and believes as long as she is nice to someone, they'll be nice back. New York City is different, and it's taken her a while to realize this. Here, there are a lot of people who only go out of their way

1

to be nice unless they want something. Arrogant businessmen, like her current fiancé, typically just want sex, power, and arm candy. She's finding this out the hard way.

Her fiancé, Steve Benson, is a 49-year-old hedge fund manager at Perry & Strauss. He's also a divorcé because of Molly. She says she never slept with Steve until his divorce was finalized, or at least when he told her that it was. They met in the Hamptons in the summer of 2013 while Molly was celebrating her 27th birthday at The Black Market, the trendiest bar that summer. The night of Molly's birthday, Steve was there with some of his banker friends, who all rented giant estates for July and August. Steve was instantly drawn to Molly's blonde hair, blue eyes, and lengthy legs, as she danced on the glass table in the corner of the club. Molly was so taken by his charm, success, and George Clooney looks, she fell hard and fast.

They got together several times over that summer while Leslie, Steve's wife at the time, was out shopping for Chanel bags and David Yurman rings. They'd meet for dinners, brunches, and hookup sessions on rented sailboats. Right after Labor Day that year, Steve broke it to Leslie he met someone new. Some would say Steve did the right thing by being honest. But, he is far from deserving sainthood. He was known around town as having a wandering libido. My experience in dealing with these sorts of investigations has proven time and time again that those who've cheated before are more inclined to cheat again.

Steve proposed to Molly less than a year later but part of his proposal was that there was to be no church, no guests, and no tented dinners, just a courthouse wedding downtown. It was quite the sacrifice for the girl who always dreamed of the fairy-tale wedding complete with crystal glasses, baby's breath floral displays, and an ice sculpture. While the engagement seemed quick, Steve still never settled on a wedding date.

Molly had become so quickly invested in him and their relationship that she had ignored all the red flags. That is, until just after Thanksgiving. I got an email from her, asking to meet. My name was given to her by her friend and one of my ex-clients.

I first met with Molly in a quiet coffee shop, not far from her apartment on the Lower East Side. It was there, in that petite, five-table establishment, that she divulged everything about this dangerous, love-at-first-sight relationship and her concerns.

"One night, while I was hanging up Steve's coat, a business card fell out of the pocket. It was for a woman who ran events at The Hotel Versailles on the Upper West Side. There was a cell phone number scribbled on the back of the card in bubbly writing....We barely have sex anymore because he's so adamant about getting to the gym. Even the type of underwear he wore changed. When I questioned him, he shrugged it off and called me crazy," she explained.

Molly could've just walked away and avoided the marital drama that was waiting at the end of the aisle, but she couldn't bring herself to. She wanted proof. She wanted my help.

I couldn't seem to be working fast enough for her. Her emotional outbursts had become so bad, I had to let her stay at my place some nights. My Hoboken, New Jersey, apartment was also Vixen Investigation headquarters. It's where I sleep, as well as analyze video, do research, interview clients, and hold meetings with my assistant, Adam. My clients enjoy the fact they get to meet with me in the comforts of an apartment rather than a stuffy office.

However, at times, Molly's appearances was starting to feel like a *Seinfeld* episode. She'd just come over, unannounced, like Kramer. This past weekend, she stopped by crying like a puppy. Meanwhile, I had just wrapped up a night with my once a year, friend with benefits, John, and was still in a sex-daze trying to make sense of what day and time it was. Her wailing at eight in the morning was hard to take. All I wanted to do was shake her and ask, "Why would you want to be with someone who clearly doesn't want to be with you?"

"I will get to the bottom of this," I told her and handed her a copy of *The Vixen Investigator's Love Manual*. "Read this. It's a series of articles and reports I've written in the past about relationships. Look," I said and flipped to the middle of the book. "Are you dating a psychopath? Here I explain what to look for and where they like to prey. And this article was one of my first on lovesickness."

"Thanks Paige...I mean Detective Turner," she said while wiping away a tear.

No matter how much concealer and blush she used, there was no hiding the pain she was feeling. Her eyes were stained red from the constant crying and she was developing track marks down her cheeks from the flow of salty tears. I advised her to stop by Dr. Gail Marks's office for a therapy session, who was actually my former therapist, about ten years ago. It was just after my 26th birthday. I was at a crossroad in my journalism career and couldn't decide if I should leave the loyal, yet ancient, *New York Day* newspaper for the brighter lights of network news. At the same time, I was dealing with a breakup from my realtor boyfriend and a growing credit card debt due to my late-night habit of ordering delivery and booking spontaneous weekend trips I couldn't afford. She was easy to confide in and as time went on and I launched Vixen Investigations, Dr. Marks was one of several people with whom I could reveal minor, if any, details about a case I was working. The thing is, after four years running the agency, I barely make a mention of the types of cases I really work on to my family and many of my friends. For a while, I wanted the practice to be more covert. But once word got out of my specialty business, it became hard. Now I do all I can to maintain a lower profile and try to stay out of any spotlight.

It's the first night I'm shadowing Steve and it's absolutely frigid. The high was supposed to be 17 degrees and forecasters were calling for six inches of snow by midnight. Adam and I were heading to The Hotel Versailles on 60th and 8th Avenue with the goal of catching the suave banker with whoever this "Caitlin" was, on that business card.

"Check this out," Adam alerted to me as we sat in the back of the ordered Lincoln town car. "I found a Caitlin Boyd on Instagram. And, look here," he continued while pointing to one specific picture on his smartphone. "Who does that look like?"

"Steve," I answered.

It was a photo of a man with salt-and-pepper hair, a snow white smile, and leathery tanned skin. He was sporting a pair of Gucci sunglasses.

Kudos to Adam for finding the picture. He was everything I could ask for in an assistant. I snatched him up, right in his prime. He had interned with me right before I quit "United America News" for passing me up for the Senior Investigative Correspondent promotion and giving it to the scandal-ridden, more famous news face, Dax Delgado. I nearly died for the network while covering the Chicago serial sniper story and that was the thanks I got. After five years and that big slap to the face, I decided it was time to leave, even if I didn't have a job lined up.

Perhaps it was meant to be, as the timing was just right to start my own business. I knew I was a good investigator since all my assignments at UAN were investigative reports. The connections I amassed covering crime and corruption cases were worth more than any dollar amount. I developed such good relationships with law enforcement over the years that now I consult with certain officials for Vixen Investigations.

Adam and I stayed in contact after his internship; it was natural he'd go on to be my right-hand man when we're out on the hunt for cheating lovers. He was exactly who I needed, with his impeccable tech and social media skills.

"How are you going to walk in those heels in the snow, Paige?" Adam questioned after noticing I was in my highest-of-high black pumps.

Adam also embodied traits of a little brother. He was cute with his rosy cheeks, brown shaggy hair, and scrawny frame. He rocked a pair of square-framed glasses that fit perfectly on his childish face. If he weren't six feet tall and 25 years old, he could probably pass for my son.

"I've dodged bullets and escaped quicksand in heels and a skirt. I think I can handle a lightly dusted sidewalk," I defended.

It seemed like the snow was falling faster when we exited the Holland Tunnel. Our Uber fishtailed around every corner as we made our way up the West Side. It was 5 p.m. and traffic was slowly starting to build. It's nights like this that make me wish I lived in the city for convenience, but I was too in love with New Jersey. It was my home state and Hoboken was an ideal spot where I could afford a two-bedroom with water views and a garage. I had easy access to the city and the ability to make a quick getaway should I need to hop in my Jeep Wrangler to get to the scene of a tryst.

"Did you find anything else about Caitlin or Steve besides the Instagram photos?" I asked.

Social media is just as useful as DNA tests for investigators these days. Everyone seems to have an account, even me with my multiple aliases. Maintaining my numerous Facebook pages is Adam's job. He'll upload edited photos to make it look like "Bethany Fry"—the alter ego I used when sniffing out dirt on Pastor Flannery—is still flipping cocktails at the make-believe bar, Grapevine, down the shore.

The snow was sticking more as we pulled up to the hotel. Given the premonition that I'd slip on the sidewalk, I made the driver help me out of the car. Adam was often aloof to such chivalrous mannerisms. I watched as he entered the hotel ahead of me like an unchaperoned child.

I had heard about The Hotel Versailles before but had never been. It was only two months old and already had the reputation for being a boutique, luxury brothel. Although I was invited to the grand opening night, I was forced to decline because of a bad case of pink eye I had caught from my niece. When I found out that New York City Mayor, Walter Wilcox, and some of his male staffers were there, I regretted missing it. It would've been worth appearing there with bloodshot, crusty eyes to catch a glimpse of Walter outside his normal setting. I was not a fan of him and the way he ran the city. I would've liked to get into a heated debate with him, just like I used to in my reporting days. I may have had an unfavorable opinion of the mayor, but not his wife, First Lady Victoria Wilcox. I found the ex-wedding gown model to be just as philanthropic as she is beautiful. Victoria launched three charities within the first two years of being the first lady. One involved free recreational sports leagues for *all* children, regardless of their family's financial status. Another charity took in homeless pregnant women and another organization she founded helps handicapped children get a chance to perform on Broadway. She was a busy woman, but always put her husband and their 18-year-old daughter, Piper, first.

The smell of new paint and lavender potpourri lingered in the air of the hotel's lobby. The entranceway even resembled the real Versailles in France, with gold-trim moldings and mirrors and antique chandeliers everywhere.

"Wow, this place is amazing," Adam proclaimed when I finally caught up to him.

The lobby was so dim I could barely tell if the velvet-covered couches were black or burgundy. Adele faintly played overhead as the after-work crowd started to trickle in. Now I knew why it had the reputation it did. It was a very fitting ambiance for those who wanted to conduct a little outside-the-marriage business.

"Good evening. Welcome to The Hotel Versailles. Are you checking in?" the clerk asked.

He was a stunning young man with green eyes and blond hair. He spoke with a French accent, which, having studied the language, felt fake. I've seen guys like him before: an up and coming model, living with a few other dudes in the East or West Village. Like many, he was probably waiting for his "big break" and dated older women specifically to mooch off of them.

"Bonjour, Claude. I'm Paige Turner and this is Adam. I am actually meeting with Caitlin Boyd about an event," I said and proceeded to lean over the lobby desk just enough to let the cleavage protrude a bit more from my red silk blouse.

"Certainly. Let me get her," Claude stuttered and motioned for us to take a seat.

The plush velvet chairs were deceiving as I found them rather stiff. Next to us, on the oak side tables, were decanters filled with strawberry- and cucumber-infused water. Black crystal chandeliers hung over our head and swung a tad every time the lobby door opened. They reflected off the mirrors, giving off the illusion of a diamond cave or even a '70s disco-era nightclub. It was nearing 6 p.m. now. Adam kept his eye on the door for anyone entering who looked like Steve.

"Paige?" a female voice asked.

I turned and looked up to see Caitlin, a tall redhead who couldn't have been any older than 24. Adam, meanwhile, was way too into his phone to notice her crystal blue eyes and perfect teeth smiling at him from above.

Adam would look so cute with her.

Even I was captivated by her looks, but in all the years I've known Adam, he's never had a girlfriend, nor talked of anyone he was interested in.

"Hi, Caitlin. Nice to meet you. This is my assistant, Adam." I stood to introduce.

"Nice to meet you. Let's go to my office. We can discuss what it is you are looking to host here."

Caitlin led us down a long, dark hallway, infused with a reddish light. I felt like I really was walking into a French brothel, not an office. The walls were cloaked with dark red wallpaper, and gold-framed pictures of classical lovemaking scenes lined the hallway. Caitlin's office was very modern compared to the rest of the hotel with its white walls and asymmetrical chairs. She had a flat screen television mounted to the wall with what looked like one of the *Real Housewives* of some city on the screen.

"Tell me a little about what you are looking to do here?" she asked.

When she shifted in her chair, the hem of her barely-there bandage dress hiked up even higher. Adam looked at me.

"Well, I am looking to have a launch party for my new book on bettering your sex life. I want enough space for about one-hundred people, an open bar for about three hours, and light appetizers. I'm thinking caviar, bone marrow, foie gras, and lots and lots of Veuve Clicquot, of course."

Could I sound more like a snob?

"That sounds like something we can work out. We offer a high-end package that comes with specific small appetizers. It would be around $20,000," she offered as if what I asked for gets requested all the time.

"What about music? Perhaps we could get Calvin Harris or Drake..." Adam began before I interrupted.

"I don't think we can afford a name like that, Adam. Anyways, I think that package is fairly reasonable. Do you mind showing us around the space?"

We followed Caitlin in and out of the hotel bars, which became packed with businessmen, sipping scotch and talking stocks and women. I overheard a tall ginger going on about a random hookup. "That girl was fucking crazy, in bed and in real life," he said. His dapper, navy blue Tom Ford suit and Salvatore Ferragamo camel-colored loafers matched his cocky demeanor. He smelled like cheap cologne and cigars as I got a whiff passing by. The sea of men dispersed and made way for us as we walked through the space. Caitlin was a clear pro at making heads turn. She knew how to work a room without even trying. Perhaps it was her red, flowing locks that made these men venture all the way up from Wall Street and the East Side for a Tito's and tonic. I looked around pretending like I was checking out the space, when I was really trying to look for Steve.

"And this room is the Boudoir. It's one of the more popular event venues." Caitlin led us into a smaller and intimate space.

"This is lovely. I can picture all my friends and followers here. Adam, what do you think?"

"It's perfect. Sexy and stylish, just like you, Paige."

"Oh, Adam...We'll keep this one in mind. Maybe my assistant and I will just hang around, mingle and figure out what feels the most comfortable," I suggested.

Caitlin agreed and handed us her card. It was the same one Molly had brought to me. We gave each other a light kiss on the cheek to not mess up our makeup.

It was now 7 p.m. If Steve didn't show in 45 minutes, we would leave. There was the high probability that he wouldn't even come here tonight, although I had yet to hear from Molly that he had returned home.

Adam and I grabbed a cocktail at the bar. The men in the hotel seemed to give off the same philandering, pompous vibe that most of my suspects embody. As I've document in my love manual, it doesn't matter if the cheater is a man or a woman, gay or straight, we all have the ability to spot a cheat.

Are their answers vague? They're probably hiding something. Do they have a ring indent on their finger? They're probably married. Are they extremely charming and flirty? They're like that with everyone; you're not special.

"Umm, Paige? Is that the mayor?" Adam motioned to the corner of the room.

I squinted but it was hard to make out the face especially standing on the opposite side of the bar. As my eyes focused in and out, I realized that Adam was right.

"Good eye. It is definitely Wilcox and he looks right at home. I'm surprised he was able to fit his head down that narrow hallway," I joked.

I couldn't quite identify the other people with him. One massive man could've been a security guard. The other two men looked like twins or at least brothers. They definitely weren't part of the administration. While pondering what Mayor Wilcox might be doing here, I failed to notice that Adam was no longer standing next to me. He often pulled these little vanishing acts and it really pissed me off. He'd usually emerge a few minutes later saying, "I went to the bathroom" or he'd come back with a vital clue to a case.

I took another sip of my Pinot Noir and eyed the crowd. I was mid-gulp when two male "typicals" approached me from my left side.

"So, is that your boyfriend you're with? He looks too young for you," said the black-haired man with the portlier frame. I looked up at him through the corner of my eye with my lips still pressed against the rim of the glass, thinking, *what he really means is he wants to sleep with me*. I sat up straight and looked at him in the eyes.

"I like them young," I said matter-of-factly. I smiled and they both looked as if they couldn't tell if I was serious or not.

"We're pretty young, you know. Where are you from?" the bald one with the scar on his eyebrow asked.

"Jersey," I answered and took another sip.

"Jersey, huh? We're from Long Island. Live in the city now. Do you consider yourself a Jersey Girl or a New Yorker?" he asked again.

"Neither. I don't associate myself with any group except woman," I replied.

"Woman, huh? That's a good group to be a part of. So, what's a woman like you doing the rest of the night?" the dark-haired man asked.

"Actually, I'm a spy and I am currently spying on a potential criminal," I teased.

I turned and placed my drink back on the bar before turning back to the bald man with the scar.

"You have a beautiful family," I commented.

He looked at me perplexed. I had noticed the picture on his phone's home screen. I smiled, stood and walked away, leaving the men in question as to who I was and how I knew about his family.

"What's with that smirk," Adam asked as I found him sitting on the plush lounge chairs in the lobby.

"Oh, nothing. Have they developed a cure for stupidity yet?" I jokingly asked as he stood up.

"If they did, you wouldn't be in business."

Our deadline had finally come and still no sign of Steve. As we prepared to leave, I furtively checked myself out in the endless hall of mirrors. I was looking svelte because I hadn't eaten and noticed the increasing puffiness under my eyes. I needed food and sleep. We headed back over to Claude to fetch our jackets. Just as I was raising the Vixen Red lip color to my lips, Adam violently shook my arm.

"I think that's Steve," he whispered.

I looked towards the entrance. Steve was standing at the revolving doors. It was as if he were cut out from the pictures I had seen of him. His teeth were whiter than hotel sheets as he stood, smiling down at his phone. I had almost expected an entire entourage to follow but he was alone.

"You know what?" I turned to Adam as Claude came out with our two, heavy coats in his hands. "I think I left my cell phone at the bar. Do you mind going to check? I'd go, but these shoes are killing my feet." Adam nodded and scurried away.

In an effort to buy myself some time, I continued to converse with Claude while keeping my gaze on Steve.

Perhaps he was texting whoever he was waiting for. I can see why Molly is so enamored by him. He looks powerful and charming just standing in the doorway.

Claude went on and on about himself. As suspected, he was 26 years old, a model, and lived on the Lower East Side with two roommates. He wasn't even French. He just learned the accent from taking acting classes when he lived in Los Angeles.

Claude was four digits into giving me his phone number when I saw Caitlin emerge from the dark hallway. Right into Steve's arms she went, looking light as a feather and as happy as a child running to an ice cream truck. Steve grinned from ear to ear as she threw herself into his chest; he grabbed her butt under her fur-trimmed coat. Their kiss went from *Gone with the Wind* passion to Vivid Entertainment sloppiness as he moved his hands all around her backside.

He doesn't even hide the fact that he's sleeping around.

Now I had my proof.

"Claude, can you check in the back and see if a glove dropped out of my jacket, please?" I asked to distract him longer.

I needed him out of my field of vision. I quickly snapped a few pictures with my mini spy camera. Because of its ultra-slim design, I was able to carry it around in the pocket of my fitted blazer. The pictures even automatically uploaded to my computer.

The lovebirds walked outside and into his town car that hadn't even turned off the engine. I discretely followed behind them and watched as they drove slowly off to 7th Avenue. I could feel the light snowflakes collecting on my head as I tried to hail a cab. One car, whose tires looked as bald as my dad's head, came fishtailing around the corner and skid to a stop for me. I tiptoed through the slush, careful not to let any of the wet mess into my Prada heels. I was more concerned about ruining them than getting my feet wet.

"I thought I was going to go sliding into the sidewalk," the cabby joked in his deep Middle Eastern accent.

"Well, you probably shouldn't be going fifty miles an hour around the turn...Just follow that Lincoln up there making the right turn," I ordered and pointed ahead.

He stepped on the gas and within a matter of minutes we were right on Steve's and Caitlin's tail. The cab swerved left and right on 7th as it tried to not spin out. In some sick way, I always got a rush out of New York City taxi drivers. The way they drove gave me a thrill like airplane turbulence or an old rickety roller coaster. Through the windshield, I could see Caitlin and Steve making out in the backseat like two teenagers. Adam had to be wondering where I vanished to so I shot him a text.

Adam Mobile (7:55 p.m.):
I'm following them. Looks like they're heading
to the east side.

Paige Mobile:
Copy

We were now heading across town on 50th, through Times Square, then Madison, and then Park Avenue. Their car came to a stop after crossing Lexington and right in front of The Kimberly Hotel. I rolled down the window that let the large snowflakes blow into my face and hair. I took a few more shots of the two of them entering the hotel.

"Drop me off on the right side at the end of the street, please," I stated to the driver.

The snow was now up to my ankles. Even the Vixen Investigator couldn't stop the wetness from penetrating her pumps. At least they weren't new. The bottoms of my black, suede leggings were also getting soaked. I hustled as fast as I could to the lobby of the hotel and stopped just before entering. My heart raced as I observed Steve and Caitlin, hand-in-hand, make their way straight to the elevator. The silver doors weren't even closed before he ran his hands under her skirt.

Molly's fear and insecurity had been justified. While she lies awake with tears in her eyes, wondering where the man she love is, I knew why he wasn't responding to her texts or calling her back. I wanted to bust down the door and catch Steve banging his mistress, but I needed more.

As I stood underneath the heated awning, I quickly grabbed the next lonely cab I saw coming down the desolate street and ordered him to Hoboken.

Adam Mobile (8:20 p.m.):
Anything?

Paige Mobile:
Confirmed. They're at The Kimberly.

Adam Mobile:
I guess that's that. Found more pics of them
on Instagram.

Paige Mobile:
E-mail them to me. Be back soon.

I flipped through the dozen-or-so pictures Adam sent as I slowly made my way to Jersey. I thought I'd be more shocked by the photos. There were pictures of them skiing together, on a boat, at the News Café in South Beach, at a Billy Joel concert. Caitlin even used #sohappytogether under all the photos. One picture struck me as odd. It was of Steve with Mayor Wilcox. Caitlin had tagged "Nobu," and wrote #birdsofafeather under it.

They were friends? Birds of a feather...flock together? That can't be good.

I thought about what else Steve had been doing behind Molly's back. The more vague and secretive a person is, the more they're hiding. I've seen it happen with lots of my clients, both men and women. Hell, it's even happened to me with my ex, Danny. I had failed to notice what he was doing behind my back—the stealing, the parties, the travel to foreign countries for "business"—because sometimes when infatuation strikes, it can be extremely blinding.

Back at the apartment and with a glass of white wine in my hand, I compiled all the pictures and notes I had gathered on the Benson/Carlson file to date. I was meeting with Molly tomorrow to reveal what I had found. Hopefully it would be all the convincing she needed.

Before turning off my computer for the night, I scanned through my unopened emails, fifteen of which were from potential new clients. It seemed like a lot of men and women had a lot of money to put down to have me chase after their cheating lovers, as if it were a sport. While it is rewarding busting the unfaithful, it is equally satisfying when I find out there is no infidelity going on.

Through the living room windows, the snow looked like glitter as it softly fell over the city. I flopped on the couch with my wine and a handful of pita chips. I knew how unhealthy it was to eat this late at night, and often heard about it from my best friend, Taylor. I tell myself it's okay because I barely ate anything all day. It was typical of us females to justify eating "guilty" things especially with magazines and morning shows telling us what to eat for this and what not to eat for that. If only they could mind their own business.

1

The next morning, the sun's reflection off the freshly fallen snow made its rays extra bright as they penetrated through my venetian blinds. I lifted my right eyelid to check the clock. I had less than thirty minutes to get myself ready for my 9 a.m. meeting with Molly. There was a faint aroma of bacon coming from somewhere. Likely the street cart below. I made my way out of bed like an overweight bear and dragged myself to the bathroom. The icy water coming out of the faucet felt good splashing on my face. The wine and salt from the chips had puffed up my eyes and cheeks like a blowfish.

Molly arrived five minutes early exhibiting a sense of stifled anger and melancholiness, all while still looking glam and down-and-out chic. I sat her down on the couch and went through the pictures I took of Steve and Caitlin. From all the crying she did in the past, she didn't shed one tear while looking through the photographic evidence.

"I need you to think back to any time in the past six months where Steve was absent for a few days straight. I have a feeling they've been together for a while, even before the Versailles opened," I encouraged.

"Does it even matter? Why even bother wasting your time anymore. What more do I need to see?" She was struggling to get the words out. I was surprised she didn't want more. "No.

Actually," she debated, "I want more. I want to see for myself. I want to bust him in the act and with you!"

Seriously? I would never bring a client on a bust. But, maybe Molly could learn a thing or two if I did take her? She's so young and naïve, how else could I get through to her?

"Listen, if it's more proof you want, I'll get it for you, but if you're looking to prove something to Steve and yourself, that's between you and him," I ordered.

"Please, Paige. Let me tag along. I promise, I'll be good. I just *have* to see for myself," she begged.

"Fine," I slowly and hesitantly said.

"Thanks, Miss Turner," she said and leaned over to give me a hug. "What should I do now?"

"Try and act like everything is great and everything is normal," I advised.

What she really needed to do was look for work. Molly had left her job as an executive assistant to be his trophy girlfriend. She had been out of work for almost two years and since they weren't married, she had no rights to any of Steve's money.

"And maybe read the chapter in my manual on going back to work after a divorce. I know you're not divorced, but you can still learn from it."

"What is wrong with men? Why do they think they can just go around hurting others and not feel bad about it?"

She walked over to the windows as if contemplating her life and every decision she has made to date.

"It's not all men. Steve's a narcissist and you will never get what you want from a person like him and you won't ever change him. It's good you're getting out now. I'm proud of you."

Molly had ignored the red flags from the beginning, and now she was in too deep. I explained to her how I had even fallen victim to a narcissist. When she heard how Danny was just as secretive as Steve, and I ignored it, it helped bring her a little peace of mind.

"Don't you get lonely? Don't you ever wish you had a husband or even a boyfriend, or just someone to share this amazing apartment with? Do you want kids?" Molly asked.

"Of course. If it happens, it happens. But I refuse to sit around waiting, hoping and praying for it, like some people," I replied.

Since getting into the crimes-of-the-heart business, I've observed in myself how differently I handle relationships. I used to dismiss a man's flighty behavior and now won't tolerate anything less than one phone call every day. If a guy wasn't into talking on the phone, I made him like it.

Molly left with her head a little higher than when she arrived. For Vixen Investigations, it isn't just about solving crimes of infidelity; it's about making my lovelorn clients feel that self-worth again. I wanted Molly to know that many men and women make bad relationship choices based off the fear of being alone. But, being with a philanderer, like Steve, is not better than being alone.

Later that evening, I made my way back into the city to meet up with my older and somewhat wiser girlfriend, Theresa. Even though she shares the same name as my favorite Saint, Theresa is no saint. With 10 years more life experience than me, I saw her more like a big sister than a friend. When drunk, I call her Snow White because of her long, dark hair and porcelain white skin. But, Theresa didn't act like a sweet princess. The only thing she had in common with the real Snow White was that she knew how to get what she wanted from men. She had a love of vodka, cursing, and making a raucous scene wherever she went. She always gave me thoughtful life advice, almost like

Confucius. She once told me, "An eye for an eye and a tooth for a tooth makes the whole world blind and ugly."

I could feel my eyes tearing up as the winter wind blew its numbing coldness into my face. With my furry Helly Hansen hood pulled up over my head and nearly covering my eyes, I made my way to the Viceroy Hotel. My cell phone said that it was only 17 degrees, but the wind chill made it feel like zero.

It took my muscles and face a few minutes to thaw; Theresa was already waiting for me in the covered rooftop bar with her $4,000 Hermès tote and a fox fur-trimmed coat. She was halfway through her Martini and it looked like she already had a glass of red wine waiting for me. The pumps I changed into in the elevator clacked on the marble tile.

"Hey, gorgeous," she said as I approached.

Theresa stood and gave me a big hug and kiss on the cheek. She seemed more pleasant and brighter than usual.

"Where the hell have you been?" I asked as I climbed myself up onto the slightly cold leather barstool. "You're like an elusive unicorn these days. I've been missing you!"

"Well...you're not going to believe this," she began.

I always hated the tease followed by a short pause introduction. I cleared my throat and took a sip of the warm Malbec to brace myself for what she was about to say.

"The reason you haven't seen me around recently...is because I am getting married." She proceeded to pull off her leather gloves to flash me a ruby with diamond halo ring.

For a brief moment, I thought maybe I was imaging she had just said what she did. I didn't even know she had a boyfriend!

"What? Married? To who?"

Seriously, I have never even seen you with a man. I thought you hated them all.

"Remember that happy hour about eight months ago? We were at Oceana and that actor and his manager were flirting with us, and we didn't believe he was really an actor?" she recalled.

I thought back for a minute.

"Wait. George? That 30-year-old guy who played the cop in that new crime movie with Chris Hemsworth and Jake Gyllenhaal?" I asked with surprise. Theresa nodded in confirmation. "You mean the actor who wouldn't stop texting you? The guy who looked like he was fresh out of college and kept name-dropping the whole night?"

"Yes," she replied excitedly and took another sip of her drink.

"Wow...Theresa. That's great! Why didn't you tell me you were dating him...or anybody?"

"I wanted to, but it's been a whirlwind. I was skeptical at first but after he bought a freaking apartment in New York, just so he could be with me more, I knew he was serious." Theresa took a deep breath as if she were about to say something even more shocking. "I'm also moving to Los Angeles," she said with a note of hesitation.

I nearly spit the wine back into the glass. The bartender with the cute face but receding hairline looked at me as if I were choking or had hated his wine selection.

"Are you okay?" Theresa questioned with genuine concern.

"Oh, God, yes! I'm so happy for you! I just wish you had said something earlier. I would've thrown you a party or gotten you a wedding gift. I feel like a bad friend now."

I gave her a big hug and ordered us another round of drinks in celebration. Out of all the women I knew, Theresa was the one I thought would never get married. She gave all men, including the ones I expressed interest in for myself, a hard time.

The bartender continued to top off our drinks as if the glasses had automatic refill switches. When 9 p.m. finally hit and the bar was packed to the walls with tourists and locals, I was ready to leave. Theresa had held off in telling me that she and George were leaving for Los Angeles tomorrow morning until we were about to leave. I guess she didn't want our last night together to be too somber. Since they were going to be doing the bicoastal living of spending time in both Los Angeles and New York City, I figured I'd still be seeing her. And knowing her, and the fact that she was a born and bred New Yorker who hated lateness and laziness, I knew she would be back here often.

As the cold winter wind swirled around, I walked myself back to 33rd Street and to the PATH train. I went through the new e-mails displayed on my phone while waiting for the train. One particular message caught my eye. In between the pitch for "Little Cockatoo: Sexy Wake Up Panty" and my credit card statement was an email from the city's first lady, Victoria Wilcox. There was something about this email that didn't leave me feeling warm and nostalgic inside. All she had written was: *"Let's catch up. I want to hear about your business."*

MONDAY

I spent all of Sunday recovering from the night before with Theresa and contemplating why Mrs. Wilcox was reaching out to me about my business. This morning, however, I was back on the Steve beat, although I wasn't too thrilled by an email received from Molly when I woke.

From: Molly Carlson
Subject: Happy Monday!!
Hi Paige!

How are you? I know that I said I would come with you today on the ride along, but I've had a change of heart. Steve and I had a really good weekend together. He took me out for a romantic dinner and we made love all night long. Maybe things are on the up and up?

XOXO-Molly

Steve must have gotten to her somehow. Please don't tell me that everything I just did for her was a waste.

Dear Molly-

You saw the proof that he was with another woman. There is the likelihood that Caitlin was just out of town this weekend. I will still pursue him tonight. Let me know if you change your mind.

-PT

The email came as a surprise, but not a shock.

Steve gives her one day of loving and she is back to thinking things are okay? Not in my book.

Whether it was the adrenaline rush it gave me or knowing Steve was a two-timing bastard, now I was determined to expose him and his filthy ways.

"I thought he was done working at five, where do you think he is?" Adam asked as the clock ticked to 5:48 p.m.

He was holding the magnum zoom binoculars I had custom ordered for him. We had been staked out in Battery Park for an hour, so far. I knew he was still inside because I had Molly call his office to check for me. We'd just have to wait, no matter how long he took.

"I still can't believe you were in a band," I commented to Adam. I was learning more and more about my often shy and humble assistant as we waited. "Why didn't you tell me? I would've come watch you. I love rock music."

"I thought the band would be my future, but then I finally woke up when my parents said they'd stop paying my tuition if I didn't start focusing on school more. I'll still rock out on the drums whenever I get a chance," he revealed.

I could tell in his face and the tone of his voice that he missed playing. Adam brought the binoculars back up to his eyes.

"I didn't want you to think that I was some fame-chasing musician who wasn't committed to Vixen Investigations. I guess that's why I didn't say anything."

I felt guilty for feeling flattered about his commitment to me. I also didn't want him thinking that he had to keep secrets from me out of fear of how I would react.

The clock ticked to 6:02 p.m. Still no sign of Steve. I went through my emails again to make sure I didn't miss Victoria's response after I asked her to let me know her availability. Nothing.

"There he is!" Adam stated.

Steve walked out with two other men and they quickly climbed into their company-owned Escalade. I revved up the Wrangler and slowly started trailing behind them as they made their way onto the FDR. I was hungry to see what he was up to now. Adam sat up straighter; his eagerness was just as obvious. I loved his enthusiasm. The Escalade veered off to the left, right near the United Nations, and then turned towards Midtown. The car finally came to a stop in front of the Hyatt Hotel, which was home to the highest sky bar in the city, Bar 47. I stopped the Jeep several feet down and watched the dapper men hop out of the vehicle.

As soon as the Escalade pulled away, I drove up to the valet, handed the young man a twenty dollar bill and told him to keep the Jeep close to the exit. I ordered Adam to stay in the lobby and wait for me because I wanted to appear single. My plastic-bottomed heels prevented me from moving fast on the slick, marble floor of the hotel.

"Hold the elevator!" I shouted.

My voice echoed over the chatter of foreign tourists and the BPM music playing overhead. I saw a hand extend out of the elevator to stop the doors from closing as I scurried over.

"Thank you so much. I just hate waiting for these elevators," I said with a slight pant.

It wasn't until the doors were closed and we started to climb floors that I realized I was in the same elevator with Steve and his two friends.

"Of course. Why wouldn't we hold the elevator for a beautiful woman," the taller and blonder of the three said.

It was just the four of us in the elevator yet I felt claustrophobic. I hated enclosed spaces and always opted for the stairs or escalator when had the choice. My ears began to pop as I watched the numbers climb to 16, then 17, and so forth. The men were whispering something behind me, but I couldn't make out what they were saying. Now that I was close up to Steve for the first time, I noticed that he wasn't as attractive as I originally thought he would be. He had lots of scarring likely from bad acne as a teenager and his skin was somewhat leathery, like he's spent too much time out in the sun. His blond friend kept looking down at my breasts while Steve and the other man talked softly.

"Are you all staying at the hotel?" I asked.

"No. We just came here for the view. And so far, it's pretty great," said the blond.

"Oh? The view of the elevator buttons?" I joked and forced a giggle to play up the cuteness. "My name is Paige...Paige

Turner," I continued while extending my freshly manicured hand out to Steve.

He shook it with an unattractive limp grip of the hand.

"Your name is Paige Turner? Like, turning a page?" the shorter and rounder of the three remarked just before letting out a loud "Ha."

I could feel my rosacea flaring up on my cheeks and neck; there was no hiding my irritability. Thankfully, we had reached the 50th floor fast. The elevator opened to a stunning rooftop that glistened under the city lights. We were so high up that looking out the window towards the Swarovski New Year's Ball made me feel a bit wobbly in my shoes. I led the three men over to a corner lounge area after agreeing to have a cocktail with them. Steve's cohorts, named Charles and Will, also worked with him at the hedge fund. Steve didn't look as interested in my company as the other two. In fact, he looked somewhat distracted.

Scoping out the scene more, I noticed heavy flirting going on between the men and the women in the establishment. I have the knack to tell if it's an actual couple or an affair-in-the-making. In one corner, I watched a Don Draper clone with a wedding ring tan line engage in a lusty chat with a girl who looked like a college coed.

Just twenty minutes in, and Steve, Will, and Charles were heavily debating last night's basketball game.

"So, do you guys have girlfriends?" I asked in an effort to change from talking about the Knicks to learning a little more about their current dating lives.

"No, thanks. The only one here that is somewhat taken is Steve. He's always taken," Charles boasted as if being single was better than being in a relationship. "I, on the other hand, am completely single." He continued with a lick of his lower lip.

Gross. I wonder what he means by Steve "always being with someone."

Ignoring Charles' suggestive comment, I turned to Steve.

"So you're seeing someone? What does she do?"

"She works in fashion. She's from New Jersey." Steve's response was rather smug.

I knew he wasn't talking about Molly or Caitlin because neither of them worked in fashion nor hailed from my home state.

"Really? You strike me as the Southern belle type," I hinted while Will let out an uncomfortable cough.

I seductively uncrossed my legs...

"What are you? Some sort of private investigator or something? What's with all the questioning?" Charles snapped like an attorney would.

"What have you heard?" I joked. "Speaking of work, I should probably get going. I have some crimes to solve," I sarcastically said and stood to adjust my dress.

Not one of the men offered to walk me to the elevator, just a casual "hope to run into you again." I checked my face in my compact as my ears began popping again with the fast decline. My eyeliner still looked good, but the bags under my eyes were growing. When I finally got down to the lobby, Adam was nowhere to be found. I could feel the paranoia building inside of me like a mom who just lost her kid inside Macy's.

"Oh, your son picked up the Jeep a while ago," the attendant said when I asked if he'd seen Adam.

"What do you mean he picked it up? I have the stub!"

I didn't even care that I was just referred to as a 20-something-year-old's mother; I was now without a ride and my assistant. Just as I started dialing an Uber, Adam and the Jeep came rolling up the street. He wasn't even fully stopped when I opened the door and pulled myself inside.

Without even an apology for his vanishing act, he delved right into how he saw Mayor Wilcox incognito come out of an elevator that was only allowed to go up to the 40th floor. He wanted to see what the mayor was up to, so Adam told the valet he was my son, and I ordered him to go home and take care of the dogs. He followed Walter's town car to his home on the Upper East Side and that was it. I couldn't help but question whether there was a link between what Adam just saw and Victoria's email. Something was up. I had to wrap up the Carlson/Benson case fast.

With the intrigue of Victoria's email lingering in my mind the next morning, I was still committed to helping Molly reveal her fiancé's dishonesty. It was my duty to protect and serve all the needs of the loveless and love-stressed. It was also my duty to take Taylor out for her birthday, which I missed. Lately it seemed I had no work-life balance. I was pretty much always on call and always had to keep my eyes open for any suspicious activity pertaining to my cases.

I decided to give Adam the night off while I took Taylor out. We were meeting at the Gramercy Park Hotel, which I found had a great man-to-woman ratio. It was also a few blocks from Taylor's apartment, which I thought would increase my chances of her showing up on time. I was correct in my prediction because when I arrived, Taylor was already waiting for me at the classy hotel. Her long, blonde, shiny locks were hard to miss, and her tight purple dress squeezed her cleavage about an inch below her chin. I called her "neck breaker" because of how quickly men snapped their necks to get a second glimpse of her.

In passing, we could pass as Norwegian sisters, but Taylor was by far the more voluptuous one.

Her head was buried in her phone as I crept up to her. If she just lifted her head up from her phone once in a while to see the world around her, maybe she'd catch eyes with the man of her dreams.

"Paige! You said seven-fifteen!" She tapped on her vintage Rolex with its slightly tarnished gold band. She smelled like lavender and oranges. "It's seven-thirty. You're the one who's late tonight."

"By fifteen minutes. Remember when you made me wait an hour last week at Del Frisco's with all those old men? I had to prod them away like hungry cattle," I retorted.

The bar crowd was decent with its guests being predominantly of the male gender. In the corner, a young Asian girl was tickling the ivory on a gorgeous Steinway piano. The classical melody combined with the dim lighting and brass chandeliers put me back into another era. My wandering ear caught the conversation of three men standing to our right. In situations like these, I liked to test my eavesdropping abilities. They were talking about a business account and they were all in town from Chicago for a meeting.

"You won't believe who emailed me wanting to "catch up," I clued. Moving my body in closer to Taylor, I whispered, "Mayor Wilcox's wife."

Taylor's eyes widened with shock.

"No way!"

"Yeah," I replied, taking a sip of water. "But I need to finish this other case first."

"I can just imagine the PR nightmare that'll cause," Taylor said while rubbing her temples.

Taylor was a publicist and very good with the press. Since some of my cases result in reporters knocking down my door, I make her speak for me. She kind of keeps them away so I can do my job.

"Well, here's to another successful sex-bust...and another potential crazy one," Taylor said, raising her glass of wine.

We continued to talk while waiting for our food to come. I noticed that the three men from Chicago were looking more like they were getting ready to leave.

"Hey, what do you think about these guys behind me?" I whispered to her.

"They're okay. I'm not really into light hair. I like darker and exotic," she replied.

"Are you serious? They're cute and I bet you the bar bill that they're from Chicago, work in advertising, are single, and they're named Felix, Abraham, and Craig. I'm going to get them to talk to us."

"I'm not placing any bets with you. It's a little too scary how you know what you know," Taylor replied and continued to reapply her lipstick.

I pretended to accidently elbow the shortest of the three, not realizing that I had bumped him so hard that he ended up spilling his drink.

"I'm so sorry. I didn't realize that was your arm," I innocently said. "I thought it was some woman's handbag."

The men went from annoyed to interested in a matter of seconds after I began talking.

"That's okay," the one with the now-stained sleeve said. "Why do you New York women carry around such big bags anyway?"

"They make up for our tiny apartments," I quipped, making everyone laugh.

A round of introductions followed and as expected, I was right about everything from their names, to their work, to their relationship status. We were soon standing in a half-moon around the bar and all our drinks and food had been placed on the gentlemen's tab. The booze was flowing and the laughs were, as well. And, just as I was about to hand Craig my phone number, Steve Benson was walking through the hotel's gold revolving doors. He wasn't alone, either. He was with his ex-wife, Leslie, and she was surprisingly happy.

Too happy for someone who has been cheated on and divorced by the man she was currently arm-in-arm with. What the hell? Is that a wedding ring? He's not divorced!

I excused myself from the group and gave Taylor the look that often signified it was work-related. Leslie and Steve lingered in the lobby as if they were waiting for someone. I took a seat on a couch near the front desk and buried my head in a copy of *ELLE* magazine left on the neighboring end table. I had bolted so quickly that I left my bag with my phone at the bar.

Taylor will just have to trust and be patient.

I raised my eyes to keep my sights still on the volatile couple. My heart thumped hard in fear that Steve would recognize me. Then, just as he and Leslie moved into the lounge where Taylor was, the three Chicagoans came walking out and a familiar voice emerged from the doorway. It was Charles. He was yapping on his phone loud enough that I could tell he was talking to Steve.

"Yeah, man. I just got here. I'm walking in now. Where the hell are you? Oh, wait. I see you now!" he bellowed.

I put down the magazine and sneakily walked around the back of the lounge and to the bar where Taylor was picking through some leftover appetizers. Steve, Leslie, and Charles were seated in some chairs in the corner and hadn't seen me, thankfully.

"Hey," I said hopping back up into the wobbly bar stool. "You have to play it cool...what happens next, I mean."

"Why? What is going on?"

"Steve, the man I've been following who is cheating on my client, Molly, is here with his wife! They're in the back corner over there. We're going to go over there and join them," I ordered.

"Okay, cool. This is like CIA stuff! I thought the guy was divorced?"

"Apparently, he is not. They both have wedding rings on. I had my doubts he really was divorced. He probably just told Molly that so he could have his cake and eat it, too. Follow me."

We gathered up our coat, bags, our complimentary glasses of wine, and casually walked over to where they were sitting. Charles continued to talk loud, which made for a good distraction. We were inching closer and they still hadn't turned to notice us. Despite Charles' obnoxious behavior, he looked cuter than he did last night. His green and white checkered shirt seemed to make him appear more youthful and brought out his olive eyes. Taylor leaned in to me.

"He's hot. Single?"

"He's friends with the cheater, but he doesn't seem to be the cheating type. I can usually tell," I whispered back.

We were now inches from them.

"Steve? Charles?" I exclaimed now, just inches from the trio. "How do I get so lucky running into you two nights in a row?"

Charles smiled wide and stood up like a proper gentleman to greet us. Steve and Leslie stayed seated. Charles gave me a hesitant hug before quickly introducing himself to Taylor. He motioned with enthusiasm for us to sit down. Steve's vibe was unwelcoming. If it were a scene from a comic strip, the bubble coming out of his mouth would be "oh shit." Leslie, on the contrary, seemed rather pleasant.

"Hi, Steve. Good to see you again. And you must be...from Jersey...?" I trailed off.

"This is Leslie," Steve interrupted. "Leslie, this is Paige. Paige Turner. Coincidently, we ran into her last night. She's a journalist." Leslie extended her hand for a very delicate handshake.

"Nice to meet you. Paige Turner. That is such a fun name and you're a journalist. It's almost like the weatherman being named Storm Cloud. I'm Steve's wife," she said proudly.

I couldn't help but shed an internal tear for her. The way she looked at Steve was of love and hope. It was painful for me to see the trust she had in him.

She had no clue what he was doing behind her back.

It was now getting close to midnight. Taylor had taken a deep interest in Charles and I almost expected them to go home together. Steve looked eager to leave while Leslie acted as if she hadn't had a night out in years. Even though Steve knew I was aware he was up to no good, I ignored him to befriend his wife. Every question I asked of their romance, Steve would grip the sweaty rocks glass and take a forced sip. Leslie never even hinted to the fact that there were any cracks in the marriage. She was either delusional or Steve did a really good job at hiding his antics. I watched Steve watch Leslie rave about their life together.

You never did file for divorce after all. That is shared time among four women. How do you do it?

I tried to hide my disgust while calculating the figures in my head.

Another successful night for Vixen Investigations. I had gotten enough pictures to prove he was still married. Now it was time to bust this guy.

3

I could still taste the alcohol in my drool as it dripped onto the soaked pillow. My tolerance appears to be waning over the years. As I pulled myself over to the night table to reach for my phone, I saw that Taylor had sent me a text at 4 a.m. detailing the "tender" and "sweet" lovemaking she had engaged in with Charles.

Good for her. Thank God I didn't have to sleep with him.

I had my "list" and then I had my "work list." I never counted sex with a source as real "sex" for myself. While it technically was intercourse, it was strictly work-related.

After debating with myself on whether I should get up, I finally did when I heard my coffeepot click on. My head pounded with every footstep as I made my way into the bathroom. It amazed me how much piss I had managed to hold in through the night. My going-out makeup still looked pretty good too. So good, I contemplated leaving it on. Today, after all, was the day I was finally putting the Benson/Carlson case to bed. With all the evidence I had, there was no reason to prolong the investigation any further. A simple text telling Molly, "It's time," was all the convincing she needed to agree with me. She was so ready for the relationship to be over, that she begged to come with me when I busted him. There was still the matter of informing Caitlin and Leslie of Steve's wrongdoings. I knew it would be hard, but Leslie needed to know. Caitlin, I had a feeling, would be dumping him soon anyway. I could tell she was the type of girl that doesn't hang around an old man like Steve that long.

As I waited for Adam to arrive, I prepped for the mission. My leather leggings were looking more and more worn as they were beginning to lose their tightness. I always wore the same outfit on a bust and even though I owned twelve pairs of these pants, they were all getting plenty of wear. Leather leggings, a silk blouse, and a black fitted blazer was the perfect outfit to look sexy in, while also allowing for my handgun if needed. The plan was to go to Leslie's early this afternoon, before Steve got out of work. Little did he know that I had secretly downloaded a GPS tracking app on his smartphone last night, while pretending to look up a recipe.

The more I learned about Steve and spent time with him and his pals, the more I understood how he was able to manipulate the women in his life the way he did. In public, Steve charmed and acted the most mature out of his group of friends. To the inexperienced eye, it makes him a catch. In reality, it means nothing, as often it's the quiet ones you really have to watch out for.

My heart raced as if I just drank three cans of Red Bull as I made my way down to meet Adam. He would be the one driving this time. First stop: to pick up Molly. Then, we'd head to Leslie's before staking out Steve's office again.

"What are you wearing?" I questioned Adam.

He was dressed in a vintage trench coach, scuffed loafers, and a dark brown fedora. He looked like a modern-day Columbo. He was chewing on a toothpick as he leaned up against the parked Jeep. He always liked to play up the detective look when we were about to nab a cheat.

"What? It's retro. I bought it at Buffalo Exchange. Cost me $10. Plus, look at all these cool pockets. They store all my belongings," he defended.

I appreciated his enthusiasm.

We hopped back into the Jeep, which Adam had perfectly heated to my preferred 74 degrees. We turned onto Washington Street, passed Carlo's Bakery with the mammoth cookies in the window, and then made our way towards the Holland Tunnel. Molly was waiting for us in the lobby of the Roxy Hotel. It was the best place for us to do a scoop up. Before leaving, I had gotten in touch with Leslie to inform her that I was in fact a detective and "had something important to tell her about Steve." Unbeknownst to me, she must have had an inkling about Steve's infidelity, because she was the one who actually responded, "He's being unfaithful again, isn't he?" Without getting into the thick of it, I affirmed her hypothesis.

With Adam carefully dodging the cobblestone and the potholed streets, I flipped through my favorite newspaper app, *The Gotham Post*, on my phone. Most of the stories reflected the quirks of Mayor Wilcox, the sexual shenanigans of the Kardashians, and the losing streak of the New York Knicks. I let out an uncontrollable chuckle at one headline about Mayor Wilcox that read, "Mayor Gets Plowed; Orders Snow Removal of Select Staffers' Streets While Queens, Bronx Streets Remain Untouched."

We pulled up to the front of the Roxy, where Molly was waiting by the door. She saw us approaching and ran out in her white kitten heels, pink fur coat, and perky coiffed mane. She didn't look as concerned and dreadful as I imagined a woman who was about to catch her fiancé in the act of cheating would.

"Hi, guys. It is so cold out there," Molly exclaimed.

The Jeep instantly filled with the scent of Burberry perfume as she made herself comfortable in the leather seats.

"Hi, Adam. I like your coat," she commented in the sweet, southern accent of hers.

Adam blushed. Molly was either distracting herself from what was about to happen, or was genuinely as excited as we were about catching Steve. I turned back to speak with her, face to face.

"How are you doing? Are you ready for this?" I asked calmly.

Molly just nodded. Perhaps it was her Pollyanna attitude that made her think Leslie would be warm and welcoming to her. I had to decline her wish to come with me when I went up to Leslie's apartment to break all the details to her.

I had concocted the perfect setup. Molly told Steve that she would be out of town, so the place he rented for the two of them would be all his for the night. Meanwhile, Steve had told Leslie earlier that he would be out of town himself. That can only leave me to believe that Steve's getting his fix with some other sugar baby tonight. The GPS tracker still had Steve located at his office. *Perfect*, I thought, as we pulled up to Leslie's on Hudson Street. I made Molly and Adam wait in the Jeep while I trekked through the slush. The instant blast of heat upon entering the lobby immediately defrosted my fingers and hands.

"I'm here to see Leslie Benson," I said to the uninterested doorman at the desk.

He studied my license intensely.

"Is she expecting you?" he asked as if trying to exercise his power. I simply nodded, yes. "You some CIA agent or something?" He inquired again without a hint that he was joking.

I should say yes to scare him a little!

"Lucky for you I am not. If I were, I'd have to kill you. That's usually how it works," I jokingly replied to loosen the tension.

It worked. He smiled, handed me back my license and sent me on my way.

For a newer building, I would've expected the elevator ride to be faster. Or, maybe it was just my surging energy that made it feel like it was moving so slow. When I finally got to the 14th floor, Leslie was already standing in the doorway with an urgent need to know what was going on. She remained expressionless as I walked over to her and then greeted me with a hug. Though she wasn't crying, I could feel her breath get deep and then stop, as if she were holding it in. She walked me inside and directed me to their large U-shaped sofa. Their home was immaculate with lots of stainless steel and black. I couldn't imagine this was Leslie's type of decor. She seemed more "shabby chic" than "hospital room." Looking around, I noticed not one speck of color except for a purple-framed picture of Steve and Leslie on a boat.

It only took fifteen minutes to explain to her what was going on with Molly, Caitlin, and the investigation. She wasn't surprised in the least, which made me wonder why she acted so lovestruck when I met her last night.

Maybe she had a plan of her own or didn't care if he slept around.

Then, I got her to open up a bit more to me. She admitted that she'd been living in a state of denial for too long and even generously offered to pay half of Molly's bill when I told her she had hired me.

"Let me go with you, please," she begged as I stood to signal my exit. "I want him to see my face when I catch him cheating on me."

Poor Leslie had wasted 15 years of her life with asshole, Steve. I felt compelled to let her join.

Molly and Leslie didn't say a word to each other as we drove and then waited outside Steve's office. It was now almost 5 p.m.

and I knew Steve would be gearing up to leave since he never stayed at work more than an hour after the markets closed.

"How long do we wait for him? Is any of this stuff illegal?" Molly asked almost out of nervousness.

Adam brought down his binoculars and shot me a look of annoyance. Spying on people and snapping pictures wasn't illegal as long as I maintained my distance. I've been trained by the best on how to do it without igniting any lawsuits. Throughout my years as an investigative journalist, I've had professional training with the FBI and still have former homicide detectives, forensic pathologists, NYPD & LAPD officials, and criminal psychologists on speed dial. Even the high-tech security and information-gathering center in my apartment was constructed with the help of my law enforcement friends.

"He's going to come out. Just relax," I replied.

The more we waited, the more the awkwardness built in the back. Molly and Leslie had still not said a word to each other. I turned the radio on in hopes that a little empowering music, courtesy of Beyoncé and Katy Perry, would relax everybody. As soon as the clock hit five, men and the occasional woman started trickling out of the building.

"There he is, ladies. Five-alarm cheater, dead ahead," I said.

The seat shook as Adam started up the Jeep. Steve hurried quickly into a town car as if he were in a rush to get somewhere.

A tryst, perhaps?

His car took off and we followed behind while maintaining a block's distance. It looked as if he were heading exactly where I expected him to: the apartment he shared with Molly on the Lower East Side.

"I don't think I can do this, Paige. This is too hard for me to handle," Molly cautioned from the back seat. Just before I was about to respond, Leslie spoke up.

"Of course you can. I had to deal with this for over a decade. We're all in this together," Leslie encouraged.

I appreciated her help. Adam and I looked at each other, happy to hear the encouragement from one jilted lover to the other. Adam stopped the car at the corner of 9th street and Avenue C, which was the block Steve's and Molly's apartment was located on. Standing near the brownstone's entrance was a pretty brunette who smiled big as soon as she saw Steve.

That must be the Jersey girl.

"I love this area of the city," Adam commented. "I think I know that graffiti writer." He pointed to a large blue and pink sketch that read, "JONUS SIX."

Nobody responded to his comments, likely because we didn't know how to respond. Instead, the rest of us watched the young girl run to Steve, jump into his arms and kiss.

This guy is the Don Juan of New York City apparently. What the hell was it about him that made all these women so in love with him? Did he have some magical penis?

Molly handed me the keys to the apartment and the four of us got out of the car. Molly and Leslie followed behind Adam and I as we walked casually to the building. Luckily, there was no doorman for us to contend with.

We lingered out front for a few minutes, so the two had enough time to get in the mood. I had to make sure they were actually having sex when I busted in there. It was all about timing.

"Let's go. I want you two to wait down in the doorway until Adam signals you to come up," I ordered Leslie and Molly.

Adam and I tiptoed up the dilapidated staircase. Everything from the creaky floors and smell of garbage and bleach reminded me of my first New York City apartment in Hell's Kitchen. It was located right next to a train trestle and every time a train went by, I feared the building would crumble down into the tracks.

Adam had the camera ready to snap Steve in action. It was devilishly one of my favorite parts of the final exposure. When we got to apartment 4FE, I lightly pressed my ear to the door to listen for any moans. I heard a girl giggle, then a manly laugh, then silence. When I heard a door slam, I concluded that they were now in the bedroom. My heart was beating so hard with increasing excitement that the thumping sound almost deafened the noises coming from inside the apartment. I loved a good bust like I loved a good orgasm.

"Isn't this so fun?!" I whispered to Adam.

"You know it. I have the coolest job."

I slowly proceeded to turn the lock and without making a sound, I opened the door. I could hear the two of them in the bedroom, but there was no way they could hear me. I tiptoed inside the small, yet renovated glorified studio apartment. As I passed by the bathroom that was strewn with clothes, I caught a glimpse of myself and in that instant I thought I looked as sly as the Pink Panther. Adam waited back in the foyer until I signaled that I was about to move in. I could hear the young girl in the throes of passion as I stood right outside the door. "YES, YES, FUCK YES! YOU ARE THE MAN!" Once I heard Steve explode in manly pleasure, I gave Adam the sign, and without losing a hint of balance in my towering heels, I kicked open the door with a loud bang.

Steve and his mistress quickly turned their heads to see me standing in the doorway.

"What the fuck?" Steve yelled.

"Who is that?" The girl wailed.

Adam ran up behind me and started snapping away like my own TMZ reporter. The horny couple collapsed to the bed and pulled the sheets over their naked bodies.

"What the fuck are YOU doing here? How did you get in here?" Steve continued.

"That's good. Adam, go get the girls now."

He ran out of the room and I turned my attention back to Steve. I flashed him my Vixen Investigation badge even though I knew he wouldn't be able to make out what it said from the bed. I had the badge custom-made in a shiny red metal. Similar to what a sheriff's would look like, except mine was heart-shaped and read "Paige Turner, Vixen Investigations" around the heart, with my slogan "Protecting and Enforcing Vows" scripted in the center.

"Leslie and Molly know about your secret life. It's over, Steve," I calmly stated while I could feel the blood from the rush surge to my face.

"Bullshit! You with the FBI or something? I can have you arrested for breaking and entering. Get the fuck out of here," Steve ordered without even realizing this was all a setup.

His mistress darted to the bathroom while I remained standing in my "pissed off" pose at the end of the bed with my chin up, eyes looking down at him, and both legs fiercely locked in place.

"I am not breaking and entering. Molly gave me your keys." I dangled them to tease. "Speaking of Molly. I think I hear her now. GUYS, I'M IN THE BEDROOM," I yelled.

Molly and Leslie emerged with Adam and stood behind me like a SWAT team. Steve pulled the sheets further up to cover his body. I walked closer to the bed, which smelled like sex.

"Molly came to me because she thought you were cheating on her. I guess your fiancé isn't as dumb as you thought. When I mentioned to Leslie what was going on, she wasn't surprised. What do you think of that?"

Steve looked at Molly, then Leslie, then back to Molly.

"Molly? Seriously? You don't even know how to turn on a light switch," he snapped.

She shook her head, struggling to say something. But all she got out was a loud and Southern, "Fuck you!"

"I can sue. I can sue you all. Like hell you will get any of my money," Steve went on, but he looked so weak and scrawny lying there under my nose.

"You have no grounds to sue these women. You're the cheat!"

Just then I felt Leslie push me aside as she stormed to the bed. She was too quick for me to pull her back. She got right in Steve's face.

"I am your wife," she hissed. "But, now I am going to sue your ass. See if you'll be able to pick up young coeds without a dime. Maybe I'll even give half my settlement to this poor girl you led on. Maybe I'll even launch a charitable support group for jilted wives."

Steve stayed silent. Molly, too, remained speechless. She was too upset to lash out again. The room became silent again. The only noise was that of Steve's hookup rustling in the bathroom.

"Is there anything else you bitches want to say? You women are so fucking crazy. You have too much free time to follow me around like this. I'm glad you caught me. Now I can be done with all of you," Steve argued.

He was a true narcissist. He justified his immoral actions by blaming others.

"They're not crazy, you're crazy. To you, all women will be crazy because you drive them to be that way," I rebutted.

Adam escorted the ladies out of the apartment and back down to the car while I stayed behind for one last word. Steve got up out of bed, tied the sheet around his waist and walked over to me. He got right in my face but I stayed forceful and stoic. I wasn't going to let a man like him intimidate me.

"Anything else you got on me?"

Any man who talks to a woman that way doesn't even deserve to live.

I continued to stare him down.

"I knew from the moment I saw you what type of man you were. Your day will come. One day, you'll be old, wrinkly and all alone. You thought your exes were bitches, well, karma is bitchier."

Steve just stared back at me. I reached in my pocket and reapplied the Vixen Red lipstick and then, as if leaving my trademark, gave him a big kiss on the cheek, leaving him with a bright red imprint of my plump lips.

Case Closed.

I hustled down the shaky staircase. I checked myself in my compact before heading back out into the street. I still looked good for having just foiled another tryst. Nancy Drew's lucky she never had to deal with this shit.

After dropping Leslie back home and Molly at a friend's house, I took Adam to Blue Ribbon Sushi for some tuna sashimi and sake. It was well earned. We discussed how this was the first case that involved multiple women. Steve was a sociopath and preyed on women like Molly and Leslie. When a person is desperate for love, they're that much more vulnerable to fall into the hands of someone who will only take advantage of them. Surely it'll only be a matter of time before Steve finds his next victim.

"So. What's up with the next case?" Adam asked.

He had just polished off four sushi rolls and contemplated another. His love for sushi was almost nauseating. The restaurant was too quiet for me to get into the details. I couldn't risk anyone overhearing me speaking about a potential mayoral sex scandal.

"I meet with V-W next week...and something tells me I may have to sleep my way through the city council to get answers," I sarcastically stated.

We laughed but a part of us both knew, there was a high probability of that happening.

4

The legalities that leslie and Molly were dealing with were now in the hands of their attorneys and after a week of some part-time R & R at my dad's house in central New Jersey, I was ready to swan-dive into my next big case. Well, almost ready. Since my escape back home, I haven't been sleeping well.

It was only 4:30 a.m. and another lucid dream had shocked me out of my slumber.

Not again.

I dreamt I was running very fast. When I looked behind me to see what I was running from, a giant tidal wave was rising high above me. I was in my old neighborhood and I feared that this giant wall of water was going to wash away the home I grew up in. Just as the wave was about to crash down on my world, my ex, Danny, appeared to be running next to me. I followed him into a cave. He didn't say a word in the dream. We kept running towards a red light and then once we got all the way to it, I woke up. I couldn't help but wonder what that dream was symbolic of. I hated how sometimes dreams play out like movies, and you always wake up dying to know what happens at the end.

"Guess I'll just get up," I mumbled with extreme irritation into my pillow.

I rolled over and grabbed my phone off the nightstand for a quick scan of new messages. I was meeting with Victoria today and a part of me was hoping she needed to reschedule. There was a random message on my Skype app that caught my eye.

Number Unavailable (3:14 a.m.):
Kryptonite tiger

What the...?
I also wondered who was sending me such a message that early in the morning. I responded with just a question mark, in hopes that I'd get some sort of response.
Maybe it was a wrong number.
Then, just as I was about to put the phone down, I caught an alert on my WhatsApp.
I never use WhatsApp. Who is this?
My heart thumped hard and I could feel my cheeks burning. Like the dream had come to life, it was a text from Danny. All it said was, "*I miss you.*"
What?? Did I somehow summon him to think about me and send me a text through that dream? Not answering that text.
I ignored the message, turned my phone on silent and rolled out of bed. I wasn't about to let Danny's emotional spam clog my mental inbox. I hadn't heard from him since we broke up five years ago. Him contacting me out of the blue only meant one thing: he needed something from me.
With a strong cup of coffee in my hands, I curled myself up in the corner of the sofa. I've opted for this particular corner, closest to the window so much, the cushion sank a good six inches whenever I sat on it.
I flipped on the TV to catch the early morning news. I always enjoy watching the hot, local weatherman because his

dramatized explanations of the jet stream and "warm fronts" moving in showed off his chiseled biceps. Even if he was usually wrong, he's a lot easier on the eyes than Al Roker.

"Mayor Wilcox will be holding another press conference today..." the cute, yet green, anchor read off the teleprompter.

Mayor Wilcox held three press conferences just last week and none of them were about anything pertinent. One presser was about putting warning labels on sugary drinks, another about middle-schoolers being taught proper condom usage, and another on blocking Craigslist advertisements of those looking for sex partners specifically on snowy nights. It was like he was distracting the media for some reason.

Who really calls a press conference to talk about blizzard hookups?

New Yorkers had mixed feeling about Walter Wilcox. Most loved him, but some hated him. Personally, I didn't care for him or his methods of governing. But for the sake of being professional I was going to have to do my best to remain unbiased.

On the other hand, I adored Victoria. I respected all of the work she's done for the city. She seemed to know how to put money to good use, unlike her husband. As much as I hated to admit that a man could have that much power over me, Adam believes Walter is what's stopping me from moving back into the city. "I would never let a man keep me from doing what I wanted to do," I'd argue with him. Adam would just smile and shake his head at me. I felt that Mayor Wilcox made the city somewhat unlivable for the average worker. It had gotten way too expensive, I ruined two bikes because of the pothole-filled roads, and the homeless population had gotten so bad, they found an "urban outdoorsman" living in my old brownstone's basement.

"...to reveal what many are calling his 'astronomical budget,'" the anchor finished.

My ears perked at the sound of the topic. I turned up the volume to hear the cub reporter state how "the FY2016 Executive Budget—totaling $123 billion—is his strategic approach to strengthen the city's future."

Did he say $123 billion?! That seems like a lot for one city for one year.

I clicked the television off and proceeded to get ready. If I didn't give myself at least an hour to get to into the city, I'd never make it in on time for our appointment. We were meeting in Tribeca, an area of the city that was about the farthest point from where she lived on Madison and 70th Street. I heard that the Wilcox apartment overlooked Central Park and had its own private elevator with golden doors.

I chose a little bistro for us that was allegedly frequented by Lady Gaga, Katie Holmes, and Susan Sarandon. I thought maybe there was something in the coffee that kept these power women going. The place was big enough so there were enough seats; I wouldn't have to fear eavesdroppers. It was also small enough that someone walking by could easily pass without realizing it was a coffee shop. With acoustic versions of all my favorite '90 s grunge songs playing, I took a seat at a table next to the window. It would be easier for me to spot Victoria rolling up. She finally did—25 minutes later—incognito. A big fur hat covered her layered bob and a pair of large Chanel sunglasses hid her almost navy blue eyes. I gave her a little smile and a wave as she scurried in and out of the frosty cold. It was my first close encounter with the first lady and I found her more stunning than on TV and in the papers.

"Mrs. Webb. It's so lovely to see you," I said and stood to give her a firm handshake.

Given that we were in a public setting, we agreed to not use her name or Walter's name in discussion. He would be referred to as "Jim" for the moment.

"Paige, likewise. I can't tell you how eager I was to finally sit down with you."

Victoria took off her long camel-haired coat and draped it over the back of the chair. She kept her sunglasses on, but I could still make out her beautiful popping eyes and long lashes.

After the brief exchange of how we were doing and placing our beverage orders of an Americano and a green tea latte, we got right to business.

"I am not going to beat around the bush. I wanted to meet with you because I think Walter, I mean Jim, is having an affair," she started.

I looked at her with deep concern to urge her to continue.

"There have just been a lot of things that have been off with him..." she trailed off and looked down as if billions of thoughts were running through her head. "I have unlimited funds and I want you to find out everything you can. You're the only one I think can help me."

Is she serious? With unlimited funds I could take down the whole administration. This may be bigger than I first imagined.

Victoria was convinced her husband was cheating but had no hard evidence for me, except what was in her gut. Unfortunately, our guts aren't always right despite what we're led to believe. She claimed that Walter had been acting distant and off more than his normal aloof self.

"Jim and I have been married for 34 years. We were college sweethearts and wed as soon as we graduated from Columbia. I know him more than I think he knows himself."

As Victoria continued to familiarize me with their relationship, I worried that getting married so young may have something to do with his recent actions. Not all college sweethearts live happily ever after.

"I never worried about the relationship. I've always been confident in our love. But, maybe since I have been so wrapped up in my own work and now that Piper is off at school, I am noticing it more. I never felt like the love was unraveling until the past few months...maybe even years. We smile for pictures and look happy in the public's eye, but once we're alone, he barely talks to me let alone have sex."

She also divulged that Walter carries around three phones. One was for his personal use, the second was a backup phone, and the third was for work. One piece of information that stuck out the most was how she had come across some text messages on his work phone that struck her as odd. While looking for a contact to send a Christmas card, she saw a message from someone named "DB." She assumed they were the initials of someone he worked with because Walter likes to use initials when storing names.

To hide whom he is talking to?

It also seemed business-related as all the text said was, "You're short $14,000...sick of this." Walter responded with a vague, "Working on it." Walter was also taking more trips to Dallas, but that didn't seem suspicious to Victoria because he was close with Texas State Democratic Congressman Harvey Trumpka. He was one of Walter's old friends from college, is extremely wealthy, and told Walter he'd support him should he ever eye a run for higher office.

The more Victoria spoke about her uncertainties, the more flamboyant she became with her hands and arms. The diamond tennis bracelets would jingle and her giant engagement and wedding rings would clank on the table. I didn't want to draw any attention, so decided to wrap our first meeting. I agreed to work with her with a negotiable rate. Victoria smiled in relief and out she went, leaving her lipstick-stained coffee cup behind.

I tried to lay low the past few days in an effort to gather as much information on Mayor Wilcox and the administration that I could. Besides a few brief encounters and exchanges with Adam, Taylor, and my unemployed girlfriend April, I spent most of my days in my office, or what I liked to call the "War Room." It was where I did my entire information gathering and data analysis, and stored all my spy gear.

Victoria and Walter were presently in California visiting Piper, who is currently in her freshman year of college at UC Santa Barbara. I was touched to learn that she was majoring in journalism and used to mimic me when she was younger. When I found out her Instagram name, Paythepiper16, I immediately started stalking her under one of my phony accounts. Based off the pictures she posted, the teen seemed to really be embracing the SoCal lifestyle. Every other picture was of her at the beach or on a step and repeat. There were even recent pictures of Victoria and Walter with her at some of these events, which also looked to be attended by George Clooney, Kris Kardashian, Bill and Hillary Clinton, and Will Ferrell.

"I've got nothing, nothing on this guy," I blurted and slammed down the stack of papers.

I put my head in my hands. Adam was over to help me go over some of the slim findings we had. He looked equally frustrated but didn't throw fits like I did.

"He seems a little too clean. His college transcripts, finances, and criminal records are all fine. The guy doesn't even have a parking violation. How does a New Yorker not even have a traffic violation or a late fee?"

Because he's New York's favorite mayor. Who knows what he is capable of hiding.

I stood to stretch my legs and walked out into the living room. We had been sitting at the desk for too long. Adam followed behind me as I paced near the windows.

"There's hardly anything on his staff," Adam added.

I had him compile a list of the people who work closest with Walter. They included press secretary, Jimmy DeFazio, police chief, Todd Mitchell, senior advisor, Leon Olson, and comptroller, Richard Brownstein. These men were all assets to me for the case. Even the office secretary, security guards, and janitors were of value. I prayed that Victoria's senses were right and that she wasn't just being paranoid.

She's not the type of woman who would get paranoid over something like this. Think she would waste her time if she weren't certain?

Besides all the social media coverage and what was free information for me, there wasn't any dirt on Walter. He had a contradicting political agenda that aimed to help businesses and build enterprise and at the same time make sure everyone got their fair share with money. He also wants to increase the minimum wage from $9 to $16 an hour. His ideas may be counterintuitive in reality but they sure sound good in a campaign speech. He'd raise taxes for new projects and nothing ever seemed to get done. The city was supposed to fix the ailing train tracks under the East River in 2008 and seven years later there still hasn't been a movement of dirt.

Do not let his politics get the best of you. It's about Victoria.
This was sure to be the most challenging case for Vixen
Investigations.

5

Valentine's Day. I have a love-hate relationship with this holiday. Not because I am single but rather how society constantly likes to remind singletons that they are alone.

With Victoria and Walter back in town I knew my free time would be close to nonexistent. I found it rather odd that New York's first couple had no plans for the Hallmark holiday, especially with the day falling on a Saturday this year.

"Okay, you're officially on the email list for the mayor's daily schedule now," Adam announced.

Though it was the weekend, he didn't mind putting in a few hours to help create my new persona to get me back into the media mix and press pool. Depending on which role I assumed, we'd then create fake Facebook and other social media accounts. While still being the Vixen Investigator, I never knew if I would have to assume the alias of a teacher, waitress, or Zumba instructor.

"So, who am I this time? Paige Turner, the sign language interpreter?" I joked, walking over to where he was sitting on the couch.

He turned his computer towards me so I can see the screen.

"Freelance reporter."

He handed me my fake press ID.

"It looks like Tuesday, Mayor Wilcox is going to be at the United Nations speaking about the safety at the city's consulates in light of recent terrorist attacks. You can pick up your press credentials at the event," Adam detailed.

Holding the warm, fresh, printed paper complete with a list of Walter's schedule took me back to when I had to cover this stuff daily for *The Day*.

"A reporter, huh? Looks like I'm going back to my roots! Politics, foreign policy, and the U.N., oh my," I joked.

The alias made complete sense. I already had the respect from my days as a journalist. After I left the business many thought I had moved to San Diego to write novels because I made it a point to stay away from the camera. I made myself unrecognizable by letting my hair grow out another six inches and tried to sex up my appearance. I went from shoulder-length, layered brown hair and a Gap wardrobe to mid-back blonde locks and a closet full of slinky dresses and tight pantsuits.

"Anything new on Piper?" I asked while putting the ID and schedule to the side.

Adam had been monitoring her social happenings.

"She seems extremely immature. All she does is post party pictures and takes a lot of selfies. Here she is at the beach. Seems like a socialite to me."

Adam flipped around his computer to show me. There were pictures of her with One Direction, Gigi Hadid, and Selena Gomez.

How does she know these people at just 18-years-old?

I typically kept children off limits in my investigations. But, Piper is technically an adult and more than willing to put her life on display. I had no qualms about stalking her if it meant getting more dirt on her pops.

"I may need you to worm your way into her social circle at some point to see if you can get anything. That is, if she comes home from spring break," I suggested.

I thought Adam would love the idea of hanging around a group of young and feisty college girls all summer.

"Nooo. Please, no. It'll be selfie central with that girl. I don't want that girl posting pictures of me, that's for sure. It'll ruin my whole vibe," he complained.

"Let me tell you something about selfies," I started while sitting across from him, almost as if I were going to regale him in some deep story. "My ex, Danny, was obsessed with selfies. He would take selfies of him doing extravagant things even though he couldn't afford to do anything. He made himself look like he was well off. I think selfies are to blame for the demoralization of society."

Adam stood and clapped, with a smile on his face. Obviously, he was humoring me.

"Ok. I get it. You hate selfies," he said. "But I think it would be cool if you took a selfie like right before busting down the door of a mistress and mister getting it on," he suggested excitedly. "Like this."

He proceeded to mimic me kicking down a door and then pretended to snap a picture of himself. His skit made me laugh so hard, I could feel it in my abs. Adam plunged himself next to me on the couch. "Smile," he ordered and took a selfie of us.

Since I made Adam spend such a romantic holiday with his boss, I decided to give him the rest of the weekend off. There is no reason a subordinate should be spending Valentine's Day with their boss, unless, that is, they're having an affair.

5:45 a.m. MONDAY

I have an hour and fifteen minutes until I have to get up. I can either lay here and risk falling back asleep, only to then oversleep, or I can just get my ass up now and go work out.

After timing it out in my head and debating my options, I chose the non-lazy way to start my day. With as much self-determination as I could muster up, I slid myself out of bed and put on what I hoped were exercise clothes. It was hard to see with no contacts and my eyes still glazed and crusted over. If I didn't leave my bedroom now, I'd just crawl back into the sheets. I grabbed my phone and headphones off the dresser, stumbled out the door, and sleepily made my way into the elevator and pressed the GYM button.

Nobody would be working out this early.

Once my phone was powered on, a slew of new e-mails and texts started to appear in my inbox. I tried to focus my hazy vision on one particular text that stood out among the rest.

Danny (4:02 a.m.):
I am in the city.
(4:45 a.m.):
How are you? I want to see you.

Geez...they all come back at once, don't they? Mercury must be in retrograde.

The text had thrown me for such a loop I accidently bypassed the gym floor and was now heading all the way down to the lobby. I repeatedly pressed the GYM button in hopes it would take me back up immediately. It did, right after two hot football-looking players got in with me.

The gym session was exactly what I needed. The day was already feeling packed, even though my only scheduled events were a meeting with Victoria and dinner with Theresa, who was in town from Los Angeles for two days. Her acting career seemed to have picked up quickly. Surely her husband had some help in the matter of her signing with an agent and getting numerous small roles.

With an hour to kill before I had to leave, I got comfortable on my white faux fur rug in front of the windows in the living room, and got into lotus pose for a quick meditation session. I was never good at completely clearing my head, but I tried.

This is impossible. How can anyone make his or her mind go blank? Even just thinking about how much I can't meditate is ruining it for me. Ugh. Enough of this. I'm getting hungry.

It may have been the shortest attempt at meditation, but I tried. I was too excited for today and tomorrow's press conference with the Mayor that I just couldn't relax.

Jimmy DeFazio, aka, Wilcox's socially awkward and high-strung press secretary, was ignoring every email I've sent requesting a meeting. One thing was for sure, I was back to being one of the groveling reporters he so often treated like crap.

No worries, though. I knew I'd at least look eye catching having already picked out my outfit: skintight black leggings, a fitted black blazer, burgundy silk blouse, and black pumps seemed to be the perfect attire. The outfit was sexy yet professional. I figured I'd also sport my thick-framed spectacles for that "fuckable librarian" look.

Miniature tape recorder and binoculars? Yes. Gun? Definitely not. GoPro cam? Yes, just have the flash off. They'd probably snatch that from me.

"Paige." The quiet voice and feel of a hand on my shoulder immediately snapped me alert.

"Adam! You scared me," I huffed. "I didn't even hear you come in."

I pressed my hand on my heart as if it would help to slow down the thumps.

"Sorry. You know I have the keys."

He walked to the kitchen and grabbed coconut water from the refrigerator and a banana. I untied my legs and tried to stand, although my left leg felt like it was in a near coma. I limped over to the bedroom to change out of my yoga attire and into a beige and turquoise dress that looked similar to what an Air Asia stewardess would wear. It was a little too pre-spring, but I was so sick of black and looking like I was in mourning all winter. Adam was coming with me to Dos Pesos on the Lower East Side for an early lunch with Mrs. Mayor. I figured it was a safe spot since the restaurant's most frequent hipster cliental would hopefully be at class.

"We should've just taken the bus, Paige. I'm getting motion sickness," Adam complained as the Jeep bounced up and down the potholed-filled streets.

Rather than deal with public transportation and risk standing on a smelly bus or getting stuck on a broken-down PATH train under the Hudson, I opted to drive into the city.

"You know how I feel about the Port Authority. It's the rotten part of the Big Apple. I just won't do it."

From my purse on the floor of the passenger seat, I heard my phone chime three times. Victoria was texting me.

"Can you check to see what she wants?" I asked Adam.

He fished around the oversized tote. It looked like he was working up a sweat in doing so.

Hopefully he doesn't stab himself on my switchblade. I think I left it in there.

"Ahh, here it is. Victoria just got there. She says she is waiting in the town car outside."

"Town car? Why would she take a town car? I told her not to make herself look too important."

"It looks like Theresa texted you, too. She says to meet her at seven at Tribeca Grill. Remember, you can't stay out late. You have that presser at the U.N. at nine," Adam lectured while continuing to go through my phone like a nosy child. "Umm. What is this text?" Adam turned the phone towards me to see. It was the text from Danny. He knew about him and that relationship and how troubling it was. "What the hell does he want now? And he texted you again this morning I see?"

"Before you even ask...I never responded...they always seem to just come out of the woodwork like a pesky termite."

What was supposed to be a 25-minute ride to Dos Pesos ended up taking over an hour. Trying to find parking spots on snow-covered Ludlow Street only added to our lateness.

The hostess inside the dimly lit establishment escorted Adam and me to their even darker and colder cellar dining area. Down the uneven steps we went, which appeared to be made of painted hard mud, perhaps when the place was first built. The walls looked like gray boulders and gave off the feel that we were in some old Mayan temple. I was convinced the underground was used to store massive amounts of wine and alcohol during the prohibition era and maybe even used as a sex dungeon. I texted Victoria to let her know we were inside. Within minutes I heard the sound of heels tapping down the faulty staircase. Adam and I had taken a seat at a corner table towards the back of the basement bar. When she emerged from around the corner, we stood to greet her. As always, she looked stunning. Her mane was perfectly coiffed with not a lowlight or layer out of place. She exuded power while walking over to us in her $1,200 Gucci heels.

After a quick welcome hug, the three of us put in our margarita orders and we cut to the chase.

"Here's the skinny. I've got nothing dirty on your husband, yet. I am not surprised, though."

Victoria leaned in closer, making the scent of her Chanel No. 5 even stronger.

"That's because he probably gets his pals to burn any evidence," Victoria interjected. "Isn't that how all politicians operate?"

The waiter placed the sweet and heavenly smelling margaritas on the table. Adam was the first to take a big sip, then me.

"I looked at past records and to tell you the truth, I need more than a suspicious text and a gut feeling that he is cheating. Hopefully you have something good for me right now."

It was important that I be straightforward with Victoria.

"I do have something that may be of interest. That's why I wanted to meet with you," Victoria started.

Adam and I leaned in more. She stared at her half empty glass as if she were looking into a crystal ball.

"I got a phone call from the bank the other day. They wanted to know if I was making purchases in Dallas. I told them, no. Walter had been going there more recently so I thought the charges were his. Until I found out what the charges were for," she hinted.

She reached into her Alaïa clutch and pulled out a piece of paper:

Coach—$400
Bloomingdales—$1,200
Tiffany's—$1,500
Yves St. Laurent—$2,300
Agent Provocateur—$900

It was a list of the purchases made on the credit card.

Women's gifts? For Victoria? For Piper?

Given the type of stores it was either Walter buying gifts of some sort, or a woman using his credit card to do some shopping. I folded the paper and put it in my purse.

"Listen, Victoria. Keep monitoring these credit cards. I mean like every day before your accountant or your husband get their hands on the bills. I need to see where the money is flowing."

"Of course. I will do my best. Walter and Richard have all these passwords and stuff..."

"Wait. What? Comptroller Brownstein?" I snapped.

She nodded.

Why is he handling your finances? It wasn't his job to handle the mayor's personal finances.

Adam quietly jotted down notes on his iPad. Apparently, Richard Brownstein and Walter were college buddies. Brownstein went off to business school and worked for the Department of Treasury in Washington for a bit and moved back to New York when he heard about Walter's mayoral run. He had promised Richard a cabinet position if he won. Richard was rumored to be gay. That was all I knew about him. In all my years in news, I never had to deal with him. Knowing that Walter's best friend was handling the city finances, it made me question the relationships he had with the rest of his staff. Thinking about it a little deeper I realized that the majority of the administration officials were all men.

The Wilcox administration was like a giant fraternity.

I had some good leads now. Rather than go back home and then come back into the city, I decided to have Adam drop me off at the New York City Public Library. I could spend the three hours compiling my notes and people watching before going back downtown to meet Theresa.

With a coffee in one hand and my tote in the other, I found a quiet nook in the lower level of the library where I felt I could have a good brainstorming session. On my custom-made legal notepad with a Vixen Investigations seal in the center, I began formulating potential scenarios of what the odd purchases were all about.

1. Walter was doing some early Christmas shopping while down there visiting the congressman. But why would he be buying sexy lingerie for his daughter? Victoria didn't look like a woman who wore that kinky apparel, either.

2. Someone—a female—got ahold of his credit card and went on a shopping spree.

3. Walter has a secret fetish and likes to dress up as a woman. Was he hiding the fact that he was transgender?

4. He was purchasing gifts for an unknown woman...a mistress.

6

Stood up by Theresa...It was moments after I grabbed a prime spot at the bar at Wilfie & Nell in the West Village that Theresa texted me that she couldn't make it. She was delayed on a film shoot.

I decided to sit by myself and enjoy a round to warm my bones anyway. Besides the eight heads at the bar, the place was dead. I scanned through my phone to make it look like I was busy reading work emails or texts. In reality, I was just scrolling my Twitter feed.

"Friend not coming?" I heard a voice say. A new bartender had emerged. "Is that Perrier-Jouët you're drinking?"

I nodded and he went forth to poor me another glass of my favorite Champagne.

"Yeah. Something came up. It's no big deal. I don't mind sitting by myself." I took a gentle sip.

"Well, you're handling the rejection quite well. Most girls I've experienced would be throwing a fit right about now."

"Well," I took an even bigger sip, "I'm not like most girls."

"I can tell. You know what. This glass is on the house. You just have to come back here more. We don't get a lot like you in here."

I smiled at him as he walked to tend to another sole patron. I am sure he was just fishing for a big tip, even though he appeared to not need it. He either did really well as a bartender or was a trust fund child. I could tell by his Hublot watch, Tommy Bahama boat shoes, and Gucci eyeglasses. I certainly wasn't wearing those brands at his age. It was all I could do to afford my $1,800 a month rent on a $550 a week freelancer salary when I first moved into the city.

Drink number three had me drifting in and out of thoughts about my first press conference with the mayor.

I wonder which reporters I'll see there. I wonder if people will recognize me. I better leave soon or else I'll have garbage bags under my eyes.

I became distracted when across the bar I heard a man mention, "Summers in Avalon."

Summers in Avalon? I grew up going down to that beach.

I began to focus my attention on these two men chatting and laughing in that beloved Jersey accent. They were both attractive with brilliant smiles. One, in particular, struck me as a younger and baby-faced version of Jason Statham. It was an instant attraction. He was with a taller guy of the same age and they both looked like they had just come from work. They sipped their vodka tonics and would occasionally check their phones. My eavesdropping also picked up on the fact that they were both single. The taller of the two had recently split from a girl he had been dating for 12 years. The other was encouraging him to move on and find someone who won't spend all his money.

Sounds like a really good friend.

As I continued the cycle of looking down at my phone, right out the window and straight ahead towards the Jersey boys, I caught them both looking at me. I veered my eyes down at my phone. When I looked back up seconds later, I locked eyes with the shorter one. He smiled after having caught me checking him out. I smiled back. He turned to his friend and engaged him in a discussion once more. It was obvious they were now talking about me. I pretended to flip through e-mails in an effort to look busy and important until I felt the presence of someone above me.

"I hope you are here by yourself and not being stood up," a male's voice said.

I looked up to see the guy I was eye-flirting with standing in front of me. I quickly closed the screen of emails.

"May I buy you a drink?"

"Actually, I was stood up by my friend. And yes, I'll take another one of these, please. Thank you."

"My name is Liam."

He pulled out the barstool next to me that was originally intended for Theresa. We shook hands. His grip was strong and his skin was soft. Closer up, I could see that his eyes were greener, like mine, than blue. From his cheeks, to his lips, to his nose and ears, everything about his baby face seemed to match the friendly and loyal vibe he gave off.

"I'm Paige, nice to meet you. Where did your friend go?"

"So you did notice us? I guess we made it kind of obvious."

"Well, I'm pretty observant. Plus, you guys were pretty loud."

I noticed that Liam's cell phone wallpaper was a picture of him and his grandparents when he was a lot younger. You can tell a lot about a person based on their phone's home screen image. It usually indicates what's really important to them. The wallpaper on my phone was the Vixen Investigations seal.

"Eh. He's going through some girlfriend issues. He'd do anything for her. Can't say the same about her. She just takes and takes from him. I hate seeing that happen."

I could sense the concern in Liam's voice and on his face as I stared into it. For a moment, I didn't even hear what he was talking about. The smell of Old Spice and laundry detergent emanating from his clothes was calming despite the surge of heat I felt building between us.

When was the last time I felt this electricity? This isn't me.

My chest was getting warm and likely turning red, as well as my cheeks. It looked like Liam was dealing with his own bout of rosacea himself. His face flushed just as much as mine.

We continued to converse all while forgetting about how late it was getting. The only thing I knew was that we were onto drink number three and Liam was really opening up to me. When I found out that he grew up only 15 miles from me in western New Jersey, I questioned if we had ever crossed paths before.

Maybe that's why I feel such a strong connection. We probably saw each other in Whole Foods or Nordstrom's.

"Maybe that's why you're not like most of the women I meet. I never meet people from my part of Jersey," he said. "You're kind of mysterious. There's something about you, Paige Turner. What's your deal?"

Without getting into the thick of my life and career, I briefly mentioned me being a journalist and reporting on everything from politics to relationships, my mom passing away from cancer, and a little about my past relationships. I could feel myself getting drunk and I didn't want to let anything slip. There was something about Liam—his sweetness, his apparent honesty and devotion—that made me want to tell him about Vixen Investigations. I didn't.

"I would love to read your articles on relationships. I am sure I could use some good advice," he said as I downed the last bubbly sip of my Perrier-Jouët.

Uncontrollable. That's how our hands were by 10 p.m. As much as I wanted to blame the alcohol, I couldn't. Liam and

I were engaged in a full-on make-out session on the corner of Bleecker and West 10th Street. He leaned his toned body against mine and kissed me harder. He knew how to utilize his tongue perfectly as he sensually moved it along my lips and in my mouth. The feel of his defined muscles as I ran my hands from his back around to his abs made my knees weak and my stomach tingle. Every sexual nerve inside me craved his body. Sex was definitely bound to happen if I let him come home with me. I could easily cave if he pushed.

No sex tonight! You just met him! You have that big press conference in the morning!

"I really have to go. I have this huge assignment in the morning," I forced out.

"Just one more kiss," he whispered into my ear. I melted back into his arms at the sound of that Jersey accent.

Every time I tried to pull away, I was easily pulled back. It was like there were magnets in our lips, in our chests and in our hips. In the midst of this unintended encounter, I had lost all concept of time and place. The surrounding apartments had turned their lights off, meaning it was late enough for New Yorkers to be asleep.

With every bit of willpower I had left in me, I hailed the only cab I saw in the area. Liam insisted on paying and gave the driver three $20 bills after he helped me into the backseat. If it weren't for the cab driver starting to run the meter during our extended goodbye kiss through the rolled down window, I wouldn't have left. Right as the car started to pull away, Liam started frantically banging on the car and yelling.

The driver stopped and I rolled down the window.

"Your number! Your number!" I could barely make out what he was saying he was breathing so hard.

"What's the matter?"

"I need your phone number. I almost let you drive out of my life without your phone number." He panted and I smiled in delight.

I carefully entered my digits into his cell. We kissed again and off I went, back to New Jersey.

Liam was already texting up a storm and I wasn't even home yet. I was the "highlight of his week," he said. Even the blast from the 30-degree wind chill when I stepped out of the cab wasn't enough to snap me out of my love spell.

The night doorman, Jason, came running over when he saw me stumbling to the door.

"Are you okay, Miss Turner? Another busy night I see," he sarcastically stated.

I grabbed his arm for balance and he walked me inside. When I got to the elevator, I gave him a peck on the cheek.

"My hero. Goodnight, Jason," I said as the doors closed between us.

I was still grinning ear-to-ear.

Exhaustion hit me as soon as I got up to my apartment. Now all I wanted to do was crawl into bed. With only the bright moon to light my path as it shined through the living room windows, I went straight to the refrigerator, chugged some water and popped two aspirin.

From the kitchen I went to the bedroom without turning a light on. I peeled off my clothes, left them in a heap on the floor, and crawled naked into bed. The silk sheets felt good against my bare skin. As I lay in bed I replayed the entire day in my head before falling asleep with a smile on my face.

I can't wait to see you Thursday.

I couldn't stop thinking about the text Liam had sent me right before I passed out. I didn't even remember making a plan with him for Thursday night, but thankfully he did.

It was almost time to leave for the press conference. I cranked up the morning news so I could hear Price Cooper and Scott Baldwin from the bathroom. They were discussing the latest happenings from overnight, the weather being unseasonably mild for late February and they even mentioned Mayor Wilcox's press conference later this morning at the United Nations.

As I curled my highlighted layers, I could also hear my cell phone start beeping to alert me of an incoming text.

Don't tell me Adam is here this early?

I ignored it until I was completely ready. I didn't want to be late so I quickly gathered up my things, including my new reporter's notebook, a handful of "Paige Turner—Freelance Reporter" business cards, my press pass, and my phones and threw them in my tote. It wasn't until I was in the elevator and heading down to the lobby when I noticed an odd text.

Number Unavailable (8:02 a.m.):
Looking forward to seeing you in the field again

Unavailable? That's the same person who texted me "kryptonite tiger."

Who is this? I responded.

Whoever this was knew that I'd be at the press conference today.

It has to be someone in the administration. The only people who get word of the press list are the ones who work with the mayor. It was the only explanation I could think of.

Now, with my heart and mind racing with intrigue, I also noticed a new voicemail message that had come in at three in the morning.

"You have a new voicemail from Danny Thompson," the robotic voice said.

My heart thumped a bit harder. I hadn't heard his voice in five years.

"Hey, Paige. It's me. I assume you're purposely not responding to me. Either you got rid of my number or have it blocked. I'm going to be in New York in two weeks." There was a long pause. I thought that was it until he continued, "I want to see you. I miss you."

I hit the delete button before I was even presented with options to replay or save the message. I wasn't about to let him put me into a sour mood. I was still riding high from my night with Liam and anticipation of being back on the reporter beat.

I hustled through the building entrance and around the corner to where Adam was waiting for me with the Jeep. I was having him drive me into the city this morning so I could get some work done beforehand. Since the Jeep was wired into a virtual roving office and mini intel center, I was able to do all my work. From the outside, it looked like any beach-cruising Jeep Wrangler. One would never know about the Wi-Fi, GPS tracking system, audio and video monitoring system, light-less headlights, and bulletproof exterior.

There was a copy of *The Gotham Post* waiting for me on the passenger seat. Adam didn't say much as he drove us down to the entrance of the Holland Tunnel. He knew my mind was somewhere else.

"How was dinner with Theresa?" he asked.

"Oh...she didn't make it," I vaguely stated without lifting my head up from *The Post*'s Page Ten. I loved to see which famous faces were out and about being scandalous.

"Really? So what did you do?"

"I just stayed and had a drink by myself. Nothing special. Hey, did you get me that list of his current staff?" I quickly changed the subject.

Adam motioned to a file folder in the backseat. While sitting in the morning crosstown traffic, I went through some of the paperwork. I was correct in my assumptions about his administration. Most of Walter's staffers were around the same age. All of them were original New Yorkers who either stayed here or left the city and then moved back to work with Mayor Wilcox. Another big red flag was that they were all men with the exception of a few female secretaries.

So much for equal opportunity.

Security around the U.N. was tight. So, I made Adam drop me off farther away on 2nd Avenue and 40th Street and just walked the rest of the way. I was one of the last people to check in at the press desk. Luckily, and as usual, the mayor was also late. It was always rare for politicians to be on time for anything, especially a 9 a.m. press conference. I caught a glimpse of the press list. It looked like someone from every media outlet, even the foreign ones, would be attending.

Must be a slow day in the news. All the mayor was talking about is security at the consulates throughout the city. Wow, Andre Hernandez is here? He was so good in bed. Hope I don't see him.

With my badge and pad in hand, I made my way into the designated conference room. I took a seat in the back corner so I could have a wide view of the audience. There was a large turnout. The police chief, the U.S. ambassador to the U.N., a few other foreign dignitaries, Walter's press secretary, and the comptroller, who was standing by whom I imagined were his wife and kid.

Why would he bring his family to something like this? The kid should be at school.

It was hard not to notice his press secretary looking distracted and overwhelmed. As I briefly conversed with the reporters sitting to my left and right, I was keeping my peripheral vision on anything I found out of the ordinary. I hadn't been recognized yet and there were a lot of new faces in the press crowd. There were a few seasoned reporters whom I remember being on the same beat with back in the day. I looked down at my watch. Nine-twenty, it said. Walter was now twenty minutes late.

"I don't think I can sit through another one of his press conferences. He seems to be a bit obsessed with hearing himself speak lately, don't you think?" I quietly addressed the Polish News Network reporter sitting next to me on the flimsy folding chairs.

She looked at me, smiled and then looked back down at her notepad. She was either ignoring me or simply did not understand my English. Having the attention span of an 8-year-old wasn't helping, as I was getting bored and antsy.

Various thoughts drifted in and out of my head. One second it was the case, then the anonymous text, then Liam, then being hungry and thinking I might be getting my period because I felt crampy and irritable.

Let's go already!

Just as I was thinking about stopping at Duane Reade afterwards for a bag of white chocolate-covered almonds, the lights dimmed a little and the podium lit up. A minute later, Mayor Wilcox was walking out. He looked peeved, almost like he didn't want to be here. He has this slight arrogant swagger that only someone in his position could master. I turned on my audio recorder and began taping.

"As you know, hate crimes are up in the city. Terrorism is a huge global threat and we're going to increase spending on security guards, cameras, and law enforcement in the area around the consulates to ensure no foreign official feels the least bit threatened when coming to our great city."

Increase spending again?

Every time I heard him say we're going to do this and then to do that, all I heard was "increase taxes."

I could see Jimmy DeFazio standing off to the far right of where the mayor was. He looked busy on his Blackberry. He was some press secretary. He seemed a lot more wrinkly and worn out than he did in the mayor's first term.

I wonder if he ignores everyone like he ignores me. He looks like he needs to get laid.

The police chief, comptroller, and two other men who looked like security guards stood behind Walter. Their eyes seemed to focus solely on what the mayor was saying or they would look straight out into the crowd. The only one who looked somewhat out of place was the lady with Brownstein. She darted her eyes all throughout the crowd as if she were looking for someone specific.

Maybe that's one of the female secretaries. She's really pretty. Perhaps the comptroller keeps her around to make him look like "The Man."

After about fifteen minutes of rambling, Mayor Wilcox opened up the floor to questions. Nobody seemed to be interested in what he had ordered the media here for because the first question posed had to do with the uprising in antipolice riots, not security. Scrutiny towards the NYPD had increased dramatically because of recent reports of excessive force used by officers during arrests.

Walter became obviously irritated as Tony Montoya, a well-known and respected veteran reporter from Channel 5, continued to probe about the controversial topic. Tony always used to call me "K-9" because of my ability to sniff out the obscure. I never took offense to being compared to a dog because of how smart and loyal K-9s are.

While still on the topic of police versus ignorant protestors, I shot my hand high into the air.

"Is that Paige Turner in the back?" the mayor said while shading his eyes from the spotlight.

All heads turned towards me as I stood. I could see the look of surprise in some of my old competition's eyes.

Bet you didn't expect to see me back on the beat.

"Yes, Mayor. Miss me?" I joked aloud.

"I thought I saw your name on the press list. Where you at now? I thought you moved so San Diego to write books or something," he continued.

"Nah. Couldn't leave. Let's get back to you, Mayor," I responded. "How do you think restraining the nation's strongest police force will actually make the city safer? Are you telling people not to call the police but try to sort matters out themselves?" The heads turned back to the mayor.

"Oh, Paige. How I missed your jabs. I am not saying that at all. I am just saying that if a situation can be rectified itself, don't call the police. It saves us money too."

"Mayor, with all due respect, a policeman's job is to protect the people of this city, even if a situation may be nothing. How can you justify the high taxes and then tell people not to call the police?"

Eyes and heads went from me to the mayor, to me and back to the mayor. I had no intention to cause such a heated argument, but it felt good to push his buttons a little.

"Miss Turner, I don't know who you're working for now but I can't get into a debate about this. Let's recall the real reason the media is here right now," he deflected.

A cloud of tension had filled the auditorium. I had gotten so in the zone, I didn't even realize the damage I could be doing to the case.

The mayor looked more and more like he was going to be wrapping up the press conference as Jimmy started walking towards the exit. It was my cue to leave too. As Walter gave his closing remarks, I gathered up my belongings, threw my reporter's notebook and cell in my bag and quietly exited through the back. I needed to catch Jimmy before the rest of the fresh-faced reporters, many being blonde girls in tight, jewel-toned poly-blend dresses.

When I got outside, Jimmy was standing next to the back exit door near the town car and smoking a cigarette. With a smoke in one hand, he was typing away on his phone with the other. I calmly walked over.

"Jimmy? Hi. I am Paige Turner, freelance journalist," I casually said. "I wanted to introduce myself. I don't believe we have formally met."

His lack of interest was apparent. His handshake was limp and his hands were ice-cold like a dead person.

"Yes. I know who you are."

He took a deep inhale of his cigarette and kindly blew the smoke away from my face. He wasn't that much taller than me. Probably about 5'10". His face looked stressed, from either the chain smoking or working with Mayor Wilcox.

I guess the cleavage-friendly shirt and do-me-behind-the-book-shelf glasses don't appeal to him.

"Well, I am back on the beat. I imagine we'll be doing a lot of work together. You'll be hearing from me a lot more."

He continued to look down at his phone. Whether he was actually looking at emails or just making himself look preoccupied, I wasn't going to let him keep me from doing my job. I owed it to Victoria.

"I was hoping to do some specials with the mayor. Perhaps a one-on-one? I sent you a few emails…"

He raised his eyes like he was holding in a laugh. His breath reeked of a dirty ashtray.

"After that little thing you did in there. I highly doubt Walter would be interested in speaking with you again. Now, if you don't mind young lady..."

How dare you! Do you know who I am?

I wanted to wring his neck. He went to walk away, but I grabbed his arm before he could completely turn his back towards me.

"I didn't mean to get so heated. It's a hot issue right now. He just wasn't anticipating my questioning," I explained. It pained me to even slightly apologize like this. I wasn't the sorry-saying type. I felt it was a sign of extreme weakness when used too much. "Actually, I wanted to do a special feature on him. I know he isn't used to those types of interviews. What do you think?"

"I'm listening. You have to be more specific, young lady."

Stop saying that!

"Here, walk with me to the car."

I followed him through the crowd of press that had all gathered around the front entrance of the building. The way we maneuvered through the crowd reminded me of college and those nights at packed clubs.

When Jimmy and I finally reached a clearing, I finished explaining that I wanted to do an exclusive with the mayor that focused on him and his family life.

"I get it. Like an exposé? That would require a lot of time and lots of clearance. What's your deadline?" he asked while looking over my head in anticipation for Walter.

"As soon as possible," I demanded.

"Yeah right," he exclaimed, finally looking into my eyes. "The guy is booked until the summer and then he spends most weekends in the Hamptons. Why don't you just email me with all the details, and I will work on it in the meantime? Whom did you say you work for, again? Which publication?"

Before even contemplating a realistic editorial, I blurted out, "*The Gotham Post.*"

"*The Gotham Post?* Huh. I don't know. They don't usually write up the nicest stuff about Walter."

FUUUUUUCK. What the hell are you thinking?

"But my piece wouldn't be slamming the mayor," I lied.

I could feel my face turning red in anxiety. Not only would I have to expose a potential cheating scandal, I'd have to somehow get *The Gotham Post* to be on board with me freelancing for them. All this after I get his staff to let me interview him.

Jimmy handed me his business card and I handed him one of my made-up reporter ones.

As we were exchanging information, the town car pulled around to get Walter. In his gray wool coat, the mayor scurried out and successfully avoided the press. I caught his eye and the look he gave back to me was stale, yet a bit flirty. I didn't know what to make of it.

Changing out of my heels and into my flats, I decided to walk crosstown. Reporters and cameramen still hung around the U.N., most likely just to delay going back to the station or preparing for their news-at-noon live shots. The fresh air and sunshine felt good while I paced myself back to the Port Authority.

I dialed Adam to let him know my ETA back to Hoboken. He had gone back to record the press conference for me so I could analyze it more thoroughly and from different angles. While waiting for me, he had been doing some digging of his own. I wanted to skip when he told me that Piper was getting a house in Montauk for the summer with her girlfriends. She had apparently posted it all over her social media.

"She has Instagram pictures of herself with three other girls with the hashtag "Montauk Summer 2015" under it," he revealed.

"We have to infiltrate her social circle," I said while crossing Lexington Avenue. "I need a mole."

"How about April!" he immediately suggested.

April was unemployed, after all. At 31 years old, she was having a hard time finding a new job and was presently living with her mom in Westfield, New Jersey. We became friends during my first year at United America News. We were assigned the same local beat those first six months. She was a rookie at Eyewitness News 8. We bonded while covering shootings, thefts, parades, and elections. That is until my career really took off and I got to cover bigger news stories. After those six months of working side-by-side, we weren't seeing each other out in the field anymore. Our friendship, however, remained strong. She stayed at Eyewitness News the entire time I was at UAN, but was laid off last summer due to budget cuts. It's been seven months and she still hasn't been able to find work.

"Hey, do me a favor and find out what the annual tuition is for out-of-state students at UC Santa Barbara. Also, books, dorms, pretty much all those expenses. I'll be home in hopefully 30 minutes," I ordered Adam as I continued my trek west.

I needed to find out how much they were paying the school for tuition. Since Victoria seemed ill-informed about her own finances, I needed to find this out for myself.

The morning felt like two days packed into four hours. If I were a napper, I would've been back in my bed as soon as I walked in my door. Knowing that I risked doing a half-ass job of anything if I continued to do work, for the sake of my body and mind, I took the rest of the afternoon off. I'd review the video tomorrow. I could work 24-7 if I wanted to, but if Nancy Drew took some downtime to hang with the Hardy Boys, I could do the same once in a while.

I decide to throw a mini dinner party and invite Taylor and April over. It would give me a chance to spend time with my friends and also gauge whether April would be cut out for being my mole.

The doorbell buzzed precisely at 7 p.m. I knew it was April because she was just as punctual as I was. It must have been a news thing.

"Coming!" I yelled.

My hair still dripped from the shower and had made the back of my Burton Snowboards T-shirt wet.

"What the hell?" I blurted out. "What happened to my brunette, Italian girlfriend?" April had colored her hair to platinum blonde. She looked like a Playmate. "Are you auditioning for *Playboy*?"

She walked in and ignored my question at first and handed me a grocery bag filled with Italian specialties from her parent's restaurant like eggplant raviolis, chicken cutlets, stuffed shells, and bread. And of course, a bag of orange-cream sugar wafers, which I planned on hoarding for myself. She walked over to the kitchen and poured herself a glass of the Cheverny.

"I just needed a change. I thought that the brown hair was getting a bit dull. Maybe someone would be more inclined to hire me if I were a hot blonde like you," she said, taking a sip and smiling in my direction, although I wasn't a true blonde; I was a light brown-haired girl with highlights.

"Girl, please...who cares what color your hair is? You could be bald and it wouldn't matter because you're smart and sharp as hell," I said.

I topped myself off with wine and we both took a seat on the couch. I turned on the news in hopes of catching the evening broadcast.

April stared out the window. I had a feeling she was regretting her blonde bombshell decision.

"Oh, April. It's not that bad. It brings out your blue eyes. What did Jordan say?"

Jordan, her devoted boyfriend, had to have hated it.

"He says he always liked the brown," she said, looking down into her wine glass. "I think he is upset because he thinks I need to change something about myself to be liked."

He's right.

Jordan and April became friends in college. They both attended Rutgers. She was the editor for the school paper and was doing a story on whether one can die from a broken heart. As part of his pre-med curriculum, Jordan was volunteering in the cardiac unit of the Rutgers University Hospital. She did an interview with him, because she couldn't get one of the real heart surgeons to talk to her. They were all "too busy." Jordan offered his knowledge and that's where the connection initially started. They remained friends through the remaining years and through her rookie years as a reporter while he was doing his residency in Philadelphia. Then, when he got hired at Lenox Hill Hospital in the city, they reconnected and so did their hearts. It was quite the love story, especially since it started over a report about broken hearts.

April and I continued to catch up while waiting for Taylor. Right as I was about to evaluate April's potential interest in working for Vixen Investigations, the doorbell started obnoxiously buzzing. It was Taylor's eager ring.

"Hellooooo...." Taylor exclaimed as she burst through the door.

"What up, girl?" I replied from the couch.

She placed her reusable grocery bag stacked with pans of her vegetarian specialties on the kitchen counter. We watched in amazement as she pulled out tray after tray of red lentil pasta with peas and tofu, roasted Brussels sprouts and cauliflowers, a vegan coconut truffle dish, and gluten-free brownies she picked up at the overpriced Simplicity market.

"How the hell did you get all this over here?" I asked as she poured herself a glass of wine and came over to join us.

"It wasn't hard. I thought I was going to drop it getting on the PATH, though. The door started shutting on me. I could've lost an arm trying to save the food! A nice hot guy helped stop the doors, though," she described while acting out the almost horrific scene.

Picturing busty Taylor running to the subway in her kitten heels while carrying two grocery bags and yelling "hold the door!" made it hard for April and me to contain our laughter.

"So, tell me more about this big case you're working on," Taylor asked before shoveling a heap of vegan pasta in her mouth.

She, too, knew very little about the new investigation. I was purposely keeping silent about it because I didn't have enough hard evidence and I didn't want to open the door to assumptions or outside opinions just yet.

"It involves the mayor. That is all I can tell you guys," I vaguely stated.

"Oh, come on, Paige! You can't say that and not give us even a tiny hint of what is going on," Taylor whined.

"Taylor, stop...you know I can't do that. With the last case, I didn't care. It was small potatoes. This is a huge deal for me. Anything involving the mayor can be dangerous," I snapped.

I stood and walked over to the windows. I could tell it was a cloudy night because I couldn't see the spire on the top of the Freedom Tower.

"I'll fill you in, in time."

"Well, if you need any help, let me know. I'm not working so I have plenty of time," April finally offered as if she had anticipated me needing her.

"Thanks for understanding. It's not like me to feel this anxious about a case. I just have a lot at stake." I went back and took a seat with my satiated friends.

In trying to change the subject, I switched gears to have them fill me in on their love lives. Taylor was still single and loved every minute of it. She embodied this constant jovialness, which made it hard not to be around her. She was a magnet for guys but usually brushed them all off. Of course, there were a few assholes I had to help her put in their place. Taylor and April were like my test dummies for Vixen Investigations before I even knew I would launch the business. I helped Taylor get over two breakups in the past seven years and April with the one right before she and Jordan got serious. I felt like I had gotten so good at combating heartbreaking jerks. In realizing this superhero-like quality I had, I started paying extra attention to the conversations of men and women when out in public. About 90% of the time, they would be talking about a relationship gone awry. Once, while I was sitting in a Starbucks working on a brief for one of my first crimes of the heart cases, I overheard a group of girls behind me talking. One was sobbing about her boyfriend, saying, "I found these texts on his phone. He was flirting with another girl and they were sending nude pictures back and forth. When I confronted him, he denied it. He said it was just porn being sent by his friend." When her girlfriends asked her if she was going to break up with him, she said no because, "I love him too much and he promised he'd delete the girl's number."

And you wonder why he gets away with treating you like that, I thought.

Then, as if summoned by a Bat Signal, the Vixen Investigator in me turned around to advise the young girl.

"Did he call you crazy and place blame on you?" I asked.

At first, the three girls just stared at me. Then, the jilted one, named Abby, nodded.

"You need to pay attention to how secretive he is with his phone. If you find he is hiding it from you more, he's probably still receiving these racy texts."

"Well...what should I do?" the girl asked.

That's when the three of them got up and joined me at my corner table. They intently listened to my wise words as I instructed her one friend to text Abby's boyfriend and pretend to be "a girl he met at TAO a few weeks ago." My new pro-bono clients did as told, and a few days later I got an e-mail from Abby saying he took the bait. He was cheating on her after all so she dumped his ass. I was so proud of her for standing up to her deceiver and she told me she had never felt so empowered.

April and Taylor had grabbed their Ubers home. I clicked the kitchen lights off and took one last look out the windows and across to glittering Manhattan. Somewhere across that river someone was getting his or her heart broken.

MARCH, THREE WEEKS LATER

Mayor Wilcox's behavior to date has left me with very little suspicious evidence to go on. Though Victoria was adamant about his secrecy, at times I found myself worrying that I would come out of this with nothing but a bad reputation. Even sex appeal, which I considered a valuable tool in my trade, had failed to sway his press secretary. Several throws at him and I got nothing but a bruised ego. It wasn't until a few days ago that I learned Jimmy never would accept my advances because he's gay. While scouring the streets last Friday night in search of an open pizza parlor after some heavy boozing with my ex-NYPD buddies, I saw Jimmy making out with another man while they waited in line to get into "Out" nightclub. I nearly slammed into the back of a police cruiser at the sight.

Within the past two weeks, besides learning about the press secretary's sexual preferences, the only other big revelation was that the former New York attorney general, Henry Parker, was found dead of an apparent gunshot wound to the head. Investigators were quick to determine that he killed himself in his Bronxville home. Mayor Wilcox expressed his sympathies in a statement after having worked with the guy his first few years as mayor.

Now, when I wasn't digging for clues, I was spending more time with Liam. It felt exclusive and nice. If we didn't see each other, we'd talk on the phone. But, my reluctance to open up was starting to bother him. After countless dates, I still wasn't ready to have sex with him. It was the longest courting phase I've had so far without sex.

To take advantage of the warm March weather, I decided to spend the morning honing my aim at Duke's Shooting Range. I hadn't gone shooting in a long time and for some reason, I woke up with the insatiable urge. The mayor's agenda was clear today with the exception of an undisclosed dinner. Victoria knew that as soon as she found out where her husband was going to let me know.

I had alerted my ex-FBI contacts that I was heading to Dukes in hopes that they'd feel like meeting me. Not surprisingly, they had been there since 8:30 a.m. I consider my three shooting buddies, and former FBI Special Agents, my Vixen Investigation consultants. There was "Chin Chin," who got his name after capturing a notorious Chinese spy back in the '80s and "Mack," who got his name from being a real life "MacGyver." He could probably fight off a bear with a paper clip, a penny, and a lighter. And Mike, my ex-agent on speed dial. I met Mike early on in my journalism career and got to know Chin and Mack when I thought about joining the Bureau. It was the physical fitness requirements, like trekking through waist-high mud and carrying a 180-pound colleague on my back while running uphill, that ultimately deterred me. That's when I realized I was better suited for an investigative job where high heels, tight dresses, and cleavage would work to my advantage. Mack, Chin, and Mike were human lockboxes. It went without saying that any information I shared with them was highly confidential.

They also gave me sound advice like telling me "do it this way," "look for this," and "pay attention to the obscure." Chin would always tell me "the truth can always be found in what may not be so obvious."

"Paige!" I heard Chin yell, while I turned into the dirt lot.

Mike and Mack were prepping their machine guns and putting on their goggles when I arrived. There was nobody at the range except for them and the range guard.

"Good to see you again. It's been a while. We putting you on the M5 or the AR15 today?"

"Both!" I said, giving him a quick hug.

Chin escorted me from the Jeep over to the shooting grounds while filling me in on his wife and children. He left the agency one year ago, after 25 years working for them. His kids were off to college and he had more suburban dreams of opening a BBQ restaurant. Originally from Houston, he was stationed at the FBI headquarters in New York City most of the time, and ended up just settling and staying in central New Jersey.

"How is the business going? I always think about you whenever I read or hear about some sex scandal in the news. I always wonder if it was you who uncovered it," he commented.

"It likely was. I have been so busy. The last case involved one man and four women. Now, I am working on a case with a very high-profile client."

"That's a huge deal. Those are the cases that take a lot of bending over backwards," he added.

"It's my hardest case to date. There is only so much information and access I have to this guy. I have to rely on his wife and all his staff the most. It's already so frustrating."

Mack and Mike had already begun firing rounds when we approached. I shoved the earplugs in my ears, which turned the semi-automatic bangs into muffled pops. Chin said something to me, but I couldn't hear him. I just gave him a thumb up. The force of the bullet as it propelled itself out of the barrel of the gun was orgasmic. With the four of us all firing in synchronicity, I imaged that we were all part of the same SEAL team, shooting at terrorists and rescuing hostages. I didn't have the best firing form but still managed to hit the target about 75% of the time.

"Nice shooting today, kid," Mike said.

"Thanks, Mike. Not my best. I felt a bit off."

Mike was the oldest of the group. Retired after 30 years, he used to be based in L.A. before returning to the New York office. Mike has been calling me "kid" since he met me a decade ago. I guess I earned that title because of how obliviously immature I was trying to get information from the FBI for a story. He was the only agent who never told me to "get lost." Instead, he mentored me and helped clue me in on what to ask and how to address law enforcement. Though he was significantly older than me by a good 20 years and had kids in college, I used to fantasize about him. Maybe it was the way he resembled Harrison Ford in those *Indiana Jones* movies or the fact that he embodied everything that made a man super manly.

A few more rounds on the AR15, a beer and some advice on the "Federal Bureau of Infidelity"—as they liked to call it—later, I decided to pack it in and head back east. It was almost 1 p.m. I had neglected my phone the entire time. When I saw several missed calls from Victoria, I assumed she had learned where her husband would be dining later. There was also a missed call from the "unavailable" number with a new voicemail.

First things first, I called Victoria back. A frantic and eager first lady picked up.

"You told me to call you if I noticed anything suspicious," she blurted before either of us could give a proper "hello." "Well, a large amount of money has been withdrawn from our bank account again."

The excitement of a new clue seemed to impair my ability to operate the Jeep as I nearly swerved off the side of the windy and wooded road.

"Fifty thousand dollars. I logged on to our account summary. I never had really looked at the transactions before and that's when I noticed the amount today," she informed.

"Any idea on what is was for?"

"It didn't say. It just showed a negative sign."

"Have you spoken to Walter about it yet?"

"No. I didn't know if I should before talking to you. Plus, he gets irate when I bring up money to him."

That's unsettling. Why does he keep her so out-of-the-loop on their finances?

"Okay. Good job on not addressing it to him. I don't want him getting suspicious or lock the account. Copy and paste it in an email to me. Any word on where Walter will be tonight?"

"He said he wasn't going out anymore."

What?!

"I have one of my charity shopping events to raise money for ovarian cancer research. He said he'd stay home since I'd be out."

Bullshit. When the cats away the mouse will play.

Feeling defeated, I stepped on the gas. I had to get home. There was no way in hell he was staying home, at least alone, while his wife is out for the night. I texted Adam, alerting him, that we may need to stake out Victoria's and Walter's place for the night.

With Route 78 relatively empty, I let the Jeep gracefully increase its speed from 65 mph to 85 mph. I was cruising way above the speed limit.

"Play voicemail," I ordered the Bluetooth.

Now I was dying to hear what message this mystery person left me.

"Hello, Paige. You're quite the sleuth, aren't you?" The robotic voice reminded me of KITT from *Knight Rider*. "I know all about you. Do you think you're smart enough to solve this one? See you at Chez Régine at nine."

The phone clicked off and my heart pounded hard. My body tingled at the feeling that I was being spied on.

How do they know what I do? Were they trying to help me or throw me off course? Chez Régine? Tonight? What was happening there tonight?

My detective instincts told me I had to be there, regardless of what happened.

"Shit! My date with Liam!" I blurted out, having just remembered that we had a date. "It's Thursday! I can just move the location. He'd understand, right? If not, I'll just have to make him," I continued to converse with myself.

Chez Régine always required a reservation a month out. It was an upscale New York City restaurant that was nothing but hype. The food was lousy as I recalled going on a really bad date there once with a man named Pierre, who I needed to let wine and dine me for some inside information on his brother, with whom he co-owned the family Champagne business. Pierre's brother-in-law hired me after he found a duffel bag full of BDSM paraphernalia buried in the couple's closet. Raymond, my client, was devastated at the thought of Lucas (Pierre's brother) cheating on him after all they went through to get their families to accept their gay marriage. I had learned from Pierre—after I let him fuck me—that Lucas was involved in an underground BDSM ring in Chelsea. So, I went undercover as a leather-and-chain-wearing sex kitten, let some Goth chick named Selena slap my ass with a paddle and tickle my nipples with a feather, all to find out that Lucas wasn't cheating on Raymond at all. Lucas was secretly teaching classes on the correct and safe way to whip and torture someone for sexual pleasure. I took my sore ass and findings to Raymond the next day.

It was almost 2 p.m. now and I was getting closer to Hoboken. Certainly Liam had the evening all planned out. Hopefully he wouldn't feel too emasculated if I changed them on us.

"Chez Régine reservations. Can I help you?" An elegant, French-sounding woman picked up the phone.

"Yes. My name is Paige Turner. I am calling to confirm my reservation for tonight."

"I'm sorry, what did you say your name was?" I could sense a hint of snobbery in the female voice.

"Paige Turner. I made the reservation about six weeks ago. I told the hostess I had a very important Hollywood executive in town and needed one of those really private tables in the back of the restaurant."

It took the girl a while to respond again. I could hear her flipping through pages of a book.

"I'm so sorry. I don't see anything reserved under that name for tonight."

"I'm sorry? Are you serious? I booked this over a month ago. How does something like this happen?"

"I'm not sure. Whom did you speak to?"

"I don't know. Another woman. I told her how important it was that we come to Chez Régine tonight because my guest is French and she was very accommodating. It's a billionaire movie investor's favorite restaurant."

There was a moment of silence before she placed me on hold. *My act better work.*

Restaurants as high profile as Chez Régine typically call you to reconfirm reservations. If I could make them feel like they goofed, then it upped my chances of us getting a last-minute reservation. Danny had attempted this with me once on Valentine's Day and it worked! He had surprised me by coming home early from one of his sketchy business trips, but we had no reservations. He pretended that he held a table for two at Yoko and got the hostess to admit that she lost the reservation, even though we never really had one. It was sneaky, but successful.

"Ms. Turner. I'm so sorry about the confusion. I don't seem to have a reservation for you, but I will make one now. Please plan on coming at nine as requested and we will have a table ready for you. We are very sorry about this."

Ha, the Vixen Investigator succeeds again!

Feeling overly confident with my skills, I stepped on the gas even more, pushing the Jeep to its limits while deliberating the mystery phone call and who it might be, as well as the $50,000 withdrawn from Victoria's account. I was eager to find out where that money was going as I waited for Victoria's email. It sounded like Walter was "pulling a Danny"—a term I use when I suspect money fraud, cheating, and pretty much any kind of suspicious activity.

When I finally got back to my apartment, Adam was already inside with all my spy gear out and ready to go. Since I couldn't be certain the mayor would be at home or at Chez Régine, Adam and I would have to split up for the night. The plan was for him to start watching Walter's digs at 6 p.m. while I went to the restaurant at 9 p.m. as instructed by the anonymous phone call.

"Won't Liam become suspicious if you're barely talking to him and paying all your attention to Walter?"

"Adam, who do you think you're talking to? You know I'm the queen multitasker."

"What if it's a setup and someone is out to get you? I think you should bring your gun."

Adam's concern was appreciated and cute at times, but sometimes he gets a little too overprotective as if he were my boyfriend. Speaking of which, I still hadn't discussed the plans with Liam. Surely he had reservations for sushi by now.

Adam left shortly after gathering what he needed for later tonight while I hopped into the shower. I could tell by my assistant's reluctance to get close to me that I was in desperate need of washing the stench of sweat and smoke from my body. I placed my phone on the corner of the sink.

"Text Liam," I voiced. With my hands filled with suds, I scrubbed my face while the phone pulled up Liam's number.

"Hi, Liam," I started. The phone began inscribing my voice. "Can we go to Chez Régine tonight instead? A good friend had to drop her reservation and wants to give it to us. Such a good place. Let me know." I finished with beads of water running into the sides of my mouth. "Send."

Thinking I had spoken as concise as possible, when I looked down at my phone, what was actually sent to Liam was nothing but nonsensical garble. Liam had actually been sent a message that read: Hi Lime can we go squeeze tonight instead egg good friend has to drop her inclination and wants to give to us such a good ace.

"Fucking technology!" I quipped. "What is the point of this dictation feature if it can't even translate right?"

I dried off my hands and face to call him instead but Liam had beaten me to it. He must have been so confused because he was calling me back within what seemed like two minutes.

"So, ignore that last text," I said as soon as I answered.

Liam laughed. The steam from the shower was fogging up the mirror to where I couldn't see how much I was blushing.

"I thought it was funny. I had no idea what you are talking about. So I just figured I'd call you. What's up?"

"That's what happens when you try to dictate into your phone while your face is covered in soap. What I meant to say was that my friend got us a reservation at Chez Régine in SoHo for tonight. Would you mind if we went there instead? She had to cancel her reservation and if she does it last minute, the place will blacklist her. It's a really good place," I cringed internally knowing how much of a lie I had just told.

Liam agreed and we planned to meet there right at 8:55 p.m. *Now that that's all sorted out, what the hell am I going to wear?*

"CASE REOPENED: Feds now looking into foul play in death of ex-NY AG," the headline of the *Gotham Post* read.

I had a good two hours to kill before leaving to meet Liam and I had yet to read the paper I lied about freelancing for.

Odd. They were so quick to dub it a suicide.

According to reports, Parker's family just didn't buy the conclusion and hired a private homicide detective of their own, who was none other than the world-renowned Dr. Michael Bradnon. I had interviewed him numerous times. If anyone could get to the bottom of Parker's death, it was Dr. Bradnon.

A buzz on my callbox.

Who could that be? I wasn't expecting anyone, was I?

"Coming," I yelled.

I heard some rustling from outside and through the peephole I saw that it was Victoria.

Victoria?

She was holding a manila folder in her hand and was donning her Chanel shades and a Tahari shearling coat.

"Victoria? Hi? What are you doing here? Is everything alright? I thought you had a charity event tonight."

She didn't answer until she was completely inside my apartment with the door closed. She handed me a file and walked over to the couch but didn't remove her coat and sunglasses. I quickly flipped through the papers in the file. It was a credit card statement. There were lots and lots of charges on one particular credit card. It was evident that Victoria definitely liked to shop: $12,000 at Bergdorf Goodman, $3,000 at Chloe, and then the $50,000 withdraw she mentioned. Except, it wasn't a withdraw. It was a transfer to another account.

"Sorry for just popping by like this and looking like such a wreck," she began, although even sans a hint of makeup, she was gorgeous. "I wanted to bring you that statement personally rather than email."

"Don't worry about it at all, Victoria. I am going to hold on to this. I need to check some of the numbers."

I didn't want to alarm her to the fact that Walter hadn't taken money out, but rather moved it somewhere else.

Was he paying someone for something?

"Do you know if Walter linked this account to any others? Your daughter's or an emergency account?" I asked.

I paced while Victoria continued to stand as if she knew she wasn't going to be staying a while.

"No. At least, I don't think so. Like I said, Richard and Walter are usually dealing with our personal account."

"Okay. I'll look into this. Do not say anything about this to your husband. Don't even bring up the subject of money," I ordered.

Victoria agreed and walked back out to meet her driver. Even more questions raced through my head. The figures couldn't prove anything except that he was possibly being financially unfaithful, as well. Walter could be embroiled in a gambling or prostitution ring. Or, maybe he was just making secret investments? It could even be as innocent as charitable donations or college funds for Piper. It was just too soon to tell.

I was putting the finishing touches on my evening attire, which included diamond stud earrings and Vixen Red lipstick, when

I could hear Adam's ring tone repeatedly going off in the other room. Worried that something big may be happening, I hurried to pick it up.

"What's up? Everything okay?" I asked in slight panic.

"Yes, yes. It's very quiet. It looks like Victoria just left for her event. There's something else, though. I got a phone call from that mystery number," he began.

My eyes widened and I straightened up as the hairs on my body did the same. The caller said a bizarre riddle like the ones I had been getting. It said to him, "What's green, destructive, and something even Superman can't combat?"

Kryptonite!

I was jolted back to the very first text from that anonymous number that read "kryptonite tiger."

Whoever was texting us somehow knew Adam was working with me. But how did they get his number?

I instructed Adam not to answer his phone should he receive a call from that number again. I also ordered him to go home for the night. I didn't want him staked out by himself any longer, especially when deep down, I knew Walter was going to be at Chez Régine.

Adam obeyed. In the meantime, I had gone from being early to running late for my date. I quickly finished painting on my face, gathered my belongings, and threw them in my clutch and made my way out.

As I inched my way in the Thursday night traffic, I decided to dictate another follow up email to Jimmy. I spoke into my earpiece as the phone typed away.

"Dear Jimmy. Following up about that one-on-one interview with Mayor Wilcox. Would love and appreciate a response ASAP. Please let me know when you would be available to chat. Thanks. Paige Turner."

"Send," I ordered the phone. It made a "whoosh" sound and off the email went.

The chances of a quick response are slim.

My eyes went from phone to tail lights in front of me and back down to the phone as traffic continued to crawl. I scrolled through the rest of the emails I had ignored all day. It seemed like endless emails from suspecting lovers.

Just as I was about to turn out of the tunnel and into Tribeca, one last email caught my eye. The subject line read, "Gotham Post Meeting Request" and it was from a girl named Connie Carter, Director of Communications.

Dear Paige,
My name is Connie with *The Gotham Post*. I spoke to Taylor Jackson about a piece you are working on and I would love to chat with you about it. Please let me know if you can meet next Tuesday.
Best,
Connie

Tuesday? That's less than a week away! I quickly typed "YES" without even bothering to check my schedule. Anything already booked that day would just have to be canceled.

When I got to SoHo, I did a lap around the block in hopes I'd find a parking spot. With no space big enough to park the Jeep, I settled on a nearby garage. It was the perfect night. At a mild 50 degrees, walking around outside was actually quite nice for mid-March.

As I neared the brick-faced restaurant, I replayed the mystery phone call in my head.

Why would they tell me the restaurant's name if something weren't going to happen here tonight?

I thought about what Adam had told me, too. Hopefully the phone call didn't frazzle him too much. I needed him on his A-game.

From the outside, Chez Régine looked like an old brownstone. That is, until you walk through the entrance's curtain, down the narrow stairs, and into the dark and cool dining room. The trick to handling stairs as narrow as a granola bar while in heels was to walk on a sideways angle. It was the only way to maintain balance and ensure that the entire foot was on the step. As awkward as I felt I looked, I didn't need to fall down the stairs and expose my privates to strangers like I did one night at Cellar Bar last fall.

My successful descent led me to a skinny hallway where, if it weren't for the hanging candelabras, I would almost need a flashlight to find my way to the hostess.

"Welcome," she said. She sounded like the same woman I spoke to on the phone earlier. "Your name?"

"Reservation should be under Dempsey. It's for nine. I am a little early."

The reservation wasn't under Liam's last name; it was under mine. I needed to figure out a way to distract her so I could get access to that seating chart for a minute.

"I'm sorry. I am not seeing anything under Dempsey. Are you sure it was under that name?"

"Yes. I am sure it is under that name. I made the reservation a while ago and was even called to confirm it."

The hostess searched through the list again with a puzzled expression on her chiseled face.

"Okay. Let me just check through some of the notes and emails here. Maybe it got deleted."

"Deleted? Please don't tell me that. I had a reservation." I pretended to get a bit more worried and angry as the hostess became more nervous and flustered. "Can you get your manager? Maybe he can help you."

She hustled to where I assumed her manager hid for the night, in between greeting guests and asking how their dinner was. As soon as she was out of sight and the coast was clear, I popped behind the desk and scanned the computer to see the seating arrangements. My eyes widened with excitement when I saw Mayor Wilcox was on the list and he was sitting in one of the corner nooks!

I knew it! I had a feeling he would be here!

Liam and I were slated to sit in what would've been the worst spot for me.

This won't do.

I clicked and dragged our names so we would be sitting next to him. Now Turner would be sitting next to Wilcox. Just then, the sound of clicking heels returned from behind a wooden door. I jumped away from the computer.

"Mrs. Dempsey..."

Did she just call me Mrs. Dempsey?

"I am sorry. We are trying to find your reservation if you can just bear with us."

"You know what I just realized. I think the reservation may be under my name and not my boyfriend's. Check under Turner, Paige Turner?"

With a smile of relief, it took her no time to find my name.

"Here you are! Your second party isn't here yet but I can seat you if you'd like," she offered.

I agreed right after making one last stop at the lady's room. I had this reoccurring feeling all evening like I had to go to the bathroom. It was either a UTI or those nerves again.

Stop being so nervous. It looks like I have a rash.

I could tell in the mirror that my rosacea was acting up, again. Maybe ignoring it will make it go away. I powdered my chin and nose to try to take away some of the shine, and pressed hard on the bags under my eyes.

"Please go down," I said.

The woman in the neighboring stall let out a cough as if to signal that she could hear me. I didn't care.

Tonight could be a game-changer. What if Mayor Wilcox shows up with another woman? No way. He's too smart for that.

"Ms. Turner, Mr. Dempsey actually just arrived and has been seated. I can take you over now," the hostess said when I emerged back from the lady's room.

I was surprised to see that he was a good fifteen minutes early himself.

Punctual and a Jersey boy. Could it be?

I was never the type to play the "fashionably late" game and I didn't like it when others did it either. It's incredibly rude. In fact, it was hard for me to be late to anything. The latest I'll ever let myself be is on time.

I followed the skinny hostess in the black wrap-dress through the dining area. We weaved through tables and around stone columns like a mouse in a maze. I swore there were hidden passages and trap doors in this place.

What is it with restaurants having dark and dungeon-like basements as if they were smuggling goods or something?

Goosebumps shot up my body as my exposed right leg accidently brushed by part of the cold, stone wall. I was curious as to what scandalous and seductive things used to go on down here. Surely there were stories to be told.

She took me by the mayor's table that was still empty. Three chairs surrounded the round table. It would be hard for anyone to spot him in the almost closed off area except for the person sitting directly across from him. It happened to be Liam. His already rosy cheeks brightened more when he saw me. He looked handsome as always in his navy blue slacks, gray button-up, and a matching sport coat. He stood up and gave me a hug and a kiss on the lips. I loved how wanting he was of me. Even in my high heels, I still needed to elevate myself a little to meet his lips.

"It's so good to see you again. It felt like a long week without you," he said while still gripping me in his arms. I looked up into his green eyes.

"I know. It's been quite a week. I was surprised to see you here before me. I was running so early and just needed to get out of my apartment."

He pulled my seat out for me and together we sat down. His smile lit up the room. I could feel my insides bubbling up. Perhaps I was anticipating a little lovemaking later or I really was falling for him.

"Thanks for changing the plans last minute. I know you wanted Nobu," I said.

The tap water on the table tasted and smelled like the streets of New York City. I quickly put it down.

"Don't worry about it, babe. I'm sure there will be other opportunities to go to Nobu. It's not that big of a deal. In fact, next time, I'd love to cook you dinner," he said and kissed me on my temple.

He had left his hand on my thigh after positioning his chair closer to mine. I felt like a virginal 14-year-old on her very first date. Usually, I wasn't into public displays of affection, but I guess our PDA compatibility was too intense to fight.

"How was your day today? What's in the news?" he inquired.

"It was fine."

Insert awkward cough.

"Just a lot of writing and stuff."

Lie #1 of the night. I was shooting guns all morning with some ex-FBI friends.

"I can't wait to read some of your writing. You should write about a Jersey boy and a cute Jersey blonde with a sexy smile, meeting in a bar after her friend blew her off..."

"Oh yeah? And then what happens?" I teased.

"Then, they fall madly in love and live happily ever after," he finished and kissed me again. His lips felt like warm, satin pillows.

We continued our heavy flirtation while I continued to watch for any signs of Walter. Liam got even more revealing and began delving into his past loves and his dreams for the future. He told me about his ex-girlfriend who cheated on him with his best friend. It made him bitter and resentful towards all girls that he became a serial player for a minute. He was quick to realize that what he wanted wasn't sexual affairs, but a girl he could "grow old with."

"So, Miss Turner. When are you going to show me around your neighborhood? You keep talking about your view. I want to see your place," he said. The sudden change of topic threw me for a loop.

"In time! I'm very picky about who I bring back to my place," I said and gave his hand a squeeze.

I could sense the disappointment he was hiding on his face. The truth was, I couldn't bring him back to my place, have him see my spy gear, the War Room and everything else that might reveal my business before I even told him what I really do for a living. What if he saw my high definition monitoring screens, case files and collection of interrogation and criminal profiling books?

"Okay. I can respect that. Eventually you'll have to or I'm going to think you're hiding like a family or bodies over there," he joked.

I kissed him playfully on the cheek. We stared back into each other's eyes right before I watched him look over my left shoulder.

"Hey, isn't that the mayor?"

I snapped my head around and let out an uncontrollable gasp.

Right you are. And I must say, I am pretty impressed he was able to spot him before me.

Surely enough, it was Mayor Wilcox and he was with two men who were both wearing big cowboy hats. The same hostess was escorting them to their designated table. Luckily, nobody else in the restaurant seemed to recognize him. When his two companions spoke, I could tell they had heavy Texas-sounding accents. From their mannerisms to their hair, thick frames, and jovialness, it was clear these men were brothers. Their giddiness proved that the three of them had to have been drinking already.

What was Mayor Wilcox doing with two Texans? They're definitely friends…or new business partners?

I kept watch on Walter's table while managing to keep the bulk of my attention on Liam. I didn't want to come off distracted or uninterested. The mayor and his chums have been here only fifteen minutes and had yet to notice me. Hopefully he was drunk enough to where he wouldn't, or even better, would forget about the hard time I gave him at his press conference.

"I'll have to bring you to the house to meet my mom and brothers the next time I go there. She's been asking about you," Liam said as I nearly choked on my croquette.

Bring me home?

"Aww, that's sweet. Hope you told her good things about me." *Whatever he was telling his family must have been a lie since I haven't even been completely honest.*

I smiled and reached for the bottle of Bordeaux, which was starting to hit us rather hard. The combination of passion and nervousness I was feeling was counterintuitive. I worried that perhaps I had fallen victim to the "love at first sight" scenario, which I knew was risky. I found myself going against my own advice as I meticulously detailed in chapter seven of my love manual.

The Vixen Investigator was in the midst of a new challenge: eavesdropping while under the influence of good wine and intense chemistry. While he continued to whisper sweet words and graze my arm with his hand, I covertly kept my ears and eyes on Walter's table. They were on bottle number three of Pinot Noir. I couldn't make out exactly what the men were talking about.

"Something, something, something, Dallas, something, hotel, something, something, Lucy," was all I could comprehend. I had yet to hear him say Victoria or Piper.

Liam had summoned the waiter over, signaling that he wanted the check. He was ready to leave, but I wasn't. I was determined to come out of this night with some damning evidence. So, I did what any private infidelity investigator would do.

"Mayor Wilcox!" I yelled just loud enough to get Walter's attention. Liam looked at me with a stunned expression. "I'll be right back."

I gave Liam a kiss on the cheek, untied my leg from his, got up and wandered over to their table.

"Hello, Mayor Wilcox." I leaned over the table to shake his hand. He looked just as surprised as Liam. His evening companions stared up at me with big grins over their face. "I've been sitting right over there with my boyfriend and I thought you looked familiar." I turned towards Liam and gave him a little wave. He had just handed the waiter back the signed bill and was getting up to come over to me.

"Miss Turner. I thought that was you. I guess I am just not used to seeing you outside your typical newsgirl character," Walter stated in a somewhat condescending tone.

Who is he calling a newsGIRL?

"Join us for a drink. Your boy toy, too. We are just about to order another bottle of this 2013 red."

It was definitely the alcohol doing the inviting. I couldn't imagine a sober Walter ever inviting press to join him on a night out, especially when that press is I.

The men scooted around in the oblong booth so that Liam and I could squeeze in on the end. The night was turning into the unexpected and I was convinced Liam wasn't used to being thrust into situations like this. He remained quiet at first, most likely out of fear or confusion.

It's not every day you go on a date with a private investigator, only to end up sharing a $1,200 bottle of wine with the mayor of New York City.

Liam seemed to warm up and relax right after we cheered to a "fun and wild night." During the round of introductions, I learned that his two friends were Rodney and Richard Roche, two oil tycoons from Fort Worth, Texas. I acted pleased and indifferent to meet them while I really questioned their connection to the mayor, who was actually heading to Dallas with them in the morning. The trip was not listed on his schedule for the week. It was either being kept a secret or it was a last-minute getaway. None of the men said why he was going down there. All I got was a "business negotiations" response when I inquired.

The four men chatted like old friends. I knew it was getting late, as we were now the last five people in the restaurant. While my company discussed the losing Knicks and new high-rise apartments on the West Side, I furtively studied my phone under the table. I had missed calls and texts from Adam, Taylor, and April. They were wondering how the night was going.

"What are you looking at, love?" Liam asked and jolted me back to the current time and place. He had caught me looking at my phone.

"Just the time, baby. I'm kind of getting sleepy," I politely replied.

"She's probably checking her emails! The girl doesn't have a life. She's always working," Walter interrupted.

"It's like all women these days. They should be home taking care of the kids and cooking dinner," Rodney blurted out.

Richard and Walter laughed in agreement. Liam shot his gaze back at the mayor and forced out a smile. I could tell it hurt him to do so. A Jersey boy in nature never lets another man insult his woman. In any other situation, I'm sure he'd uppercut a man in the nose for talking like that.

"Well, I can tell your wife does A LOT of cooking for you," I snapped back at Rodney.

Walter and Richard burst out laughing. They knew I was referring to Rodney's massive indulgence gut. My snarky response even got Liam and the passing waiter to giggle.

"You're a feisty one. Don't mess with this girl! That's why I love New Yorkers and being the mayor of this city," Walter arrogantly stated while aiming a wink directly at me.

Dinner finally came to an end around midnight. The five of us stumbled out of Chez Régine. I didn't think any of my male companions, including Liam, would be able to make it home without a stop at the ICU to get their stomach pumped. Since I had switched from wine to water two hours ago, I had sobered up and decided to go back to my home and put Liam in an Uber back to his place. We all stood outside like an awkward date determining how to say goodbye.

"You folks sure you don't want to go out for another round?" Richard loudly offered right as their giant tinted Suburban pulled up.

"Nah. I think I have to call it a night, boys. I'm ready for bed," I said as Liam continued to drape his arm over my shoulder.

"You know. I think you have the right idea, sugar. Fellas, I'm ready to go to bed with Paige too," joked the mayor.

My stomach churned. Liam looked down at me through the corner of his eye as if to ask, "Do you want me to kick his ass for you?" I had to play along. The fact that Walter would make such a comment in front of my boyfriend showed just how careless of a man he was. So, in an effort to tease and give the mayor a little something to remember me by, I made sure to give him a little cock-grab during our hug goodbye.

"Whoa, now. I hope you didn't take my comment that serious. But if you're interested..." he whispered into my ear. I slowly pulled myself away from the hug and gave him my fake "I want you" eyes.

"Goodnight, sir. Looking forward to working with you," I smiled and returned to Liam.

"You're welcome in Dallas anytime!" Rodney yelled just before shutting the door of the taxpayer-funded car service.

Anytime?

The air felt light and crisp, like right after a day of showers as Liam walked me to my car. I grabbed his hand and gave it a little squeeze.

Did the mayor act like this all the time? Did Victoria have ANY idea he was like this? Should I even mention the way he acts with me?

The questions raced through my mind as we approached the garage. Conflicting thoughts ransacked my brain as I went through all I had heard tonight, and at the same time I was experiencing a surge of chemicals I hadn't felt in a long time. Despite being in a parking garage, that didn't stop Liam and me from engaging in clothed and vertical sex acts against the Jeep. He had me up against the driver's side. I could taste the fine wine on his lips the more intense his kiss became. With one hand grabbing my lower back and the other on the back of my neck, he pulled me even closer. With every light grind against my pelvic region, I could feel him getting even more excited.

This is the worst possible time for this. He's drunk and you're in a parking garage and now you have to get up super early!

"I should let you go," I whispered.

He didn't budge, just let out a little moan. I gently pushed his hands down and off my hips.

"What?" he innocently asked. "Are you okay?"

"Yes...I'm just...I don't want to do this, yet."

"I'm sorry," he said, taking a deep breath and releasing me from his grip. "You're right. This isn't the time or the place."

"Soon," I said and gazed back into his hazel eyes.

He came in for one deeper hug. With my face smashed against his North Face jacket, a huge part of me didn't want him to let go.

You smell like cookies and puppies.

We took one more kiss before parting. I watched as he walked out to the street and into his Uber. How could I feel so elated and overwhelmed at the same time? It was a very successful night. I owed that mysterious caller a bit of gratitude for tipping me off to his location tonight. Whoever was feeding me hints obviously wanted the mayor to be caught...doing something.

I should've been more tired than I was at 1 a.m. driving home. Perhaps I was still revved up from the night. Getting closer to the Roches would be key in my investigation. As the mayor's friends and business partners, they had to know stuff about him. While I pretended to be distracted on my phone at one point in the night, I overheard them talking about money, real estate, and oil. It made sense to me now. Mayor Wilcox had investments in the Roches' oil and real estate businesses. It was apparent he was sitting on a pile of money that Victoria had no idea about. He was, at minimum, having a financial affair.

As I pulled down into the garage under my apartment, I heard my iPhone vibrating intensely from inside my clutch. Expecting it to be Liam wishing me "goodnight" when I saw the word "Unavailable" on the screen, I nearly drove straight into the garage wall. My heart raced in anticipation of the text.

Unavailable Mobile (1:13 a.m.):
How was dinner? Fun boys aren't they?
Hope you have a good pair of cowboy boots.

Dinner? Cowboy boots?

Shivers ran up and down my spine. Whoever this was knew that I had ended up eating with the mayor. While still locked inside the Jeep, which was now parked underground, I dialed Adam. After four tries he finally answered.

"Adam! You won't believe the night I just had," I gushed. "I'll explain it all tomorrow morning on the flight."

With the exception of a faint groan like I had just waked him, Adam remained quiet.

"I need you to book two tickets to Dallas ASAP, leaving tomorrow morning, first class, any airline," I requested. "I would do it but my phone is about to die and I'm not up to my place yet."

"You're still not home? Can't wait to hear about the night. I'll forward you the flight info as soon as I book it," he muttered.

Maybe it was the anticipation of Dallas, the mystery caller, or learning that Adam charged nearly $9,000 on two first-class tickets to DFW that sent my insides into a tizzy. I was still without a plan of what I was going to Dallas for and where I was specifically going to look. Sometimes not having a plan puts me in a better spot in the end. I was just so confident that shadowing Walter away from the confines of The Big Apple and his administration could reveal some juicy information.

"What's the matter? You look rattled," Adam observed while shoving his carry-on as much as he could under the seat in front of us.

Watching him maneuver his bag made me realize I had forgotten to pack underwear and a toothbrush. I looked at him.

"I don't know. I can't put my finger on it. Maybe I'm still in shock over the flight costs, tired or...maybe it's just something else."

"What did you want me to do? We're lucky there were seats left," Adam defended.

"It's not the money. I guess my intuition is trying to tell me something and I can't figure out what it is. Like it's saying 'Don't go' or 'You're going to find out something huge.' "

We sat back in our cushiony leather seats that cost me $4,500 each. As people continued to board, I quietly detailed the night to Adam. In code, I told him about seeing the mayor at the restaurant and drinking with him and his Texas friends. I felt inclined to leave out the part about me grabbing Walter's junk and Liam and I getting hot and heavy in a parking garage. Adam tended to cringe when I brought up using sex to bait an alleged suspect, but understood that seeing the mayor in a state like that and getting new assets for the case is like finding a leprechaun standing in a patch of four-leaf clovers under a rainbow. It's hard to get that lucky.

Four hours and 34 minutes later, I was awakened by what I thought was violent turbulence, or perhaps a terrorist on the plane. To my relief, it was Adam's aggressive shaking.

"We're here, Paige. Can't believe you fell asleep."

I didn't remember much from the flight. I must have passed out right after takeoff. Even Adam knew how rare it was for me to fall asleep on a plane. I always liked to designate myself as the onboard air marshal should anything happen, like the captain passes out or someone tries to storm the cockpit.

"What has Liam done to you?" Adam sarcastically asked.

I turned my head slightly towards him and gave him a groggy glare.

Adam and I bolted off the plane as soon as we got the green light from the crew. I always insisted on sitting in the first three rows of the plane with a carry-on under our seat—not over our heads—so we could always make a quick escape.

"Where exactly are we going?" Adam asked while hustling behind with his Herschel backpack slung over his shoulder.

"Not sure yet. Those Texans I told you about live in Fort Worth and work in downtown Dallas. I think I'll just have a cab take us to The Westin Dallas Downtown for starters."

The Texas sun was scorching hot as we stood outside waiting in the taxi line. I was not as prepared for this kind of heat in the middle of March and neither was Adam. We were both way overdressed in our morbid black fashion that New Yorkers knew how to rock so well. I could feel the beads of sweat penetrating my dark gray T-shirt, I quickly shed my leather bomber jacket and threw it in my tote. There was absolutely no breeze and the sky looked a bit ominous. Every now and then, a whiff of cow dung—from feedlots nearby—would waft through the air.

"Welcome to Dallas," the cab driver said with a deep Texan drawl. He immediately came around from the driver's side and with a tip of his Stetson, proceeded to help Adam and me with our bags.

"Thank you, sir. We're heading to The Westin Dallas Downtown," I kindly stated.

"The Westin it is. And please, call me Chet," he ordered with a smile as big as my forearm.

Chet held the door open for us as we climbed inside and he ran back around to the driver's side.

"I'm Paige Turner and this is my assistant, Adam McKay. Nice to meet you, Chet."

We were now cruising towards Dallas. Chet was quietly humming to the tune of Toby Keith playing on the radio. Remembering that the Roche brothers had given me their business card, I dug around for it in my purse. Buried underneath my Ray-Bans and a reporter's notepad, I pulled it out. As torn up as it was, all I cared about was that the phone number was still legible. I immediately texted the number in hopes of a quick response.

Maybe they were here by now. That is, if they made it out of New York City.

Less than a minute after hitting SEND, Rodney's name appeared on my screen to signal his incoming call.

"Rodney, baby!" I answered. Adam quickly looked up at me from his laptop.

"Paige Turner. You just couldn't get enough of us Texans that you had to fly your pretty self down here," he boasted.

His voice was so loud through the phone I thought Chet would be able to hear the entire conversation.

"You bet. I told you last night that I was also heading to Dallas today. You offered me a ride on your jet but I told you I didn't think you'd actually make the flight because you guys drank so much," I lied.

I knew I could tell him anything because the likelihood of them remembering was near impossible.

"Wow, I had way too much to drink. I don't remember any of that. I remember you being really pretty in that blue dress. And you had that boy with the funny accent with you," he continued.

"Ha, you better watch what you call 'funny.' That's New Jersey, for your information. I was hoping we could continue that excitement this weekend while I am in town. What are your plans for the weekend?"

It wasn't the case of actually wanting to hang with the guy, I needed to; he was a treasure trove of information.

"Well, we have some meetings today. Then probably going to the Mavericks game later if you want to come. We have a suite at the American Airlines arena."

"That sounds perfect! What time is the game?" I exclaimed.

Basketball was a sport, so naturally I hated the idea of wasting hours of my life watching really tall men run back and forth trying to throw a ball into a net.

"My assistant and I are staying at the Westin Downtown. How about you send us a car so we don't end up late?" I subtly suggested, thinking he probably would.

I turned to Adam, who had been watching me speak with Rodney the entire time. His eyes widened at the sound of "Mavericks," especially since they were playing the New York Knicks tonight. Adam had a child-like obsession with Carmelo Anthony and held a nerve of resentment towards me for busting the former coach in a cheating scandal two years ago. It was rumored that former Coach Darvey was sleeping with the wife of the star player on the Golden State Warriors, Antonio Rush. The Warriors' owner hired me to conduct an infidelity investigation. It was one of the easiest busts of my career in vow enforcement, as Darvey took no caution in trying to hide his affair.

After hanging up with Rodney and with a glowing Adam by my side, we flipped through some of the pictures I had snapped so far of the mayor and categorized them. We both observed how Walter seemed to pal around with the same men, all the time.

As we were going through the pictures, I felt an intense vibration coming from my phone, which had fallen in between my legs. It was Liam.

"Hi, baby. I was just thinking about you," I answered. My face got warm and I could feel myself blushing like a little girl crushing on her first boy.

"I was thinking about you. I had to take the day off. I am so hung over."

His voice was scratchy like he had an oncoming cold. In a way, it made him sound sexier. We chatted briefly. I knew I had to keep it short. He had no idea I was in Dallas.

"I'm thinking tonight...you come over, we watch Netflix, I cook you some meat or pasta," Liam started before I quickly cut him off.

"It's really not a good night for me. My assistant and I are neck deep in material we need to go through for this ca...I mean story I am working on," I interjected in the most sorrowful voice.

"Oh...okay. I didn't realize you even had an assistant. How about Sunday?" Liam continued while trying his best to hide his suspicions.

"Sunday is fine," I agreed. There was a brief moment of silence, as if he wanted to ask or say something more, but didn't. "I hope you feel better. If I were there, I'd help nurse you back to good health," I teased.

"Ha, alright, alright. Enough or I'm going to have another problem in my pants," he joked. "Have a good day."

We hung up just before approaching the hustle and bustle of the downtown area, or at least what's considered a hustle in Texas. The buildings were far from what I considered skyscrapers.

After dumping our luggage in our suite, we decided to hit up a local BBQ favorite nearby. There was a food truck within walking distance from the hotel. It had to be good given the line and the aroma of barbequed meat, which was downright intoxicating.

"So, what's the plan for tonight and tomorrow?" Adam asked, breaking the silence. He took a big sip of his lemonade.

"The Texans I met last night, they're good friends of Walter's. They know stuff, Adam. I can probably get them to divulge even more. The one seemed to really love me."

"Well, who wouldn't?" Adam sarcastically replied. "I'd be concerned you were losing your game if at least one of them didn't fall for you by the end of this."

"I'm sure they'll treat us very well here. I got you into that game tonight. No other boss would do that for their staff, F-Y-I."

My unexpected gift to Adam gave me a sense of relief for dragging him down here so last minute. He didn't say it, but I knew he would be missing his first rehearsal with his old band that had been contemplating performing together now that all the musicians were out of college. I caught an email exchange between him and three of his bandmates. They wanted to bring back their old hit songs like, "I Knew from Day One," "Rainy Day Swell," and "Manhood." Knowing I made him miss that and he didn't even give me an ounce of complaint verified once again how much of a saint Adam was.

The car that Rodney sent to the hotel arrived right on time. Adam was ready and waiting for me inside the suite while I threw all that I needed for a good night of fun and snooping into my purse.

"How does my ass look in this skirt? I haven't worked out in a while," I asked just as I stepped out into the living room, where Adam looked worrisome at his smartphone.

"Everything alright? You look concerned."

Adam looked up, not realizing what I said. He didn't say anything, just held up the screen of his phone. I walked over and grabbed it from his cold hand. Within the two hours after finishing our late lunch, he had been texted three times from the "Unavailable" number again. The first text asked how the flight down was.

How did this person know we had arrived?

The second text asked if I had fucked a Roche yet.

What was this person implying and how did they even know my scheme?

The last text simply said, "See you tomorrow."

See you tomorrow?

I switched off his screen. I was becoming too creeped out. Adam seemed a bit uneasy himself. We vowed to ignore the texts; I refused to let fear slow us down.

It was first class all the way from the moment we got into the Mercedes town car to being escorted up to box 53. The Roches had the suite's fridge stocked with beer, wine, water, and Pepsi, which gave the impression they were expecting a packed suite. Rather than wait for the suite attendant, I popped a bottle of Albariño and poured myself a nice hefty glass. There was a large leather couch, a generous-sized closet that smelled like oak, and framed pictures of the Roches with Mavericks players hung on the walls. There was also a flat screen TV for those who wanted to watch the game from the comforts of the couch. I took a seat just behind Adam in one of the private stadium seats.

At every mini break, Adam and I strategized our mission for the night once the Roches arrived. No matter how much planning we tried to do, it would be hard to get a sense of where the night might end up. When I told Adam that I might have to go home with one of the brothers, he wasn't the least bit supportive. In fact, he tried to tell me it wasn't necessary for me to sleep with "everyone" for the sake of work. I took a slight offense to his comment but decided it was better to let it go than attack his insult. I just knew that with the Roches being such heavy drinkers, it would be simple to seduce some information out of them.

It's amazing what you can get from a man in exchange for legs, a butt, and the potential for sex.

"Did you miss us?!"

A loud voice yelled from the entrance. Adam and I turned sharply to see Rodney and Richard burst into the suite like two raging bulls. Rodney was also holding a bottle of 2006 Screaming Eagle Napa Valley Cabernet Sauvignon, valued at over $1,000, in his hand like a water bottle. As annoyed as I was that they made us wait nearly an hour, I did my best not to show it.

"I was starting to think you boys left us hanging," I stated.

According to them, their wives were giving them a hard time for going out when they had already been gone all week. Even though they were married, the Roche brothers came across as forever-bachelors.

The second half buzzer blared and Adam and Richard hustled over to the edge of the suite to catch the remaining game. Meanwhile, the suite waiter brought in more BBQ pulled pork, chicken sliders, some kind of cheese and rice dish, and baked beans. I could barely even stomach looking at the food but Rodney had no reserves about piling his plate high with the cuisine.

The Roches were getting louder and more inebriated as the night wore on. There were only two minutes left in the game and the Knicks had somehow brought themselves up from a 22-point deficit to now being tied at 110.

Please, I need overtime. I've got nothing new from tonight, so far.

Rodney left the other two and was heading towards the refrigerator. I quietly got up from the couch and followed behind him. When he opened the door, I snuck my hand around him while making it a point to let my breasts press up against the back of his arm. It made him jump.

"So, are you surprised to see me here?" I said in a near whisper.

"Hey, pretty girl, I am so happy you are here," he said in his deep Texas drawl.

He put his heavy arm around my shoulders as if I was one of his long-time buddies.

"Last night was a blast. Liam is still recovering back home. I had no idea you were so close with Mayor Wilcox. What's the scoop there?"

With his arm still draped over my shoulder, I led us both back over to the leather couch. He plopped down fast as I slowly and seductively removed my blazer.

"It's really hot in here," I said despite the goosebumps on my legs.

Rodney blatantly looked at my breasts with his glazed-over eyes. I could sense his arousal with my busting C-chest. I placed my cell phone on the coffee table in front of us, which I had inconspicuously placed on record.

"Walter? Yeah, we go way back...money stuff. Probably a good twenty years."

He put his arm up behind me to either stretch it out or try to pull me in closer. I smiled and batted my eyes in a welcoming gesture. The way he spoke of their relationship made it seem like they had a very long history together; probably even longer than Victoria knew.

The Knicks had successfully scored enough points to lock in overtime. I looked over at Adam and Richard, who were sitting and chatting. I turned my attention back to Rodney.

"How far back do you go with the mayor?" I asked while casually putting my hand on his knee.

I proceeded to take a sip of my water and puppy-dog eye him. Rodney glanced down at me through the corner of his eyes with a look of intrigue.

"Wait a second, girlie. Aren't you some reporter chick? How do I know you aren't doing some kind of undercover story on me? I think you need to sit on my lap and make me feel a little better."

My insides churned as I inched my way onto his lap with a forced smile. I could feel his bulge harden a little.

"Undercover? Please. I'd like to get under your covers," I joked. "Plus, I have a hard time faking anything in my life."

Rodney let out a childish giggle like he'd never been teased before.

"I was only kidding. I like you. You're a smart little cookie. You ask a lot of questions. I never would've thought that about you," he rambled and took a big swig of beer.

"So, you were talking about how you know the mayor? I'm just so intrigued." I ran my fingers up and down his arm teasing him to the point of nearly getting him fully erect.

While continuing to caress him, he spilled some more about what Walter was like before he became mayor. Rodney revealed that he would come to Dallas a lot because he was looking to invest in the oil industry. He bought a large plot of land not too far from where the Roches lived—just outside Fort Worth—that was ripe with oil and gas. The Roches helped him with the purchase, mineral rights, production, and all the rest of the necessary arrangements. He couldn't help but add that Walter likes to get out of the city as often as he can. When he said, "Walter likes being the mayor and all, but for him, the role is more about power."

My blood boiled hearing such details but I stayed sitting on his lap.

"Why does he keep serving if he hates it so much?" I asked, with my arms now wrapped around Rodney's neck.

I could tell the game was ending after a loud roar from the crowd and then the buzzer blared again.

"He's got way too much to lose. That's for sure," he said.

Too much to lose? What was he talking about?

"I told him to come and hang tonight, but he is back at the house with..."

WITH?

And, just before Rodney could finish telling me who the mayor was "at the house with," Richard and Adam came rushing over to fill us in on the game and completely info-blocked me.

"Sorry, New York. You lose!" Richard boasted before crashing down on the couch next to us.

Damnit! I was so close to getting a major clue.

I looked up at Adam, who was visibly inebriated. My alone time with Roche informant number one was officially over. I shimmied myself off his thighs and stood up.

"Hey, give Carmelo a break. He's just coming off a sprained ankle," Adam rebutted.

"Is Melo's ankle to blame for Lopez's greasy hands?" Richard replied.

While the two of them continued to analyze and fill Rodney in on what he had missed, I snuck out of the suite to give Liam a call. He was either ignoring me or asleep. I decided not to leave him a message. I couldn't stand the idea of him having a taped lie of mine on his phone.

Just as I clicked off my phone, a stampede of basketball fans came swarming out of the suites like water through a broken levee. I pushed my way through the hordes of people to make my way back to the Roches and Adam, who were knocking back shots of tequila.

"Hey, fellas, let's go somewhere else!" I loudly suggested.

"Hell yeah! Let's go to Giddy Up for some line dancing and bull riding," Richard announced before tossing his empty crystal shot glass into the air and sending it over the balcony.

"Sounds great. Pour me one of those, will ya?"

I proceeded to grab one of the glasses and Richard topped me off. I knew I'd have to be more intoxicated to deal with these boys for the rest of the night.

Oh my God, I'm paralyzed... and blind!

It was the first thought that entered my head waking up the next morning. I tried fluttering my eyes open but the mascara from the night before had glued my eyelashes together. I continued to analyze my surroundings to reassure myself I was back in my hotel room, alone in bed and not covered in vomit. I couldn't remember anything after shot number four of Patrón in the Suburban.

I forcefully turned my stiff neck to the other side of the room. The fluorescent green light from the digital clock showed 9:45.

9:45?!

I couldn't help the sensation that I was running late although I had nothing to be late for. I guess the idea of sleeping until midmorning even on a Saturday seemed wrong. Having succeeded in lifting my heavy head off the pillow, I peeled myself off the queen-sized bed, carefully positioned my feet on the floor, and stood. I could feel the stiffness of my leather miniskirt, which I had apparently slept in. My shirt was off but my bra was still on. I reached my hands to my head and pressed on my temples while moving the skin in a clockwise direction.

My phone!

The instant panic made my head throb as if I was just hit with a metal baseball bat. I scanned the room. It was nowhere to be found and the blurriness from leaving my contacts in all night didn't help, either. Everything I recorded, from my chats with the Roches, photos, and who knows what else were on that phone. I dumped out my purse which was already half spilled out on the floor. I searched under my bed and everywhere else I could think of. The room was a mess.

Did I bring anyone home last night? Why is the lampshade hanging on the doorknob? There's no vomit in the garbage. That's either a good thing, or a bad thing. I'm never drinking again.

Then, I found it. Right below the doorknob on the floor was my cell phone. My heartbeat returned to normal. I could see from the cracks in the blinds that the sun was going to be strong today.

Where is Adam??

Panic ensued yet again. I went next door to his bedroom. He wasn't there. I bolted to the living room, hoping he was passed out on the floor, at best. Stunned, he was sitting upright on the couch, curtain and blinds open, and looking bright-eyed while dressed in his Ralph Lauren polo khakis and navy boat shoes. He was on his laptop too. There was a heavenly aroma coming from the kitchenette. It was the coffee he had brewing and the breakfast sandwich he had ordered from room service.

"How the hell are you up before me?" I grumbled while sloth-fully making my way to the coffee pot.

"You don't remember anything last night, do you?" he asked, matter-of-factly.

"Uh...No."

This can't be good.

I went over and sat next to him with a hot cup of caffeinated goodness in my hands. He smelled nice and clean, like lavender soap, while I could only imagine what farm animal I smelled of. Adam hit the slideshow and the pictures of the night before started cycling through. One-by-one, there were photos of me riding the mechanical bull in my bra and skirt with my thong sticking out. Those were preceded by images of me making out with Rodney, me screaming at some girl, and then taking more shots.

"I don't even know how to react to this," I commented.

Adam was failing at his attempt to hold in his laughter. The brothers looked even more plastered than me in the pictures.

"You and Rodney then left for a little bit. I didn't know where you went, but you were back in about 45 minutes," Adam continued to detail.

Forty-five minutes? Did we hook up? What the hell happened?

After Adam alerted me to the fact that I had disappeared with the one brother, I quickly went for my phone. I had yet to analyze it and thought maybe there would be evidence on there. I opened up the photo gallery to some new pictures of Rodney and me. There were at least 30 selfies of us kissing, smiling, and making stupid faces and one of me pretending to strangle him. There was also a new audio recording on the phone that was taken about the time Rodney and I disappeared for that short while. I must have remembered or accidently hit record on my phone when we were alone.

Still sitting next to Adam, I replayed the audio. There was country music playing in the background. Then, Rodney and I could be heard talking and there was the occasional sound of lips smacking. It sounded like there was a lot of flirting going on too. "Things really are bigger in Texas, aren't they?" I heard myself say, followed by some giggling.

"Wow," I said to Adam.

What we heard next was what really stuck with me. It was I saying, "I want to do an exposé on Walter and his family." Then, Rodney responded with, "You need to do a book on his family life, not an exposé."

A book? His family life didn't seem that complex. What was he talking about?

It took all morning and afternoon to feel like myself again. Adam had to continue to fill me in on some of the details throughout the day, in addition to how I committed us to joining the Roches at their house this evening for a barbecue. I must have also demanded a ride to the party because promptly at 5 p.m., we were being whisked away in a town car. While eating more barbecue in the hot sun was not that inviting to me at the present moment, I was anxious to see how these men lived and if Mayor Wilcox would be there.

When the car rolled up to Rodney's compound, a massive security gate and a large stonewall surrounding the front of the property prevented us from going any farther. It was the type of wall you'd expect along the Texas-Mexico border, not someone's house. There was a sign carved into the stone along the gate that read "La Casa De Roche." The driver punched in a code and, like magic, the gates opened and up the driveway he went. Adam and I each stared out our windows in amazement. I was more taken by the level of security surrounding the place than the opulently manicured landscaping. Cameras, locked gates, codes: it was beginning to feel like I was entering the grounds of Pablo Escobar.

No wonder Walter likes being around with them so much.

A guard stood at the entrance, ready to take us through the marble-floored foyer. From there, we zigzagged through the kitchen with its oak cabinets, double oven and brass cookware hanging from a large rack overhead. We were then led outside to a beautiful patio and an in-ground pool. People, casually dressed in polos and khakis, were scattered about. Rodney and

Richard were easy to spot. And, standing right with them was Mayor Wilcox and to my surprise, Comptroller Brownstein.

What's he doing here?

Richard yelled in our direction and summoned us over with his big, Sasquatch-like hand. I gave Adam a little nudge and we proceeded over to the group. With my head held high and a "nice to see you" smile plastered on my face, I greeted everyone. Mayor Wilcox didn't appear as open and friendly as he did two nights ago at Chez Régine.

"Why if it isn't Paige Turner. Reporting for duty down in Texas? What brings you down here?" Walter questioned while raising his voice slightly as if to demonstrate he still had authority over me.

"Hello, Mayor. I take it you don't remember anything from Thursday night?" I hinted while reaching out to shake his hand.

It was a slow and firm shake, as if he was trying to tell me, he remembered.

"Oh, I remember bits and pieces. Mostly the good bits," he slyly said with a perverted smile.

"Let's get you both something to drink. It's rude to not have a drink in your hand. But, I think we better keep Paige away from the tequila and any mechanical bulls," Rodney joked while grabbing me around the shoulder to escort me to the bar.

I could feel myself sweating underneath my white T-shirt and denim pleated skirt. The sun beating down on the stone heated the patio another ten degrees, at least. The poolside bar had just about every kind of top-shelf liquor I knew of, and more. A busty blonde girl who looked like she was still in high school was behind it serving the drinks. She poured me a glass of Sancerre and I tipped her five dollars.

We walked away. I wanted to bring up the night before to learn a little more about what the hell happened. Instead, I decided to rave about his castle-like home with the Venetian columns in the front, the marble floors, gold-finished moldings, and Italian fountains along the sides of the house.

"Eh, the house needs updating," he responded. "I just try and please the wife. It is all her doing. Well, not *all* her doing, I did pay for it. She just decorates and all that crap. Oh, I need to introduce you to her first."

Rodney's constant quick-changing thoughts made me realize that not only was he obnoxious and a womanizer, he apparently had ADD. I followed to where his wife was standing with a few of her other friends, who could've all been clones. The majority of the women at the party were over-tanned blondes, with lashes the length of my pinky, lips the color of Valentine's Day, and all were sporting some of the biggest diamond rings I've seen this side south of 47th Street. They were obviously all wives of oilmen, or men with money, in general. Pamela was the prettiest of the group, who also happened to be Rodney's wife.

"Pam. This is my buddy, Paige, from the big city. Say hi, Pam," Rodney ordered.

His Barbiesque wife came in to give me a big hug as if I was a long-lost cousin.

"Nice to meet you," I forced out.

"It is a pleasure to meet your acquaintance, Paige. It is just like my dear Rodney to pick up complete strangers and turn them into his best friends," she gushed. "So what brings you to Dallas?"

She batted her butterfly lashes at me and smiled. Her teeth were so white, I thought they could light up the night.

"It was just the funniest thing. I was coming down to gather some information on a story I am working on, on the best cities to travel as a single girl, and figured I'd connect with your husband, as I am sure you all could offer me some help."

The lie came out like silk and naturally she took the bait.

"I'd LOVE to help you with that. Dallas is great and there are some amazing men in this state. I mean, just look who I snagged," she exclaimed with such exuberance I wanted to barf.

Oh Pamela, he's not that much of a catch, if you ask me.

Pamela didn't look like an angel herself, though. She had this "I'm doing the landscaper" kind of vibe about her.

"Yes, you really lucked out with Rodney. They don't make them in New York City like they do down in Texas."

"Speaking of New York, our good friend has a place up there in the Hamptons. Do you ever go? We love it," Pamela continued.

The women all nodded in synchronicity.

"Yes, of course. The Hamptons are the place to be in the summer. Where is your friend's place?"

"I'm not sure," she answered, before turning to her blonde friend. "Betty, where's Lucy's place?"

Lucy?

I turned to Betty too, but before she could answer, Rodney and Richard came sneaking up to the group like a wrecking ball to pull their wives away. All the other women then scattered faster than a billiards table.

Wait! Who is Lucy?! Damn.

Two hours into the evening and the men were now much louder, the women more catty, and I more bored. Adam had made some new friends and was shooting hoops with them on the opposite side of the house. I assumed they were husbands of the other women. I stood by the table strewn with veggies, cheeses, and crackers and continued to keep my eyes on the mayor and the comptroller. I took a few secret snaps of them on my camera phone as a way to document their existence here. There were some other women and kids who had arrived and were now scattered throughout the property. Brownstein had one woman standing next to him who looked familiar. There wasn't much touching or kissing going on between the two of them. When Walter walked away from the group, that's when I made my move after him. He was heading for the bar.

"Mayor Wilcox?" I said as I moved in closer.

His cold demeanor proved that talking to me was the last thing he was interested in doing. For some reason, he didn't want it to look like we knew each other.

"What happened the other night...the way we were all acting...that's all off the record. Ok?" he said as he took the Dewar's on the rocks from the server.

Walter's tone sounded more like a threat than him asking for a favor.

"Of course, Walter," I hesitated. "You've known me long enough. I'm not into selling myself out just to get some exclusive details for a smutty rag," I said and gently touched the back of his upper arm.

He grinned. We slowly walked away from the bar and back to the buffet table, where nobody stood. Walter carefully selected the red and yellow julienned peppers while avoiding the green ones. The snap of the pepper in his mouth sounded like a rubber band smacking against bare skin. I could almost feel the sting just thinking about it.

"However, I do have a proposition for you," I began. "I reached out to your press secretary a while ago about doing a feature on you and the family. You are the city's favorite mayor, after all," I ass-kissed.

"Really? Jimmy didn't mention anything."

That asshole!

"Interesting. I'll have to follow up with him then. Anyways, I want to do a feature on you, Victoria, and Piper. I'd write about your family, your home, your relationship, your mayoral affairs..."

"Mayoral affairs? What does that mean?" he interrupted almost in defense.

"Like the day-to-day of being the mayor of the greatest city in the world."

I smiled and he relaxed his shoulders again while boldly putting his hand on my lower back.

"Email Jimmy. Tell him I'm down," he said.

He let his hand graze up my rump before heading back to his group. I stood there watching him haughtily walk away as if he had just bedded the hottest Cowboys cheerleader. Then he suddenly stopped and turned back towards me.

"Who did you say you are working for now?" he asked.

"I didn't. *The Gotham Post.*"

My heart raced as the words exited my mouth. I knew how he felt about the paper.

"I'll tell you the truth, Paige," he said while swishing the ice around in his drink. "I could really use a nice write-up about me and the family. It seems like all I get written up about is bad stuff. The last thing I need is a reporter looking for dirt on me. You understand?"

I stood and took a few steps towards him until we were eye-to-eye again. I put my hand on his shoulder.

"Oh, Mayor Wilcox. We both know there's not a speck of dirt on you," I stated while already contriving my attack plan in my head.

I winked and smiled again. He reciprocated with the same look. We were now friends. At least he thought we were.

11

Tuesday the following week and I was back to the daily New Jersey-New York City grind. I felt ready and eager for my meeting with Connie and another executive from *The Gotham Post* today. Coming off the impromptu trip to Dallas, I now felt I had uncovered some more hidden secrets of dear Walter. A lot of people knew him down there. It was almost like he was harboring a second life, but then again, just having a group of friends in another city doesn't mean anything.

"Hey, Tay. I'm heading over to meet with Connie right now. Any advice on how to approach this woman?" I decided to give Taylor a call for some last-minute guidance on what to expect.

Taylor let out a few phlegm-clearing coughs. It was 1 p.m. and she was clearly still sleeping. Probably a late night press event.

"Well, she likes strong but not too pushy women. Women who can get an interview. She likes really big stories, so I am sure whatever you present to her, she will love. And if you expose a big scandal and her paper gets the exclusive, she'd be indebted to you."

Taylor's advice was constructive. The problem was, I couldn't tell Connie the story I was really working on.

"Just lie like you always do," Taylor surprisingly added.

"I don't always lie!" I refuted. "I embellish the truth—at times—to get the actual truth."

"Love you...good luck," she said and hung up.

I took a deep breath. I was still feeling anxious...for the meeting and to see Liam later tonight. It would be the first I've seen him since getting back from Dallas since Adam and I ended up staying later than we originally planned.

"I'm here to see Connie Carter with *The Gotham Post*," I announced to the guard.

He motioned me back so he could snap a picture, then handed my ID back and I proceeded through the metal detector.

Oh shit, my lucky pocketknife!

As expected, I was instantly asked to step to the side by not one, but two security guards. It was my lucky cheetah print pocketknife I bought with my dad at a flea market when I was a teenager. I carried it around with me on occasion because it was my first badass purchase. I watched one of the guards pull the knife out of my bag with his latex-gloved hand.

"Oh, that was a gift. I forgot I had that in there," I innocently stated.

"You can't take this with you. It has to stay here," the guard ordered.

As much as I wanted to grab it from him and run, I wanted to avoid making a scene.

"You can pick it up on your way out."

The guard handed me the stub and I continued to the elevators. It was just a young, pensive-looking man and me waiting in the lobby of *The Gotham Post*. He looked like he could be vying for an internship or his first job in news.

Every two minutes, I'd hear the click clacking of high heels echoing down the hallway. They'd get closer and closer and then fade away. I looked down at my Rolex: 2:13.

"Paige?" a forceful voice said.

It was Connie. She was a lot older than I imagined.

"Right this way, we can go into this conference room," she offered.

Her hair was long and the toll of decades of bleaching was clearly visible. She smelled like classic Chanel and I wondered why she wasn't retired down in Casey Key, Florida or at least working at *Vogue* instead of a rag like *The Gotham Post*. I took a seat at the large oblong table in conference room number four.

"So, how do you know Taylor," she started.

Should I tell her the truth or make up something?

"She is a good friend and colleague. She invited me to a press event of hers several years ago and that's how our friendship started," I explained. "And yourself?"

"I know her through a client she had featured in the paper during Fashion Week, once. This goes back years, but the girl is good at staying in touch, that's for sure."

I couldn't read if that was a good thing or a sign of irritation.

"To be honest, I typically ignore requests like hers, but I really did find your idea interesting. We rarely do soft stories on political figures. As I'm sure you know being a reader of our paper."

She stopped, swiveled in her chair a little and raised her hands to her chin as if she was rubbing an imaginary beard.

"But, I feel like we owe it to Mayor Wilcox. He is a pretty popular guy and gets coverage all over the country. Plus, we've been pretty rough on him throughout his time in office."

"Yes, *and* they live a pretty lavish lifestyle. I've seen their home uptown. I think if I were to cover him and the family in the right way, it would go over very well for your audience. They could either learn to hate him more for the money he has, or like him better when they get to learn about the family."

I felt like I needed a shower pitching myself like a used car salesman.

"True. Not to mention, I know about your work. You're quite the established journalist. I honestly wondered what had happened to you after you left UAN."

Rather than get into the grittiness of my exit at the network, I said a humble "thank you" and detracted back to the exposé on Walter. We went over my idea for almost an hour before Connie called in Juliet, another managing editor. After mapping it all out for them, including my ideas for the editorial and photo side, I was pretty confident in the fact that they were going to let me do the story for them. They even approached me with a rate of $5 a word, with a desired word range of 2,000 to 2,500. It was chump change to me, but that's not what I cared about.

Jay's Organics, my favorite vegan restaurant that was located on the corner of 6th and 14th, was the perfect place to rejuvenate my body with their fresh-squeezed "mental booster" juice. I still had some time before I went to Liam's place but not enough to go back home. The restaurant was rarely packed and usually quiet. Its bright and earthy ambiance also made it the ideal place to get some work done. I chose the seat by the window that looked right out to the intersection. It was the perfect place to people-watch the circus of sexy, nerdy, ugly, crazy, and flamboyant-looking folks who all came through this area.

While sipping my power juice, I got busy composing another email to Jimmy, who had been ignoring me still. Just after hitting "send," I noticed my cell phone signaling an incoming call. It was from an "unavailable" number. My heart raced. Anticipation, excitement, and a bit of panic washed over me as I thought perhaps I was going to be given another lead.

"This is Paige," I quietly answered, expecting to hear that robotic voice.

"Hi, Paige. Connie and Juliet from *The Gotham Post*."

Every muscle and nerve instantly relaxed, although I was a bit upset that it wasn't the mystery caller and surprised at how fast the paper got back to me.

"We discussed the idea with the rest of the team and we'd like to contract you for the piece on Mayor Wilcox," Connie announced with a hint of excitement. No matter how hard she tried to maintain that stoicism, I could tell in her voice that she was thrilled about the piece.

"That's great news! Thank you so much," I exclaimed into the phone.

"Fabulous. We look forward to your updates throughout the next few months and hopefully that July deadline works for you," Connie continued before I politely interrupted.

"Likewise, and I promise I can get you what you need and more within the allotted amount of time. But, there is one thing." I waited a minute as Connie and Juliet got silent. Perhaps they weren't expecting any demands from me.

"It's about my byline. I can't use my real name as the author of the piece."

Silence again. For an instant, I thought they had hung up or were waiting for more. I continued anyway.

"I can't get into why. It's a demand that I think is for the best for me and for the paper."

"If that is really what you prefer," Juliet said almost empathetically and surprised that I wouldn't want my name attached to such a piece. Luckily, they didn't ask any further questions and agreed to use "Gotham Post Staff" in the byline.

The pressure was on now and I had no time to wait around for responses from Mayor Wilcox's staff when I already knew that Walter was down for this. I was losing my patience with Jimmy and decided to give Walter's office a personal call. I took the last sip of power juice, gathered up my belongings and made my way outside. I didn't want anyone to overhear my conversation with the mayor should he actually answer his phone.

I found a quiet spot around the corner from Jay's Organics. The phone rang and rang and just as I thought I would be greeted by a voicemail message, an unexpected answer.

"Hello, Paige. You're relentless, aren't you?"

It was his press secretary. Jimmy had intercepted the call.

"Jimmy? I thought I was calling Walter's personal desk number."

"You did. But do you think he actually answers his own phone?"

That phony! Walter told me in Texas the number went straight to his personal cell if he wasn't at his desk.

"How did you know it was me?" I continued with my barrage of questions.

"Caller ID, sweetie," Jimmy answered.

I didn't appreciate his sarcastic tone. While still wondering how he was so quick to identify my digits, I cut to the meat of why I was calling. Without getting too into how and where I spoke to Walter, I told him that the mayor agreed to the exclusive for *The Gotham Post*. Jimmy seemed doubtful at first. That is until I lied and told him Walter said I would make a great press secretary for him one day. Perhaps Jimmy felt a bit threatened by me or realized that he wasn't dealing with any ordinary reporter. Whatever it was, he promised that he would get my request cleared in a "reasonable amount of time."

We hung up.

I win.

Things seemed to be aligning just as I needed them to.

I decided to walk from the restaurant to Liam's apartment, to buy some time. I didn't want to arrive too early. Just as I thought about stopping in Bittay's Wine Shop for a bottle of fancy red, the ringing of my cell phone caught me off guard. I pulled the cold phone from the purse and looked to see who it was. The word "unavailable" flashed on the caller ID. My heart raced a bit faster.

Connie again?

"Hello?"

I knew someone was there, but there was no response. I increased my walking speed a few paces.

"Who is this and why do you keep leaving me messages?"

"You're very inquisitive aren't you?" The robotic voice taunted. "How was Dallas? Abnormally hot this time of year, wasn't it?"

I stopped walking. Frozen, I stood in the middle of 36th street. I had the eerie sensation that I was being watched. I remained silent to force whoever was on the other end to talk.

"Do you like costume parties? I do. I know of one coming up. It's a hard list to get on. But, I'm sure you can make it happen," the voice teased.

"What party? Where? Hello?"

But, whoever was playing this game with me had hung up. The mysterious caller had yet to throw me off course. Whoever it was kept pointing me in the right direction...so far at least.

Costume party? What costume party were they talking about?

My walk turned into a soft jog as I texted Adam to research any upcoming costume parties. If it were a private party, it would be harder to find. There was a chance it could be listed on Plusone.com, the snobby party website where anyone who is anyone hopes to get their picture posted. It was the only way to prove you were at a VIP party, because we all know there is no proof without a picture, these days.

I turned off the phone and dropped it in my bag when I finally arrived at Liam's. It would take all my strength to not reach for it tonight.

The aroma of tomato sauce filled the air and only got stronger as I approached apartment 30SE. I delicately tapped on the door. Liam was shuffling around inside. His footsteps got louder as he approached the door. Before I knew it, there he was in the doorway with his rosy cheeks, green eyes, and perfect smile. The way the light shown behind him made him look Godly. He childishly pulled me inside and kissed me hard. I was now pretty sure we wouldn't be doing much eating.

His apartment décor spoke volumes. Just by the way it was decorated with photos of his family, his friends, and his deceased black Lab, it was easy to see that Liam was a loving man who valued his relationships. There were slight hints that he was a Jersey Shore boy, as he had randomly placed beach and surfing artwork hanging on the walls. The furniture was pretty standard for that of a bachelor, with the most important pieces being the large leather sectional and a mounted HD television. He had a variety of books stacked on one of his bookshelves, with everything from *The Art of the Deal* and *Killing Jesus* to *The Heroin Diaries*.

"Here, you choose what you want to watch," he said and handed me the remote.

I really didn't know what to put on. My instincts had me wanting to put on the 6 p.m. news or *Forensic Files*.

What's something Liam would want to watch?

"*Seinfeld*?! This is the best episode, when George stops having sex because he thinks it makes him smarter," he exclaimed from the kitchen.

"I went through dry spells and I never got smarter," I argued for fun. "Must be the opposite way for girls."

Relaxing back into the seat, I watched him pour me a glass of Pinot Noir. His apartment looked out to the East River and that iconic Pepsi Cola sign in Long Island City. He must do pretty well in banking to afford a place like this. The apartment had to have cost several thousand dollars a month. He sat down next to me and handed me the wine.

"What should we drink to?" he asked.

How about to the success of the mayoral affairs case?

"To us," I joyfully answered.

No sooner after we took our first sip were we kissing intensely on the couch. I could taste the marinara on his lips from him sampling it. Liam started undoing my blouse while pulling me on top of him. My tight jeans made it a bit difficult to straddle him, so I stood, slowly removed them, and resumed position. He gripped my lower back with his meaty hands and pulled me in as close as he could. I wrapped my hands around the back of this head and kissed him even harder. Without leaving his lips, I ran my hands under his shirt, down the sides of his torso and around to the back. I could feel every ripple of his six-pack. His pulse was racing as fast as mine as he began moving his fingers under my red laced underwear. His touch was electrifying. He continued to gently rub my upper, inner, and outer thighs before slowly working his way up to my breasts. He undid my bra. Now I was in nothing but a skimpy pair of panties. It was clear what we both really wanted: each other. I abandoned all the concerns I had towards him and gave in to my desires. I couldn't hold out any longer.

My eyes fluttered open to hazily see the time on the digital clock next to the bed: 7:20. I thought about the night that was. I was still smiling. Liam remained passed out next to me in what looked like a failed attempt to spoon me. He looked cute lying there with a little drip of drool streaming from his mouth. His cheeks were still glowing and I yearned to kiss the top of his bald head but I didn't want to wake him. I knew I had to get up soon; the thought of leaving his warm, comforting bed was unappealing.

I gently reached over his sleeping body to grab my cell phone on the night table. No missed texts or emails, just the calendar alert reminding me about my meeting with Victoria back at my place. I dropped the phone down onto the carpeted floor beside me and snuggled back under Liam's arm instead of getting up.

Just 5 more minutes.

"When can I see you again?" Liam asked.

We were both standing by the door. It was like he wasn't going to let me out without an answer. After two more rounds of morning sex, I was now running later than I'd wanted to. Liam had the luxury of going into work late and staying later. I did not. If it wasn't for Adam's repetitive calls, I'd probably still be cloaked in Liam's arms.

"I don't know. We'll figure it out. I'll see you when I see you," I teased.

"Ugh...I HATE when you say that," he whined.

I smiled, stood on my tiptoes and gave him a kiss goodbye. I'm sure he wanted to hear "tomorrow" or "whenever you're free" like I did, but I really didn't know.

I hopped into an Uber, which was waiting downstairs for me. As I stepped out of the building and into the sunny street, I was nearly blinded by the reflection coming off the East River. I had an hour to get home and look presentable for Victoria.

There was minimal traffic out of the city and I was able make it home just in time to change, comb my hair, and make a pot of coffee. My brain was still in a thick sex-fog when Victoria finally arrived. She looked stunning as always as she made herself comfortable in her usual spot on my couch before filling me in on her latest observations of Walter. According to Victoria, he was still acting distant. My ears perked up right as she began telling me of his anxiousness to get away to the Hamptons.

The Hamptons?

"Isn't it a little early for the Hamptons? It's not even April yet," I inquired.

Walter liked to head out to the Hamptons in the early spring to pick out their summer rental. It was tradition for Victoria to stay behind because Walter liked to go out there alone to find the summer home of their dreams and then surprise Victoria and Piper. I found the routine quite odd. If he was heading out there, that meant I would be too.

Victoria continued to elaborate on Walter's recent late-night office habits. Several mornings these past few weeks, she'd find him passed out on the couch with his personal laptop closed on his stomach.

Personal computer meant, personal server, which meant nobody had access to that information. It was the only place he could really have full privacy.

As we continued to sift through the latest findings, when Victoria handed me her latest credit card statement, my eyes were instantly drawn to three transfers of $20,000 to three different accounts. They were made through PayPal. Rather than alarm Victoria about my suspicions, I took the papers and didn't alert her to my concerns.

Following our meeting, I felt like I had a bevy of new information to go on. In addition to what Victoria told me, I was still on the lookout for any upcoming costume parties. The lead from the mystery caller was the only knowledge I had of it. Nothing was found on Plusone.com, Adam hadn't heard anything through his grapevine and neither did Taylor, who was always tied into the party scene.

While typing up notes and analyzing some recent headlines about the mayor, my cell phone started repeatedly beeping.

Rodney Mobile (1:15 p.m.):
See you soon, going to be up in the
Hamptons in a few weeks. You around?

Hamptons? Few weeks?
The out-of-the-blue text was a welcoming surprise. Surely if the Roches were out there, so would Mayor Wilcox.

Paige Mobile:
Rodney. I've missed you!
Is that an invite? Where you going to be?

Rodney Mobile:
East Hampton.
Party Time!
Will let you know.

Party time? Like a costume party? Change of plans.
Adam was originally tasked to become part of Piper's posse as her new "gay best friend" when she returned home for the

summer in a few weeks. That wouldn't work now. I needed Adam with me but also someone with Piper, 24-7. I couldn't ask Taylor or Theresa for they already had too much on their plate. There was only one other person who I could assign the mission to.

This is the perfect opportunity to bring April on board.

I was certain her boyfriend would have some reservations about her participating in my investigation where her task would be to act like a drunk and promiscuous sorority sister. April used to be a powerhouse drinker and partier when we were younger. That is until she and Jordan started seriously dating. She went from Robert Downey Jr. circa late 1990s to his sober, Iron Man days in a matter of days.

"I have a proposition for you," I said to April before even letting her finish her "what's up." "I'm going to be spending some time out in the Hamptons with Adam in the next few weeks. The issue is Adam was supposed to be my mole in Piper's social group. She is back from school in a few weeks...How would you like to be that mole? I will pay you," I offered.

With the exception of a few "huhs" and "okays," April didn't react much.

"Are you sure you want me to do this? I know nothing about the case except for what you told me. I'd hate to mess something up and then blow the whole investigation for you," she responded with hesitation.

"April, there's nobody more perfect for this role than you. Remember when you went undercover with those mob wives?" I encouraged. "I want you to work with me."

I could sense her mulling over my offer. But finally, and as I expected she would, April agreed to be the Vixen Investigation mole.

APRIL

I had been working myself like a race horse...and enjoying some quality time with Liam. We had nearly doubled our weekly time together. It seemed like we couldn't spend more than one day apart. Sex had become more intense and we were doing it so often—some days up to four times—I decided to go back on birth control. Even though I still hadn't opened up about Vixen Investigations, the relationship felt secure. At times, I'd pick up on his suspicions. Like, when he called me one night while I was staked out near the mayor's house. It was just after one in the morning. Adam was driving the Jeep while I snapped the pictures of Walter exiting his building through the loading area. Rather than ignore Liam's call, I answered. In the middle of our lovey-dovey conversation about him "not being able to sleep because he missed me," Adam started loudly commenting about Walter taking a file from a guy on the street. It was a rather thick file. Concurrently, the sound of Adam's voice in the background stunned Liam to the point he thought I was sleeping with another man! I blamed the noise on my loud neighbors, thankfully putting out that spark. Although he believed me and even apologized for making such an accusation, I felt like a complete asshole.

I've yet to find out what that file was that Walter accepted from the unidentified man on the street. All we could make out from those photos was that the man was short, stocky, and dark-skinned.

The month was nearing its end and the unseasonably warm spring seemed to have kicked many New Yorkers into an early summer mode. Weeks of stalking hadn't revealed anything new and the mystery caller still teased me about the upcoming costume party. It was the one riddle I had yet to solve. Until last night. Adam and I were analyzing and categorizing photos and prepping April on her tasks as my mole. After feeling like this costume party was nonexistent or we had missed it, out of the blue, I got an email with a subject line that read: INVITE: Lord Max's Annual Summer Kickoff Soirée. Right in the middle of the paperless post it also said "costume required" and it was taking place in the Hamptons this Friday.

Coincidentally enough, I already had plans on being in the Hamptons this weekend after Victoria alerted me that Walter was heading out there to find their summer home, as well. I now had a massive burst of energy knowing that in less than 24 hours, I'd be out in the Hamptons partying, spying, and hopefully accumulating some major evidence in the case against Mayor Wilcox.

By 8:30 the next morning, Adam and I were back outside the Wilcox home. Parked under a "No Parking" sign, I kept my eyes focused on the entrance of Walter's building while Adam kept watch for any cops. They say what happens in the Hamptons, stays in the Hamptons. Not when the Vixen Investigator is involved.

"My intuition tells me there are buried bones out there," I hypothesized to Adam, breaking the silence.

"And the earth always gives back. Isn't that what you always tell me?" he responded.

"Hey, I'm picking up on some movement in the window by the front door," I said while zooming the binoculars even more.

Then, as predicted, Walter made his way through the revolving door and into the tinted Escalade parked in front.

"There's our man," I exclaimed with composed excitement and handed Adam the binoculars.

Mr. Brownstein and a security guard also got into the vehicle. The security guard threw a bag into the back.

Not a lot of luggage for three men and an entire weekend.

"Adam, take a note," I ordered. "Suspects have no luggage. They may keep goods out there."

He did as told as we watched the SUV start to slowly pull away. I started up the engine but before putting the Jeep into Drive, I put on my Ray-Ban aviators and tipped my fedora a little farther down so it was slightly covering the corner of my eye. The goal: to look unrecognizable.

"Who do you think you are? Eliot Ness?" Adam sarcastically stated.

"Yup. And New York City's favorite mayor is my Al Capone."

13

From 68th Street and Park Avenue where we were held up, we were now heading east towards the Midtown Tunnel. It was right when we were crossing Lexington that I remembered Pamela Roche telling me about their girlfriend who had a house in the Hamptons.

"Their driver drives like a maniac," Adam observed.

The government vehicle weaved left and right in front of us. It looked as if it was trying to maneuver through the cars that were actually obeying the speed limit. Once we got through the tunnel and eventually onto the Long Island Expressway, the anxiety from the traffic subsided and my adrenaline was revving up. Walter's driver must have been doing at least 85 mph in the carpool lane. I lingered back in the right lane, doing 75 mph.

"Hey, listen to this." Adam was engrossed in a copy of the *The Daily Record* I had grabbed when we stopped for gas and coffee before heading into the city. "Lord Maximillian to host annual presummer costume rager at Water Mill estate tonight."

"Let me see that."

Adam turned the page towards me. Lord Maximillian, as he liked to be called, came from diamond money. His family owned several diamond caves in South Africa and he'd inherited the family business. He was a sleazy, aging 62-year-old with caps that were too white, skin that looked like a tangerine-colored catcher's mitt, and he always had blonde babes with him, even though he was gay. I've yet to find a picture of him where he doesn't have a beautiful woman on his arm. Adam and I both knew that this wasn't going to be some pinky lifting, classy soiree. This was going to be a balls and tits out, "pass the ecstasy" kind of event.

Nearly two hours later, and much further east, the Escalade began to veer off the expressway, towards Bridgehampton and right into massive gridlock. I managed to keep up with the speeding SUV and was rolling in the traffic just a few cars behind. There was no way Walter could speed off.

Blue lights started flashing from a little strip on the roof of the SUV. The vehicle turned out of the right lane, onto the shoulder, and continued going up the street and passing every other sucker, like myself, stuck in traffic.

"They can't do that!" Adam yelled. I looked at him and then back out the windshield. "He is way down there, now!"

"Of course he can do that. He can do anything he wants," I replied loudly while mentally trying to figure out what to do next.

Crap...

We continued to creep along with the other cars. I could see that the two young men and two young women in front of me in the BMW M3 were already boozing it up. The mayor's SUV was way out of sight, now, and I had no idea where they had exited.

Rodney! He must be out here by now.

When the line of cars came to a stop, Adam and I switched places so that he could drive and I could make my inquiries. I dialed Rodney. At first, there was no answer. But less than a minute later, he was calling me back.

"Rodney! You out in the Hamptons yet?" I answered with feigned excitement.

"Hey girly. I was about to message you. My bro and I are here. We left the wives at home. Needed some time away to see my Yankee friends!" he boasted.

I had forgotten how loud and irritating his voice was.

"What about Walter?" I pressed.

"Walter should be out there now or any minute. They left a while ago. I think he is with Dick," he continued.

Who is Dick?

After my barrage of questions over where they were staying, where they were going and whom they were with, I was able to piece together a plan for later. Rodney had given me the exact address of where they'd be in East Hampton and, as suspected, they would be at Lord Max's presummer soiree too. First stop, the East Hampton hideaway.

The one thing about the Hamptons and the eastern end of Long Island was if you didn't know the ocean was just a few blocks away, you'd think you were in the middle of some small town in New England. All the properties were heavily wooded, which made it a lot more difficult for me to spy from the street. Even my custom high-powered binoculars couldn't cut through the thick brush that blocked the house Walter was allegedly staying at from the street.

I parked the Jeep in a nearby marina parking lot and Adam and I walked the quarter-mile to the house. The driveway was long, but luckily there was no gate or wall to climb over. It didn't look like there were even security cameras. I found it rather odd that the mayor wouldn't have more security. Adam and I found a small clearing in the woods near the house that gave us a pretty good view of the back windows. I could see the Escalade in the driveway along with a black Range Rover, a silver Porsche, and a red Bentley. Despite the hundreds of thousands of dollars parked in the driveway, the house looked rather unkempt, like gardeners or landscapers had yet to be hired for the summer.

I was able to see some movement going on through the big bay windows in the back of the house. It looked like three men and two women. They were just standing around the island in the kitchen. I couldn't make out their faces. The glass was way too spotted and the sheer curtains didn't help the matter. Two of the men had their arms around each other's waists and they'd appear to kiss every now and then. None of the other folks seemed to mind. It was as if they were used to the gay couple displaying their affection in public.

Then, I noticed a woman standing off to the side and the third man who had his arm around the lower waist of the second woman. This one, I could tell, was wearing a bright red halter jumper. It was so bright, I could see how well it hugged her perfect hourglass figure.

I cranked up the focus on the binoculars even more. This woman had a black or very dark brown bob hairstyle. If she weren't already in costume, then she was living in the wrong era. I assumed it had to be her attire for the night.

"Make a note for me, please...in case these photos don't come out clear enough," I began dictating to Adam, who was hastily jotting my words down. "Two men embracing...man with arm around women with dark-haired bob and red jumper...also... write down, swing set, old grill, and trampoline in backyard."

The phone pinged at 5 p.m., which usually meant it was time to take my birth control pill, but also that we had been on watch for an hour. Once the group scattered, there hadn't been any noticeable movement. I could tell Adam was getting a bit antsy, so I sent him back to the marina to get the car. I didn't want anyone getting suspicious of the Jeep being parked there after sunset.

It was getting darker and cooler. Nighttime fell faster in the woods and I knew that whomever was in that house would have to be leaving soon. I looked down at my phone, which I had placed on silent. Three missed calls displayed on the screen: *The Gotham Post*, Liam, and an "unavailable" number. All left me voicemails.

"Hi, Paige. Connie here. Our sister company, News 6 New York, is interested in doing a joint feature with us on this piece. It wouldn't require extra work on your part; we'd just be video-taping the interview so they can air it later that day. Give me a call. I'll be in the office until five."

On air?! What if Walter doesn't want it taped? Just worry about it later.

I took a breath and then played Liam's voicemail. It was hard to even concentrate on his words as I had become so distracted by the thought of having my article go from print to television.

"Hey, beautiful."

His words instantly calming.

"I wanted to see if you're around tonight and/or tomorrow. Actually, and selfishly, both nights," he continued. "I have a friend's birthday party tonight I would love to take you. If you can't tonight, then tomorrow it could just be you and I. Maybe we can try for Nobu again. Or I can cook for you. Call me back...where are you, by the way?" he innocently asked before hanging up.

As much as I wanted to call him and hear his voice, I ignored it for now. I'd text him later. My nerves started firing up again as I prepared to listen to the message from the mystery caller.

"You'll find the answers you need in the desk," the robotic voice said.

There was a long pause and I could hear some breathing and then nothing.

Anything else? That's it? What the hell did that mean? What desk?

Suddenly, it felt like the woods were caving in on me. I had missed my chance to get out while I could still see and now I had the sinking feeling like I was being watched, again. With every rustle of wind and snap of a branch, the hairs on my body stood a little straighter.

I started gathering my belongings. Chatter was coming from the house. I lifted the binoculars. I could make out the people now! They were exiting through the garage. Walter Wilcox, Richard Brownstein, Jimmy DeFazio, the Roches, a slender blonde with a boob job, the bobbed-haired woman in the red halter and last, and surprisingly, Police Chief Mitchell. There were more, two of whom I didn't recognize.

"Wait a minute," I quietly said aloud. "That man. He kind of looks like the guy who gave Walter that file on the street."

He was short, stocky, and dark-skinned, just as I remembered. His face was most unrecognizable. Before the motley crew hopped into the Cadillac I snapped some zoomed-in photos of the man's face in hopes my facial recognition software might put a name to his mug.

"Hey, you out front?" I whispered into my phone to Adam, who I felt was taking a long time to fetch the Jeep.

"Sorry. I got distracted," Adam shakily said.

I could tell something was wrong.

"Adam? You okay? What are you talking about?"

"Someone had left a photocopy of a picture under your wiper blade," he blurted out.

"What? A picture of what?"

While trying to make sense of what he was telling me, I could see the giant SUV begin backing out of the driveway.

"A family...the mayor's family."

"Just...hold on to the picture and listen to me, I need you to swing back around here right now and follow these guys. They're leaving to go somewhere and it's way too early for that party. We'll worry about the picture later," I instructed Adam.

The SUV roared away. I giant-stepped my way out of the brush to make sure no thorns got lodged in my stretch pants and trench coat. The house was now dark. Everyone had left. My blood pumped harder the closer I got to the home. When I finally reached the grass, I scanned the corners of the roof for any faint lights to make sure there weren't any security cameras installed.

I was golden. The house was much bigger up close and I was barely tall enough to see inside what I assumed were the living room windows. I pushed two large rocks against the cement exterior. It was just enough height to allow me to peer inside. Without touching the ledge, I examined the inside. I had to be careful not to disrupt any dust that may have accumulated on the outside of the house. The room was empty with the exception of some beer cans and an open bag of potato chips on a cheap-looking coffee table. It would be easy for someone to think the place was abandoned. Two couches faced each other and I could see by the open floor plan that there was a small kitchen table with four chairs and a pool table.

After snapping some pictures, I carefully made my way to the opposite side of the house. There was an old, tin garbage can, that I moved under the window to stand on.

My legs shook as I tried to maintain my balance all while making sure not to leave any traces of myself behind. I couldn't tell what room I was looking into with the curtains drawn.

Looks like an office.

Through a skinny crack in the curtains, I spotted what looked like a pathetic bookshelf with three books. There was also an old rolltop desk that reminded me of the one my mom used to have. She used to sit at it day and night while typing her manuscripts on her vintage Remington Standard typewriter. I could almost hear the sound of her vigorously clicking away on the keys.

Just as my mind drifted to that place 30 years ago, the garbage can gave way and down I fell into the dirt. The tin can fell over, its contents spilling out beside me.

Thankfully, a small pile of mulch helped cushion my fall. I stood, brushed the dirt off my pants and shined my flashlight over the trash to make sure none of the discarded banana peels and Chinese food landed on me.

What's all this?

Condom wrappers, empty bottles of lubricants, and a few other pieces of kinky sex paraphernalia were scattered about. I grabbed a stick and started poking through the trash. There was also a pair of furry handcuffs, a man's G-string with a hole cut out in the front, a gag ball, and some sadomasochist-type toys I didn't know what was used for.

Geez, do they hold orgies or something here?

I snapped some pictures for evidence, and rummaged through the rest of the disposed goods hoping for more than some bondage wear. Amongst the trash—a crumpled piece of paper. It looked like a receipt. I slowly opened it hoping that the sound of crinkling wouldn't alarm any wandering wild animals. I shined my flashlight over the faded writing. It was a receipt for $900 from Agent Provocateur. The ink displaying the date and place was too far gone to make out when and where this was purchased but I could only suspect that it was in Dallas and right around when Victoria came to me with her questionable credit card statement and list purchases.

I folded up the piece of paper and tucked it away in my back pocket. Using leaves as mock gloves, I carefully pushed the garbage back into the can. If anything, someone would suspect raccoons over the Vixen Investigator rummaging through their trash.

I had lost all track of time. I could continuously feel my phone vibrating in my bag, but ignored it. I had to answer to the adrenaline surging through me.

One of the small basement windows was slightly open.

It's either my lucky day...or someone conveniently left it open for me.

Still careful not to leave any imprints of myself, I covered my hands in more big leaves, and forced the window to open completely. I took off my trench and fedora and carefully dropped them down onto the basement floor below. Then, I shimmied myself through the window and executed the perfect two-foot landing. With a quiet thud, I was now inside the pitch-black basement, which was empty with the exception of some clear storage bins with linens inside. I tiptoed my way up the stairs, which led to the kitchen. There were some suitcases with DFW to JFK tags on them. No names, however. I figured they were the Roches'. I proceeded to the office. The three lonely books on the shelves were dusty, but something about the irregular subject made me ponder who would read such material; *Chemicals and The Human Body: The Everyday Chemicals that Can Kill Us, How the Mob Got Away with Everything*, and *How to Win Friends and Influence People* by Dale Carnegie.

Such a random collection.

Thinking about what the mystery caller said about "the desk," I began analyzing every nook and cranny of the rolltop. There was nothing on or even inside it. Feeling defeated and mislead, I pressed on and made my way up to the bedrooms. My heart thumped with every footstep. Each one put me one step closer to a possible clue. All the bedrooms had perfectly made queen-sized beds, with the exception of one room. It looked used, like it had been slept in.

Someone slept here last night.

In the connected bathroom, there was a brush with some brown hair strands in the bristles and a reddish purple MAC lipstick. I grabbed a few strands of hair left in the brush and since I was short of time, grabbed the entire tube of lipstick and tossed it in my purse. In the trash, a bag with a label on it for a brown-haired wig caught my eye. It looked like the style the woman with Walter and company was wearing.

With the bedroom appearing like the only room in use, I planted one of my wireless and self-destructing audio recorders and a video recorder under the bed and on the door hinge to the bathroom. It was the only angle that would give me a complete view of the entire bedroom. These devices were so micro one would mistake them for a fly. I had them custom-made for me by my ex-Secret Service friends, and the best part about them was the self-destructing feature. The audio and video would stream and automatically save to my smartphone and computer. Then, once I was done with the equipment, I'd tap the destroy feature on my phone—masked under the name "menstruation tracker" in case my phone ever got stolen—and the recorders would melt. To the unsuspecting offender, my melted device would look like a simple ink stain.

With not much time to spare before the party, I hurried out of the house. The fools didn't even lock the front door. Down the driveway I hustled to where Adam was waiting. I quickly brushed off the broken leaves and dust from my pants and out of my hair and hopped into the Jeep.

"Find anything?" he asked, while pulling away before another car coming by could see us.

"Oh yeah…condoms, banana hammocks, and wigs, oh my," I sarcastically replied. "And you?"

Trying my best to multitask, I pulled the visor down to smooth out my hair and reapply my lipstick and eyeliner.

"Umm…ok. I'll let you explain later. It looks like they're having dinner at Kennedy's right now. I think they reserved the entire restaurant because they were the only ones in the parking lot," Adam informed.

Knowing we had some time to kill, we found ourselves a small pizzeria and ordered some slices to eat in the car. We'd hold it down in the Jeep until it was time to crash the party.

"So, here's what I think," I started. "The mayor is going to be at this party, in disguise, I imagine. He's with a few of his staff, including two women." I took a big bite of pizza; the cheese scolded the roof of my mouth. "One woman is in a wig, but her face looks familiar. I think I've seen her before."

"Was it one of the guys' wives or girlfriends?" Adam asked.

"It could be, but the Texans didn't bring their wives up here. Unless it was one of Brownstein's or the security guard's," I theorized.

"Maybe they're with the Roches."

"Nah. They're obnoxious and flirty but they're just not the cheating kind."

Neither one of us looked "1920s chic" as we approached the estate for the costume party. But, with me in my trench coat and Adam in my fedora, which I let him borrow, I figured they'd think we were old school detectives or something.

After getting near interrogated by the svelte brunette girl at the "check in," Adam and I were finally allowed through the home's mechanical gate. She had given us each a white wristband, which apparently meant we were important enough to have access to the entire grounds.

The music bumped louder and louder as we approached the backyard. A mix of swing, house, and rap echoed over the property. The closer we got to the actual house, the easier it was to see how much it resembled an actual castle. A miniature moat wove its way through the landscaping. We were led to the heated pool in the back, which was where the bikini-clad girls were swimming around. It was only in the 60s, and yet, you'd think it were a hot evening in July.

"Let's scope out the scene, get a drink, and try to find the mayor," I said to Adam above the music.

Surely, Lord Max was paying off the neighbors and the police department or the noise would've had this party shut down as soon as it started. We took a seat in the exclusive area for white wristband-wearing attendees on one of the horrendous-looking vintage sofas.

For a man of such wealth, you'd think he'd try and modernize the place a bit more.

Everything from the wallpaper, to the chairs, to the smell screamed outdated. Between entering, taking a quick lap, and finding a resting spot, we had yet to find Walter and his crew anywhere. I texted Rodney to let him know we were here. He didn't respond.

Odd. He's always quick to respond.

Adam and I people-watched while sipping our Bellinis. An obvious cross-dresser walked by in leather chaps and eight-inch stripper shoes.

"I thought this was supposed to be a '20s party?" Adam questioned carefully to not insult anyone who might overhear him.

"We must have missed the part that said stripper attire optional," I sarcastically replied.

Adam laughed so hard he nearly spit out his drink.

"Come on...let's take a walk," I said and led us back down to the pool.

We found a good spot on two lounge chairs. The night air was crisper and cooler now; the steam from the water helped keep me warm and started to make me sleepy. I eyed the crowd and finally, standing in his gaggle of followers, I spied Walter. They were all in costume. If it weren't for the woman in the eye-catching red halter jumper, I may have missed seeing them.

With the near-nude girls wading around me, I continued to observe Walter's group. They were drinking heavily. Some were taking shots with one hand and sipping Champagne with the other. Every now and then, Walter would reach for the woman in red's hand. But she looked unwilling to hold his as if she were mad.

Wait a minute. Now I know that face. It was the girl from that party in Texas who was with Brownstein. What was she doing here? And why was Walter trying to move in on Brownstein's girl?

The realization made my heart race. The new details hit me like a narcotic and I wanted more. The puzzle pieces were there but I was having trouble putting them together. I saw Rodney look down at his phone. He clearly had it and was ignoring me. Suspicions grew. I heard Adam say something, but was in my own world. When I saw Brownstein put his arm around Jimmy DeFazio's lower back and proceed to give him a kiss on the cheek, the shock nearly sent me into the pool.

WHA?? Brownstein and DeFazio are together?

"Paige?! Did you hear me?" Adam got a little louder and stared at me as if concerned.

"What? No, sorry..." I turned to him.

"I am going to go to the bathroom, be right back."

I just nodded and turned back to the scene playing out in front of me. Adam stood and walked off towards the house. Brownstein and DeFazio were still holding each other's lower backs and Walter was standing suggestively close to the woman in red. They looked more like a couple than she and Brownstein. Lord Maximillian came sashaying out of his castle like a court jester on cocaine and approached the group. He was in nothing but a pair of leather booty-shorts and a cape and his boyfriend was following behind him wearing a white tank top and cutoffs. He went right up to Mayor Wilcox and hugged him! They looked like good friends.

Adam was taking forever in the bathroom. I wondered if he had gotten lost. But, I didn't dare leave and take my eyes off Walter and his friends, who still held it down in their corner near the replica statue of Michelangelo's David. Lord Max danced off and just after he did, Walter gave the girl in red a huge kiss. He could've broken her neck back.

Holy smokes, it is his mistress! Why aren't the other people doing anything? They all know he's a philandering asshole! Shit!

I snapped as many photos as I could and left to find Adam.

"Where the hell were you?" Adam was standing near the front of the house looking down at his phone. "Who are you texting? I can't have you conducting personal business at a time like this. Let's go," I ordered and tugged his arm, nearly flinging the phone out of his grip. "We have to get back to the house before Walter."

"Sorry. I got talking to the drummer of the band that's about to perform and then my bandmate, Ronnie, texted me about a gig we just got booked for," Adam explained with an apologetic, yet excited, tone.

I wasn't even paying attention to what Adam was telling me. I kept thinking of Walter kissing that young girl and what little effort he put in, in hiding his affair. Now I had real proof that New York's mayor was seeing someone else and his buddies were all aware.

Why would a man of his caliber and his power risk it all like this? Did he want to get caught?

While driving us back to the estate, I had Adam upload the pictures to the MacBook. He was fiddling around on my computer right before turning the laptop towards me.

"Paige, take a look at this."

With the face recognition software, Adam was able to match the face of the woman at the Roches' house to the face of the woman in red. As suspected, it was the same woman. The comptroller was pretending to be with her as a ruse, when in fact, he was really gay.

How clever.

"We're going to find out what is going on. I know it," I said while stepping on the gas even more. The adrenaline and the discoveries made me feel like I could tackle just about any obstacle. Nothing could come between me and the truth.

The roads leading back to Walter's hideaway were dark and eerie this late at night. I pulled up to the edge of the driveway and Adam and I switched seats so I could change into my night spy gear. The pumps became flats once again and I threw my hair into a ponytail. The black face paint I smudged under my eyes and on my cheeks was unnecessary but looked cool. I exchanged my fedora for a Volcom beanie that, for some reason, was in the backseat.

"You look ridiculous and sexy at the same time. Only you could pull that off," Adam stated.

"I can't have my cover blown," I replied and adjusted my hat in the visor's mirror. "Don't crash into any deer and keep your phone on in case you fall asleep so I can call you. Copy?"

I took a deep breath and hopped out of the Jeep to make my way back to the wooded hideout.

I waited. Every five minutes that passed seemed like an hour. I meditated to pass the time, but all efforts failed with every snap of a branch. I thought about Liam and how I still hadn't texted him back. The minute of sorrow and guilt quickly dissipated as soon as I saw the Escalade turn up the driveway. It was now close to midnight. I pulled out my night-vision binoculars. Mayor Wilcox and the same young girl got out. That was it.

When the SUV backed away and finally drove off again, that was my cue to move in a little closer. I could see the couple's motions through the curtains. The lights flicked on in the bathroom, then went off. They flicked on in the office, then back off. They flicked on in the upstairs hallway and then off. The lights went on in the apparent used bedroom and stayed on. I couldn't make out what was going on now. I'd have to rely on my audio and video recorders for the rest of the evening.

While keeping the light on my phone as dim as possible, I activated the devices to switch on. I pushed the earbuds into my ears, which silenced any cricket, snapping branch, or potential serial killer that may be rustling around in the woods.

"That was some party. So glad to get out of this itchy wig," I heard the female voice say. The video was a bit grainy, but I could see, after she pulled off the wig, her long brown locks fall to the middle of her back. She was beautiful and looked a lot younger than I first thought.

"I like you with the short hair. It looks a lot like my wife's," Walter said and then laughter from the both of them.

Walter pulled the girl in for a kiss.

"When's it going to be my turn?" she whined.

"Stop it. I am trying to do everything I can to make this work," Walter answered.

Next, she released herself from his hold and walked into the bathroom. Walter proceeded to take off his clothes stripping down to his boxers.

He's pretty fit for an old guy.

The young girl reemerged into the picture and this time, she was completely naked. Her breasts and butt were as perky as a 23-year-old's. Walter was sitting on the bed facing her while she got down on her knees and started giving him a blowjob. As much as I wanted to turn it off, I couldn't. They were still talking. I could hear Walter moaning and then there was the occasional "slurp."

"I should be the first lady of New York," I heard her say in between having her mouth around his penis. He pulled her up and they kissed before moving fully onto the bed. Walter proceeded to conquer the young damsel.

I turned off the audio and the grainy video that resembled poorly produced porn from the '80s. I had all the proof I needed. Now, who is his mistress?

14

SATURDAY

A whirlwind 24 hours. Adam and I ended up driving back home right after the Hamptons' mission. We didn't get back to Hoboken until nearly five in the morning. I was near delirious driving home. When I finally got to my place after dropping Adam off, I flung open the door of the apartment and expected to immediately crash on the couch, black face paint and all. However, my OCD kicked in and I started uploading all the photos, video, and audio to all my computers instead. Fatigue finally set in around 9 a.m. That was the last I looked at my clock.

"Paige...Paige, get up. You have drool going into your keyboard."

Adam was violently shaking me awake to the point where he may have thought I was dead if it weren't for the waterfall coming out of my mouth. I rose slowly off my computer. I could feel the ridges in my face left by the buttons. Focusing my eyes on him was hard with my contacts plastered to my eyeballs.

Was that all just a crazy dream? Did I really see Mayor Wilcox banging some young girl who wasn't his wife? I smell coffee...I need that coffee!

"Coffee? "What day is it?" I mumbled.

"It's Saturday, Paige. It's 3:30. Here..." Adam placed the coffee on my desk. "There is an extra toasted bagel for you in the kitchen."

"You're the best assistant ever."

I dragged myself into the kitchen. I needed carbs desperately.

"What?" I asked with a mouth full of bread and cream cheese.

Adam was doing a very bad job at hiding his humor in watching me inhale my breakfast.

"It's the face paint, right?" He started giggling. "I'll take care of it. I'm not embarrassed. Go ahead and laugh," I said as I continued to masticate the toasted goodness.

Now I know why he thought it was so funny. I look like I just escaped a police chase after robbing a bank.

I finally caught a glimpse of myself in the mirror.

I fiercely scrubbed my face thinking that perhaps the dark marks had become embedded in my pores. It took five tries to finally get my skin looking Norwegian again. The lack of sleep from the past several days was starting to show. I sent Adam home for the rest of the day, turned off every computer, monitor, and device with an "On" button, packed up some spring clothes and headed for my dad's. Some time and peace in the country was exactly what I needed to recover and recharge.

MAY

Deciding to give myself some time away from the throes of adultery was a much-welcomed mental break. Dad had gotten a new German Shepherd, Zelda. She was fun to run around with. We didn't talk work, but instead, sat outside on the deck, drank vintage wines, and reminisced about the summer of 1996, when forty hot-air balloons landed on our property. We laughed about how Mom would get drunk and overcook the chicken and then complain about it being overcooked. Whenever I visited, I'd stay in my old room. My dad had left most of the house untouched. As much as I loved staying there, it was hard at times, as the memories would get too heavy. I'd think too much about my mom and get upset.

Things had gotten tense between Liam and me after going MIA on him a few weekends ago. But with much explaining, apologizing, and convincing that I wasn't cheating on him, Liam and I ended up back in our routine of spending most of our nights together; at his place of course. Each lovemaking session was as sensual as a romance novel scene. But, I continued to wear that scarlet letter inside. He still didn't know the truth about Vixen Investigations.

Adam and his band had lined up some new gigs and they were getting rave reviews. The *Asbury Park Press* even defined the group as "The Black Keys meets Soundgarden." It was quite the accolade.

Walter was back to his daily press conferences. I had found attending them to be a waste of time. There was a lot more under the surface that I was getting close to. I could feel it. Now that I had also agreed to *The Gotham Post*'s request to tape the interview, I felt that I needed to precisely strategize my method of taking Walter down.

The week before Memorial Day weekend I had a few things lined up: a tour of City Hall and a sit-down meeting with some of the communication officials about the upcoming interview. But sitting in my office that Sunday night, I couldn't seem to concentrate. While studying facts and trying to piece together information, I'd occasionally look up at my collection of worn Nancy Drew books. Despite there being no pictures, I was always captivated by Nancy's inquisitive mind and ability to sniff out clues.

She didn't even have the internet...

Suddenly, my phone going off in the other room snapped me out of my daydream. I hurried to my purse but missed the call. There was a voicemail that made my heart thump harder.

"How do you find a missing kid?" was all the mystery caller had said in the voicemail.

Another riddle...

"A missing kid?" I questioned allowed. "What the heck does that mean?"

I stormed back to my computer without a thought of what I wanted to Google. Surely, all that would come up would be a missing children's database. I typed in the exact question, hoping to trigger a quick response that made sense, but instead up popped a list of articles and foundations that'll search for missing and exploited children.

Nothing seemed to make sense. I clicked to page two and halfway down the search revealed a link to the website for Amber Alerts.

Amber? A name?

I jotted down "Amber" on the legal pad next to me, and as many other acronyms for the name.

Ambr, Mber, Amb, I wrote. Then I went onto Facebook and searched for the name Amber. A trove of names came up.

This won't help.

On my phone, I searched the name on Instagram. In separate browser windows, I searched for the name under the acronyms I came up with. I had likely thousands of names and faces in front of me and one by one, I went through all of them.

My eyes strained scoping out the hordes of unfamiliar faces. Narrowing the search to New York City wasn't helping either. I was starting to feel my eyes dry out until a familiar face caught my attention on Instagram. It was under the name "@Ambralrt" with the handle's owner being "Amber Wright." I clicked on the name. LOCKED.

"Damnit!"

I was convinced it was the same face I saw in the Hamptons with Mayor Wilcox. She needed to accept my request. I logged out of my Paige Turner account and back in as my alias, Kim Sharp, who, according to the fake account, is a bartender at Martell's Tiki Bar down the shore.

I waited and hoped that it wouldn't take days for her to accept me. While tooling around on my computer and phone, I had unknowingly and uncontrollably been tapping my pen so much, it had left a sizable ink blob that resembled the shape of a kiss on the pad of paper.

Wait...kiss? Lipstick!

I had forgotten about the MAC lipstick I snatched from the Hamptons house.

Might it hold a clue?

I scrambled around the apartment looking in every bag and coat pocket. No luck. I called Adam even though I promised to give him the day off without interruption.

"I need you to check your pockets...anything that you may have brought with you when we were in the Hamptons," I ordered.

He was rehearsing with his bandmates, but took five to search for me.

After turning the apartment upside down, the lipstick remained lost. I plopped down on the couch and put my head in my hands. Frustrated, and tired. I felt like I had hit a brick wall. My phone vibrated in front of me.

"Hey, Adam, any luck?"

"No. I remember you throwing a few items into the glove box right after you covered your face in that black paint." Adam's words rejiggered my memory.

"You're right, I did. I probably thought it was my ChapStick!"

Eager to find out, I hustled down to the Jeep. When I unlocked the glove box and the door flung open, out rolled the MAC lipstick and that random photo I had forgotten about that was left on my windshield.

"YES!" I yelled so loud it set off the neighboring Acura's alarm.

Perhaps it could tell me something. Back in my bathroom, I pulled the cap off the lipstick, revealing the half-worn-down stick of the "Femme Fatal" color. I wiped off the top layer and applied it to my plump and dry lips. It was a good-looking color. Something I'd wear myself. After perfectly applying the shade, I snapped a few selfies.

Back to the computer I pulled up pictures I had taken of the mystery woman with Walter, enlarging the woman's lips. I didn't need elaborate technology to match a lip shade. Comparing my lips with hers, I knew that it was the same reddish color. To my right, my phone flashed an Instagram alert: "@Ambralrt has accepted your request."

Finally, a lead!

I opened up the account, owned by a girl named Amber Wright. There was no doubt that it was the girl I had been looking for. I now had a name. The lipstick color matched other pictures. There were photos of her with two women resembling the Roche brothers' wives, except this picture was years old.

I Googled "Amber Wright" to see if anything else came up. Nothing.

I heard my front door open and a familiar voice. But, my face was too focused on the screen to care who it was.

"Everything okay?" Adam asked while standing in my office doorway.

I turned sharply at him with a smile on my face.

"I have a name. Amber Wright," I announced.

He pulled up a chair and together we scanned the web.

"It looks like there are a few Amber Wrights from Long Island on People Finder," I said. "Let's see if we can pinpoint who this girl is."

We scanned all sorts of websites and databases for almost an hour. I failed to notice the bag of Chinese takeout Adam had brought over. The salty smell grew more intense, with a stain of soy sauce and grease slowly seeping through the bag.

"Look," I pointed out to Adam.

An Amber Luciana Wright from Long Island seemed to be a likely match. Her father was Peter Wright and according to the information, this girl was 28 years old.

"That girl we've been seeing with Walter looks to be about that age," Adam observed.

I was too much in thought to even hear him because I was too focused on the name.

"Wait a minute. Those girls in Texas kept talking about their friend Lucy. You think Lucy is short for Luciana?" I turned and looked up to Adam.

We looked sharply at each other. I needed a full background check on this girl stat. I shot Chin Chin a text asking for him to run a detailed check on the name and within minutes, he responded with a "10-4."

"Look," Adam said, summoning me over to his phone.

When he typed "Lucy Wright" into Google, almost every social media channel revealed a page for the name. Then, Adam proceeded to show me her Facebook, Twitter, and Instagram accounts.

This girl secretly went by her middle name as a diversion for some reason.

"That's definitely her. She must use various names to mislead anyone who might suspect her of anything," I announced confidently.

Lucy Wright's pages seemed a lot more sophisticated than the Amber Wright ones. @Ambralrt was an obvious old account. Lucy seemed like an elitist with her fancy photos of sailing in Sag Harbor and skiing in Aspen. There was one, more current, photo of her sipping a mimosa outside on the beach.

I know that spot. That's Shutters in Santa Monica! But who was she with? Who was taking all the pictures?

"Is that...the Roches' wives?" Adam observantly asked.

"It has to be. It looks just like them," I agreed.

"They must be longtime friends. I mean, look at this picture from the Amber account. It looks just like a younger version of all three of them," I analyzed. "This has to be the girl they mentioned."

Despite feeling invincible, I was no match for the increased security around City Hall the next morning. Armed guards lined the perimeter, while blacked out SUVs stood along the street. I was dressed in my typical "I mean business" getup as I handed the guard my license. His intimidating stare was no match for my cleavage-bearing blouse. He smiled at me as I passed through the metal detector.

I sat down on the stiff chair in the sterile lobby.

I wonder how long Jimmy will keep me waiting this time.

Two hot men, who looked like detectives, were seated nearby. Their scent of Old Spice subtly stimulated my nostrils. The scent immediately made me think of Liam. It distracted me enough to where I was visualizing Liam's face while reading a copy of *The Gotham Post* I had purchased at the neighboring bodega. The headline of the paper read, STONED VAGRANT: "COX LOVES US."

No wonder he hates this paper.

"Homeless population voice love affair with Mayor Wilcox, while taxpayers complain about increase in vile hobo activity," the subtitle read.

"Miss Turner?" I heard.

A short portly woman was standing in the entranceway to the hall. I raised my hand like a schoolgirl during roll call.

"Follow me."

I followed behind her as she led the way down to the office where Jimmy was on the phone. He motioned for me to sit down with his free hand and then held up his pointer finger to say, "one more minute." I patiently waited in the old, hard, wooden chair as he finished with his "uh huhs," "yeahs," and then finally a "your ass is toast" and a slam of the phone.

"Hi, Paige. Sorry about that. Good to see you again," he greeted and shook my hand.

I still couldn't shake the image of him and Richard Brownstein making out under the fluorescent spotlight at Lord Max's castle.

"Let's take a walk," he said, standing quickly as if he feared his office was bugged.

I followed him out of the office and down the aging and musty-smelling hallway.

"Have you ever been in here before?"

"City Hall?" I asked, almost dumbfounded, as if he were just trying to make conversation.

He didn't answer me so he obviously didn't care. Further down the hall he led to where a guard stood stoic in front of Walter's office.

"I thought I would give you the tour rather than my intern," he said.

"Thanks. I really appreciate all your help with everything."

A little ass-kissing couldn't hurt.

"Where is everyone? It seems rather quiet for a weekday morning. Does Walter have an event?" I prodded.

"Lunch," Jimmy curtly replied, like he didn't want me to ask any more questions.

The towering guard looked down at Jimmy and me as he opened the mayor's office door.

"My colleagues will be back shortly and we can go over the parameters of the interview then."

He whispered something to the guard, who left, leaving Walter's trusty press secretary and me with full access to his office.

"I can't let you take pictures in here, because we only let media use the official stock photo provided by our staff," he mentioned, as if it wouldn't be a problem, "but, feel free to take notes...maybe it'll help inspire your questions for him," Jimmy said almost suggestively.

I strolled around the room. I could smell the history and the corruption. There was a big oak desk, leather chair, ceiling-high bookcases, and the official portrait of the mayor, one of his family and another "Never Forget" painting, marking September 11th.

"Very nice. I guess it is how I expected it to be," I commented to Jimmy, who was standing in the doorway. Or so I thought. When I turned, he wasn't there.

"Jimmy?" I questioned louder while popping my head out the door.

I looked left and right. He wasn't anywhere to be seen. In fact, there wasn't anybody in sight.

He really just left me alone in the mayor's office to freely roam around?

I immediately started scouring around for clues.

"You'll find the answers you need in the desk."

I remembered the mysterious caller's words. Not knowing how much time I'd have, I quickly got behind the desk and started opening the drawers. There was nothing inside but pens, random files, and bags of Swedish Fish. Pissed that I hadn't found more, I slammed my fist hard on the top of the desk.

What was that?

Something had fallen on my foot. It appeared to have come from a concealed cubbyhole underneath. I bent down and picked up the fallen picture. Encased in the cheap silver frame was a photograph of Walter and Lucy. I snapped some pictures of the framed photo. It was obvious it was supposed to remain hidden.

I ducked down under the desk and felt around the cubby. I pulled out an envelope which was filled with developed photos, most of which were of Walter and Lucy and their random friends. Just about at the end of the pile, there was a picture I never would've imagined. It was the same photograph of Walter and Steve Benson, my ex-client's fiancé, that was posted on his mistress Caitlin's Instagram.

What is going on here?

I reached back and pulled out a few more miscellaneous papers. As I carefully started to remove a letter from the opened envelope, I could hear the sound of footsteps growing louder.

Fuck!

I shoved everything in my tote bag to go through later, stood, and smoothed out my pants and blazer. My breath slowed down just as Jimmy returned.

"Sorry...too much coffee and fruit this morning. Don't tell anyone I left you, that warrants some kind of unglamorous disciplinary action," he said but his tone wasn't of someone who actually cared. "Come on, let's go to the conference room and wait for the rest of the staff."

We spoke and negotiated the details of the interview for less than thirty minutes. The group seemed more interested in getting done for the day and starting their Memorial Day Weekend early than talking about the project. Their lackadaisical mentality ended up helping me in the end. I was pretty sure they didn't even realize what they were agreeing to. When I mentioned a camera crew coming, they thought it was a "wonderful idea."

We agreed that the interview would be done in the mayor's office, which I thought would make for the perfect setting. I was also, and generously, allotted one hour with no breaks to do what I had to do. However, because of his "packed schedule," I couldn't do the actual sit-down interview until Thursday, July 9th.

That gives me six weeks to be on my best behavior, so he doesn't end up changing his mind.

While it was over a month away, my photo shoot of Walter and Victoria's home was only in two weeks. The four-week gap between the shoot and the interview was plenty of time for me to garner more clues for my big interrogation.

My Memorial Day weekend plans had gone from alone time with Liam to following him and his friends down the shore, and bringing my work with me. I rounded up Taylor, April, and Adam and willingly decided to drop $1,000 on a beach house in Point Pleasant for the weekend. I needed to strategize the upcoming weeks with my crew. Since Liam and his friends were going to be down there, as well, I figured I'd be able to kill multiple birds with one stone.

The Friday morning traffic was minimal as I expected it to build later in the day. We made the all-important stop at Wawa for coffee and breakfast before getting on the Garden State Parkway.

"I can't believe how this case has fallen into place for you, Paige. I mean, what were the chances you'd meet the people you did and get the opportunities you have?" Taylor observed while sitting in the backseat.

I looked at her through the rearview mirror, catching her mid-bite of her egg, vegetarian bacon, and cheese sandwich.

"You have cheese on your chin," I teased, instead of responding.

We all laughed as Taylor slapped my shoulder.

"You know how entertaining it is for me to watch you eat and put makeup on." April laughed in agreement with my comment. "By the way, it's not about luck, Tay. I've sacrificed a lot of time, sleep, and romance for this case. It all comes down to me knowing what I'm doing and having associates like you guys," I bragged.

"You always taught me that success doesn't come without some sort of sacrifice," Adam added as to not let me forget the sacrifices he has made.

"I'm just glad to be doing something meaningful. It sucks being out of work," April chimed in.

I felt like the luckiest employer having my best friends working for me.

Point Pleasant was bustling. Ice cream parlors displayed their "Open for the Season" signs and the little seafood restaurants had their outside seating all set up. The sun's force on my shoulders as soon as I hopped out of the Jeep felt more like 90 degrees and not the 75 predicted. We threw our stuff inside the rental house while designating our rooms and then promptly hit the beach with two large blankets and three bottles of chilled rosé.

"Aaaah, if only work meetings could be like this all the time. Here's to a great summer and a great outcome for you and Vixen Investigations," Taylor declared, raising her plastic cup.

"And, Victoria Wilcox. I wish the best for her after all of this," I added before clapping our cups together.

The salutation was promptly followed by simultaneous sips of wine and nibbles on cheese, crackers, and hummus. Adam, having the only cell phone signal on the beach, turned on Pandora.

"Ha, imagine that. The first song to come on. Hall & Oates!" Adam announced.

He couldn't help but notice the irony, as did I. He began singing the lyrics in a voice that I never realized he had.

"*Private eyes, they're watching you, they see your every move,*" he belted out.

"I don't know. I always felt my theme song was, *Every Breath You Take,*" I sang but didn't sound a smidge as good as Adam.

The wine continued to flow as the sun fell even more to the west.

"So, Paige. We get to meet your Jersey boy this weekend?" April inquired.

"Yes...hopefully. He's a sweet guy and has that Jersey attitude I like. I'm just going with the flow for now," I divulged.

"Tell us..." Taylor moved in closer as if she wanted me to reveal the size of Liam's penis or something. "What's the one thing you've learned in your dealings with all these philandering men and women?"

I could tell she was looking for something extremely juicy. April moved in closer, as well, as if I were about to reveal some top-secret, highly classified information. Adam looked at me but acted like he already knew the answer.

"The one thing I can tell you is, it all comes down to the person's character and moral values. Every person is different. Every relationship is different. You just have to be with the right person."

"That's so...not exciting," Taylor quipped and took another sip.

I was the first one awake the next day. Lita, the weekend house-maid, had a big, fresh pot of coffee calling my name when I walked out to the kitchen in my silk pajamas.

"Your paper, Miss Turner," Lita pleasantly offered and handed me a copy of *The Gotham Post*.

Today's headline: "POT HOLED: Report Reveals City Streets Still Haven't Had Potholes Fixed Since Winter."

I flipped to Page Ten, hoping for all the weekend's Hamptons gossip. As expected, there was a picture of Mayor Wilcox, Piper, and Victoria smiling and waving while walking on the beach in Amagansett.

I guzzled down two cups of coffee and continued to scan the paper. When I got to the sports section, I tossed the paper in the trash. I never read past the horoscopes.

Life finally started revealing itself from the depths of the hallways around 10 a.m. and then by 11:30 a.m., we were all up and ready to begin the meeting. Surrounded by glasses of orange juice and plates of fruit and bagels, I delved into the details and expectations. April's only mission was to hang with Piper as much as possible. Adam would be my right hand, as always, as well as my photographer for the tour of Walter's home. All I wanted Taylor to do was keep the paper at bay, so I could focus on what was left of the case.

The discussion continued to the point where I felt like we were on a romance panel for a version of *Meet the Press*.

Topic this Sunday: Philandering Bastards.

I wrapped the strategy session by 2 p.m. with a vow that we were never to speak of the case unless we were with each other and in private, from here on out. Most importantly, we'd see it through, until the very end.

The rest of the lazy Saturday afternoon was spent baking in the sun and was later followed by a quick catnap around 4 p.m. After some much needed primping, the four of us left to meet Liam and his work friends at Shore Bar for a few drinks before heading back to Liam's beach rental. Everyone was getting along, including Adam, who seemed to have taken a liking to Liam. Maybe it was that Jersey Boy bond. During the night while we girls were dancing, Taylor told me that she thought Liam was "good for me." Their approval was appreciated and crucial. When friends and family give their "okay," it speaks volumes.

Despite the growing distance I sensed in him, sex later that night was as safe and secure as it always was. When he worked his naked body over mine, I really felt like we were one. Still, I worried how he'd take to my profession...and to me lying about it this long.

As I slept soundly in Liam's arms, I could tell, and hear, that Taylor had really hit it off with one of Liam's friends. The occasional thud against the neighbring bedroom would jolt me awake.

SUNDAY

Adam and April ended up taking early trains home in the morning. Taylor and I opted to stay with Liam and his friends and spent the day hanging on the beach, playing Frisbee, grilling hamburgers, and drinking Coronas. I felt like I was in a country music video where everyone was young, carefree, and running around in bikinis and trunks. I was trying to enjoy the moment even though the case occupied my mind.

"Babe. Are you okay? You look distracted," Liam observed as we sat on a large rock by the jetty. Every so often, the frigid water would splash my feet, giving me goose bumps.

"Yes. Just work stuff," I deflected.

"You and work. Can you go a few hours and just enjoy yourself? I feel like you're never fully here."

"I am just under a lot of pressure right now...it's really not up for debate," I snapped but instantly felt bad about my tone.

I could feel myself getting bitchy. I turned to catch his face staring out into the Atlantic.

"I didn't mean to snap at you."

"You're right. I don't understand. I haven't said anything because I don't want to pry, but I haven't seen anything of yours published recently. It makes me think you're lying when you tell me about work."

Gosh, it sounds like he was reading from my manual.

"Can we just talk about it later? I don't want to get into it now," I reiterated.

Liam let out a deep sigh.

"Fine. I just hope...I just hope you're not wasting my time."

He slowly stood and kissed me on the top of the head before going back to join his friends.

I'm not wasting your time.

15

JUNE

The infidelity case against Mayor Wilcox was thickening. April had succeeded in becoming best friends with Piper, which was evident from Piper's social media posts. Over the past two weeks, it seemed like every day and night, Piper and her girl squad were doing something scandalous. Her erratic behavior was bad press for Walter and Victoria as she was always in Page Ten. Meanwhile, I had made it my mission to make the mayor my pal ahead of the interview. I became a regular amongst the political press pool and always made sure to sex it up. My strategy seemed to be working. Walter had taken such a liking to me that he'd always call on me first at press conferences. I ditched the tough questions in exchange for softballs.

With Wilcox's home photo shoot a couple of days away, Walter and Victoria had invited me over for dinner the night before as a way to say "thank you." It would be the first chance I'd get to have complete alone time with him and the family. I had to hand it to Jimmy, while he still maintained that strung out disposition, he had gotten a lot more lenient with me over the last few weeks. It was almost as if we were buddies. He started confiding in me about his sexuality and how hard it was for him to meet men in the city. Of course, I understood where he was coming from. I was still in a relationship funk with Liam.

185

I tried to see him as much as possible while keeping work as nine-to-five as I could.

"April, over here!"

Summer was officially here and every day was scorching hot. I started doing more of my work on my building's roof, which had a pool. I hadn't seen April in a week and invited her over to go for a swim. As she neared me laid out in my lounger chair, I couldn't help but notice how skinny she was getting.

"You look like you lost weight," I observed as she plopped down next to me.

"That's because I am out all night with that party animal. None of them eat. Did you know that? They starve themselves so they get drunk faster and on less alcohol," she exhaustedly stated.

I put my laptop aside and turned towards her and her protruding hipbones.

"Okay, you getting sickly was not part of the plan. Here," I said pushing my cooler towards here, "eat some hummus and crackers. There are some sushi rolls in there from Whole Foods. Want me to order a pizza or something?"

I watched her inhale the crackers and hummus as if she hadn't seen real food in a month. She didn't say anything.

"So, anything to brief me on besides your weight loss?"

She sat up and pushed her sunglasses down to the edge of her nose to look at me.

"Piper hates her dad. I have no doubt about that."

"What makes you say that?"

"The girl pays for everything. She just puts it on her dad's credit card. Every time a bill comes she says something along the lines of, *You can thank my dad for this*, or, *my dad owes me a lot more than this bill*. And, she is so unappreciative."

"Well, she is acting out."

"It's more than acting out. There is like a sense of resentment," April said before lying back down onto the chair with her face towards the sun.

"Has she questioned anything about your background?" I asked.

"Nope. She still thinks I am a freelance fashion journalist."

"Ha...good."

I let April doze off as I got back to organizing some notes on my MacBook. As she slept, I watched her phone light up with back-to-back phone calls and texts messages from Piper. It was getting so annoying. After call number four, I grabbed the phone. April has had more Red Bull vodkas and dancing in high-heel club nights in two weeks than I've had in the past decade. Piper would have to party without her.

WEDNESDAY

The night before the photo shoot. I didn't even have an appetite but I'd have to fake one for dinner with Victoria, Walter, and Piper. I couldn't wait to see how they acted in front of me as a family.

Standing outside the mayor's building in my beige, used Louboutins and sunburst yellow DVF wrap dress, I checked myself out in the glass windows one last time. I texted Liam to remind him that I'd be over later tonight and made sure to let him know how excited I was to see him. Since Memorial Day weekend, I was trying hard to not be so shady. It was up to me to salvage whatever was remaining of the relationship. I didn't want to lose him.

An aged doorman, who looked like he could've been doing this for 60 years, escorted me through the marble-floored lobby, to the gold-plated elevator, and up to the Wilcox floor without saying a word. The elevator doors opened right to the family's foyer. It was opulent. Fancy paintings and sculptures immediately graced my eyes. Directly ahead in the living room housed a floor-to-ceiling window so large, it made it look like there was no window or wall separating us from Central Park below.

This place must cost like nine trillion dollars.

"There she is!" Mayor Wilcox exclaimed with a suggestive hug and light kiss on the cheek.

Victoria followed behind and gave me a hug, as well. I had to hand it to her. Throughout all of this, she has maintained strength and has done an exquisite job of not leading her husband to suspect she hired a private eye.

"Hello, Mayor, Mrs. Wilcox. Thank you so much for inviting me. Your place is stunning."

"Eh. The view gets old," Victoria sarcastically stated. "Come, we have wine and caviar in the living room."

Their home reminded me of The Hotel Versailles with its velvet couches, dark red moldings, and gray-toned walls. They even had a similar black chandelier hanging above the dining room table. There was a plate of caviar, oysters, crackers, and cheese on some fine china on the mahogany coffee table. I was starving, so without hesitation, I started stacking my plate with the small appetizers. Victoria didn't even sit down. She left Walter and me alone to "use the bathroom and check on Piper."

"So, Mayor. I am excited to do this feature story on you. Thank you so much for the opportunity," I said and crossed my freshly waxed legs.

"My pleasure, Paige Turner. I can't tell you how annoying reporters are. It's like all they want to do is dig up dirt on me," he said while cockily sitting back into the couch.

"Well, there are a lot of young and hungry reporters out there that'll do anything for a story."

Walter moved his body forward, bringing himself to the edge of the couch now and leaned in towards me.

Can't this guy sit still for two minutes?

"Wouldn't you do anything for a story?"

He grinned while eyeing me up and down.

"You know I would, Mayor," I teased back.

He took a spoonful of caviar, placed it on a crostini, and took a bite. Stale bread and black fish eggs rained down to the carpet below, creating a mess.

"You like caviar, girl?"

"No thanks. I am fine with the cheese," I answered as he scooped another teaspoon of fish eggs.

"Now, Paige." Walter returned to his reclined pose but kept chewing.

I could see black specs of caviar caught in between his capped teeth.

"If it weren't you doing the story, you know I wouldn't have done this. I can't stand the *Post*."

"Well, sir. I am honored that you let me do this."

"I like you, Paige. I always did. You may have heard around the rumor mill about another term?"

He shifted his position again and was now leaning forward with his hands fisted together over his legs like he was about to say a prayer or take a dump.

"Here's the thing. You embody genuine trust, Paige. I don't want people seeing videos and photos of how I live and thinking I have nothing in common with the common man," he began while sounding like a used car salesman. "They think I'm one of them. And you know what? I am one of them. I thought we could play up the fact that I've worked really hard to get where I am today."

What is this guy up to?

He reached his hands over the fish eggs and grabbed my hands as if he wanted to pray with me. I played along, leaned in closer to him, and let him hold them.

"You report a nice, sappy piece about me and the family and I will make you my press secretary."

I should've known. A bribe.

"What an honor, Mayor. I will make you look like the patron saint of New York City," I lied and flashed him a brilliant smile.

Victoria returned with Piper moments after Walter and I came to our "agreement." Their daughter looked reluctant to join us. From the living room, we moved to the dining area, where a hired-chef had plated out beautifully constructed Cornish hen, roasted root vegetables, sautéed kale with garlic, and a coconut risotto. The delicious food couldn't take away from the awkward family dynamic. Victoria barely made eye contact with anyone except her glass of Malbec. Piper moved the food around on her plate and would take a bite in between checking her Instagram. I artfully scanned the walls and bookshelves, looking for anything would help me spark a conversation.

"Piper, are those all pictures of you?"

I pointed to some framed photos hanging on the wall of the dining room. She let out an "mmmm" without even picking her head up to see what I was referring to. I walked over to analyze the perfectly placed pictures. There were many of the three of them at the beach, at Disney World, and just looking like a normal, happy family. There were pictures of her a little bit older, in middle and high school and even some more recent ones of her in college.

"Who is this, in this picture?" I asked.

Out of what might have been thirty photos scattered on the wall, just one had someone in it that wasn't Piper, Victoria, or Walter. Piper turned to see whom I was referencing.

"Oh, that's my old babysitter. She was like family for a while...until Mom fired her."

"Piper!" Victoria snapped. "We don't need to get into this at dinner," she scolded.

"What? It's true." Piper huffed and turned her attention back to me. "Mom dubbed her Loose Lucy, because she thought she was bringing random guys here while she was supposed to be watching me."

The three of us sat, stunned.

"Anyway, dinner was swell, but I have an event," Piper sassed.

She stood and threw the balled-up napkin on her full plate of food.

"Dad, I'm taking the Porsche and the credit card...F-Y-I."

Walter didn't say anything. He just took the gold card from his wallet and pulled the keys from the pocket of his brown sweater vest and dropped them in his daughter's groveling hand. Victoria got up to help the maid clear the table, leaving Walter and me alone again. All I could think about was that name.

Lucy?

"Sorry about that." Walter said, almost embarrassed. "I guess she's the one female I've yet to control."

It was my queue to bounce.

"Well, she is still young. Don't worry about it," I consoled. "I actually have to run. I just realized I have to let the dogs out."

I slowly stood and started to see myself out. Walter followed my lead and walked me towards the door. Passing by the kitchen, I saw that the chef was piecing together some sort of chocolate mousse brownie and caramel confection. I said a quick goodbye to Victoria. The look in her eyes begged me to stay, but I was just way too anxious to hang around after realizing Walter was banging the old babysitter.

"You're unbelievably tense. You have about six knots I just worked out of your back," Liam remarked.

Later that night, while stretched across his lap, he was doing his best to give me a massage. He didn't give the best rubdowns, but I appreciated the effort. Nothing would be able to get the kinks out of my back right now.

"Hey, why don't I call out tomorrow and we can spend the day just chilling out in bed, ride bikes and go out for brunch?" he suggested.

Yes!!

"I can't tomorrow." I was slow to let the words leave my mouth as Liam exhaled in disappointment, probably figuring it was just another excuse. "I have a photo shoot in the morning, remember?"

I turned myself over so that my back now rested on his lap and I could look up at his face. He kept his eyes straightforward on the screen as if trying to avoid a conversation. I took a deep breath, using my abs to pull myself upright and grabbed his face to make him look at me. I kissed his limp and lifeless lips hoping for some sort of response.

"I promise this chaos will be over soon," I urged. "You've never dated a prive...a reporter before, have you?"

He didn't say anything.

"Sometimes I get assignments I can't talk much about. Sometimes they get really intense and there isn't much I can do about it," I defended.

Liam looked like he was holding back words. I wasn't sure if I wanted to hear what he had to say, anyway. I decided to take a more physical approach since it was obvious he didn't want to get verbal. I kissed him harder, letting him know that I wanted him. Slowly, he started coming around, this time kissing me back. I stood up and held his hands. Then, with minimal force, led him to the bedroom. He willingly followed.

I awoke the next morning to a cold and vacant feeling. Not to mention a note that had replaced Liam's naked body on the pillow next to me.

Babe—Couldn't sleep. Went for a run.
Have a good shoot.
-L

I got up, showered, and shimmied into one of the dresses I had left at his place. I didn't know if I would see him before leaving.

Maybe he doesn't want to see me.

Thanks...
xo-Paige

16

Adam and April were both waiting for me in the Starbucks a few blocks away from Walter's home. Although April wasn't taking part in today's shoot, she had been demanding to see me in person. She had to "tell me something big." Funny how whenever a girl in her 30s teases you like that, your first thought is, *oh my God, you're pregnant.* Since I didn't have lots of time these next few weeks, she agreed to meet Adam and me before the shoot.

As I neared Starbucks, I could see the both of them acting very chatty and jubilant through the window. April was glowing.

"Hey, hey!" I exclaimed, sneaking up behind them.

"Paige!" April squealed.

She stood and hugged me as if we hadn't seen each other in years.

"April...you're scaring me a little."

I gave Adam a questionable look over April's shoulder. He motioned to his ring finger. I looked down at her hands. Right there, in the middle of her unmanicured pinky and middle fingers, was a sparkly emerald-cut diamond with a platinum band and two halos.

"Holy shit!" I blurted while grabbing her hand for a closer look. "It's magnificent. It's like the size of my eyeball. Did you expect this?"

"I had no idea. I thought Jordan was just taking me hiking. When we got to this beautifully cleared area in the woods, he got down on his knee and proposed!" She gushed.

"Wow. Good job Jordan! And what a ring," I exclaimed, grabbing her hand again to take a look.

"I hate to break you guys up, but we need to go," Adam interrupted while tapping on his watch.

"Don't worry, Paige. I am completely focused on you and this case. I have no intentions of marrying the man for at least a year." April felt the need to reaffirm her commitment.

A sudden sense of déjà vu overtook me as I stood, once again, in the Wilcox foyer. Though I was expecting to see that stunning view of Central Park, this time, long white curtains were up. Like, they had been installed overnight.

What the hell?

Instead of Walter and Victoria greeting Adam and me at the door, we were being kept back by a linebacker-looking security guard until Walter was ready. I assumed it was his personal security guard, the same one that was with him in the Hamptons. It was like I had gone from being a family friend to a crummy press person overnight.

"Did you used to play for the Jets? You look very familiar," Adam naively questioned the guard.

Whether or not he was serious or just trying to make conversation, the guard didn't answer. He stared down at Adam as if to say, "I can crush you with my thumb."

"Paige Turner! Is that you?" Walter blurted from around the corner.

He wasn't alone. Jimmy DeFazio and his senior advisor, Leon Olson, were with him. Walter gave me a sweaty handshake this time, while Jimmy and Leon just smiled.

"Nice to see you all again."

We followed the men over to the living room and took a seat. There were some papers scattered on the coffee table in front of us.

"I need you to sign these confidentiality agreements first," Leon said, pushing the papers towards me. "You have free rein of the house, with the exception of the bedrooms and please, no shots of Central Park. The shades must stay drawn."

I get it. You just don't want people to see the insanely expensive penthouse you live off a "mayor's salary."

"What about Victoria and Piper? Where are they? I was supposed to take some family photos," I asked.

"They won't be here for the shoot," Walter answered matter-of-factly.

I felt conned hearing his words.

What else would they try and pull at the last minute?

"But, the piece was supposed to be about you and the family," I argued back.

"Yes. Well...things change," Leon responded.

Bastard!

When the parameters were agreed upon, Adam went to work. First, we took photos of the interior, then some with the mayor in his office. He posed as if he were doing work at his desk and then him, contemplating his life as he stood looking at a vintage map of New York City. The expensive statues and paintings that hung in the foyer last night were gone, almost making it look sterile. Pretty much anything that screamed "wealth" had been removed. The photos taken today would tell a fictional story of a mayor who lived a simple and frugal life.

"How about one with me on the phone looking really concerned, like I was just informed of a potential terror attack?" Walter suggested.

"Genius!" Jimmy declared while throwing up his arms. "And maybe put your glasses on and furrow your brow a little bit more to look distressed."

"Yes, that's perfect. Just like that. Show the city who is boss," Adam instructed.

The mayor took Adam so seriously but I knew my sarcastic assistant was just jerking his chain. Walter was getting really into it; I had to keep from laughing.

This is the most ridiculous thing I've ever seen.

Leon was too fixated on the time to see his boss pretending to be Kylie Jenner or Kate Upton.

"Alright, we're done here," Leon finally interrupted. "I think you have about all the pictures you need."

It didn't look like Walter was ready to wrap. It had only been an hour. Adam took some last few pictures before giving me a "thumbs up" to indicate he was done.

"Well, Mayor...Leon and Jimmy. I want to thank you for letting us come here to do this," I said.

After packing up his camera, Adam excused himself to go to the bathroom. Leon and Jimmy went into the living room to make phone calls. I went into the office with Walter.

"I'm sorry I didn't get to see Victoria and Piper. Will they be back later?" I asked.

"No, no. They decided this morning to head out to the Hamptons for some mother-daughter time. I'll be staying here...all by my lonesome. Have some work to tend to," he revealed.

With his tone and suggestive smile, it was obvious what he was really trying to say: "Why don't you keep me company?" I wondered what work he actually had.

Back at my place, Adam uploaded the pictures to the computer and filtered out all the photos that were pertinent to my case.

We stopped on one particular image. It was the picture I had seen the night before of Walter, Victoria, Piper, and Lucy. Adam had managed to get a few zoomed-in shots of the photo hanging on the wall. Then, another crucial image. During the modeling session in Walter's office, Adam captured some snaps of papers that had been left out on his desk. As we zoomed in on the paper, it was clear it was a phone bill. I enlarged it to where we could get a read on the telephone number of the account. I jotted it down along with the email address, wow4nyc2005@ mail.com.

"Now look at this. Don't you think this is odd?" Adam pointed out.

One of the desk drawers was slightly ajar and inside was several files. While Walter thought Adam was taking pictures of him at the computer, my genius assistant was really zooming in on the files' tabs with printed names.

"Leon Olson, Jimmy DeFazio, Richard Brownstein, and Todd Mitchell. Aren't those his staffers? What do you suppose is in those files?" he asked.

I got up from desk chair and started to pace the office.

I don't know. But I need to find out.

By the time Adam and I were done sorting out the pictures, Chin Chin had gotten back to me on the phone number from the telephone bill. Turns out, it was registered to Walter and was a Dallas phone number. I thought maybe it was one of Walter's private phones, so I gave it a call to confirm.

"Hello?" A young woman's voice answered.

"Good day, ma'am. This is the Florida tourism board calling about an exclusive offer on some brand-new time-share opportunities in Venice, Florida. Is this Abigail?" I pretended in my most salesperson-sounding voice.

"No, this is Lucy. You must have the wrong number."

She hung up and my heart raced so hard I could feel the thumping in my throat. Walter had gotten her that number. And, the email address must have been a private one he set up years ago specifically for it.

Who uses mail.com anymore? It's so outdated.

Walter was more than her sugar daddy. This has been going on for a while. At the time it was set up, Lucy would have been in college. There were more clues down in Texas. I had to go back and dig for more.

"You're traveling again? Geez, Paige, when did this come up? I thought we had plans this weekend," Liam moaned.

Lying naked under his arm, I thought that breaking the news to him after we orgasmed would've softened the blow. Thursday was quickly turning into Friday and I was flying back down to Dallas in about eleven hours.

"Baby, I know. It was very last minute," I soothed while looking up into his eyes. "I just need to wrap up this story. I'll still be home to see you this weekend," I promised.

I could tell in his eyes he didn't believe me. I've made similar promises before. Without any sort of response or even a kiss goodnight, he rolled to his side of the bed facing away from me.

With all the running around I had been doing the past several weeks, I was actually looking forward to the four-hour flight and being unreachable. As the plane taxied out to the runway, I shoved the earbuds that were plugged into my seat's television and put on episodes of *The Big Bang Theory*—just one of the features on the American Airlines flight. Back home, my team was diligently working on their tasks. April was out on Long

Island with Piper living it up at *Surf Lodge* in Montauk and *1 OAK* in Southampton. Adam kept it local to monitor Walter. Taylor was also doing all she could to keep *The Gotham Post* out of my hair. With three weeks to go before the interview, I couldn't deal with the paper's perpetual nagging for photos and updates.

Rodney and Richard were aware of my quick jaunt to Dallas after surprising them with a "guess who's coming to town" text. Despite our lack of communication lately, they were quick to invite me over for dinner when I got in. They even arranged for a car to fetch me from the airport!

If all goes as planned, I'll be back home Saturday evening and in Liam's arms by midnight.

"Paige! So good to see you! Come here!" Pamela gushed as if we've been friends for years.

It seemed like just last week I was at the Roches' estate. The butler escorted me to Rodney's wife, Pamela, and Richard's wife, Tracy, who were both sitting outside by the pool. Pamela's waist must have been 20 inches around. They were both in skimpy sundresses and floppy hats and sipping on what was likely a Skinny Girl Martini.

"Aren't you excited for another barbeque dinner?" Pamela sarcastically questioned. "Tracy, you remember Paige? She was here a few months ago. A friend of our hubbies. She is back in town for more work, isn't that right?"

I took a seat in the wicker chair and was promptly served an identical drink to Tracy's and Pamela's.

"Yup...duty calls. Where are the men anyways?"

They have such a large presence; I can usually detect them a mile away.

"Oh, they're out hunting something. They should be back soon. They said no later than four," Tracy said while tapping on her diamond-encrusted Rolex.

The Roche wives could've passed for twins, with the bleach blonde poufy hair, size D implants, swollen lips, and bulging blue eyes. While discussing superficial things like white versus black pearls and flying on private planes and trips to Turks and Caicos, the butler would repeatedly come over to refill our emptying drink glasses. The more we drank, the more chatty the girls got.

"So tell me, how did you meet Richard and Rodney?" I began. "Are you both from Texas?"

Pam and Tracy looked at each other as if to tell the other one to speak.

"Well, we're from up north, went to Texas Christian, and met Richard and Rodney right after graduating," Pamela explained.

I took another big sip of my drink. Two down. The sun was setting behind us and the patio umbrella was slowly becoming ineffective. I could feel the strong hot rays on my back.

"Yes, but how did you meet them?" I pushed harder.

They gave each other that same look again.

"We don't usually tell people this, but, since you're a good friend and seem genuine...we actually met them online," Pamela admitted.

Online? Oh really?

"No way!" I cried with feigned exuberance. "I didn't know online dating was a big thing down here. Do tell!"

Richard and Rodney online dating?

"It was a different kind of dating website. Have you ever heard of the site Rags and Riches?" Tracy timidly asked.

The brief and casual mention made me nearly regurgitate my drink back into my glass.

"You mean the sight where rich men solicit young women in need of money? I thought that website was shut down years ago," I questioned while trying to not come across too accusatory or insulting.

"It did following that massive data breach. All the user names were leaked. Luckily, we met our men in the site's glory days. It's like, it was meant to be," Pamela boasted.

"You know, Texas Christian is a very expensive school. And with all the loans and our sorority fees, the three of us were all kinds of desperate," Tracy defended.

Doesn't that go against the school's morals? How "Christian" is being a sugar baby?

"I'm sorry, did you say "three of us"? Who was the third?"

"Yes. Me, Tracy, and our sorority sister, Lucy. She lives in New York City now. Did you meet her when you were here last?" Pamela unknowingly divulged a swath of information in that one detail.

"Unfortunately, I didn't meet her. But I would LOVE to," I exclaimed.

"You'd like Lucy." *I'm sure I would.* "She has the life..." Pamela started before Tracy interjected.

"I beg to differ, Pam. Actually, she has to keep her relationship under wraps because it's pretty high-profile," Tracy let out in her high-pitched voice. "I'd rather be in a relationship that I didn't have to hide."

Pamela and Tracy continued to serve me info like I was ghostwriting their memoirs. It turns out that none of the three women knew whom they were getting involved with until the second date. That's because Rodney, Richard, and Walter used fake names and profiles on the website. It seems almost sinister that Walter would bring his Rags and Riches mistress into his home and hire her as Piper's babysitter, later on. Tracy even confessed that she and Pam wanted to sue the men for fraud, but after learning about the Roche's net worth, they opted to continue on with the relationships.

What would possess Walter to sign up for such a sleazy website like that? Was he really that unhappy in his marriage? How did he know Lucy was on there?

Rodney and Richard finally returned an hour after they said they'd be home. After finishing with the platter of barbeque meats, casseroles, and thick slices of bread, I ended up spending the night at the Roches' in one of their guest bedrooms. As much as I didn't want to impose, Pamela insisted, so I obliged.

The next morning, instead of wasting time perusing the grounds of TCU and nosing around Sorority Row, I spent the few hours I had before my flight palling around with Tracy and Pamela. The two women dropped an easy $5,000 on a new Chloé purse, $2,000 on a leather bomber jacket, and $350 on a swanky brunch at Le Beau Pain. With endless funds courtesy of their husbands, these women were well taken care of. But, walking behind them as they window-shopped on the hot Dallas streets, I still sensed emptiness inside them. Money, trips, and endless "stuff" can only do so much to satisfy a person's soul.

Back in that same small seat of the American Airlines flight back to Newark Airport less than 24 hours later. I had successfully accomplished what I wanted and would still be home in time to see Liam.

The plane was full and because of the late booking, I had to settle for coach. Careful not to let anyone see, I angled my laptop screen towards the window so I could conduct my research a little more privately. The inflight Wi-Fi sucked but was just enough to allow me to Google *Rags to Riches*. I scanned old headlines. When the website was hacked years ago, media outlets published the email addresses of alleged users. I remembered how big of a scandal it was. Thanks to the Internet and the fact that nothing ever disappears these days, I was able to pull up some old articles on the hacking. One, in particular, linked to the list of email addresses. I downloaded the 340-page document containing the user accounts. It seemed like millions of users and they were in no particular order. Still, I scanned every single one of them.

It wasn't until we were flying over Philadelphia, and I was on page 324, when I saw an email address that made me do a triple take.

Am I really seeing this?

wow4nyc2005@mail.com: the same e-mail that was on Walter's phone bill. He had managed to bypass anyone getting wind of this. I had more than I needed to take down Walter. It was time to free Victoria from her husband's deceitful grip.

Once off the plane and through the gate, I threw myself into the first cab I saw outside of the terminal. I had the urge to celebrate.

"Forty third and third," I ordered the driver.

I opened my Seamless app, clicked on Insomnia Cookies, and had two double chocolate chunk cookiewiches sent to Liam's place with a note: *"Sweets for my sweetie. See you in 30."*

SUNDAY

Five in the morning. Too early to be awake, yet something did not feel right. Liam was still out cold next to me. His chest would rise and fall with every breath he took, like light rolling waves on a calm sea. For that moment under the cool Ralph Lauren sheets, I thought about how lucky I was to have met someone so right, considering all the wrong men I am surrounded by on a daily basis. I kissed him on the cheek, careful not to wake him, and quietly slid myself out of the bed and tiptoed into the living room. The sun's rays glistened off the East River while sailboats slowly made their way downstream. I clicked on the news, making sure to keep the sound at the lowest level. Channel 4's token Asian anchor was going through the usual top stories, including a shooting in the Bronx, a hit-and-run in Queens, a theft in Harlem, and expected subway delays.

Coming up next, "Mayor Wilcox caught with his pants down," she said.

What?! Please don't tell me someone leaked something...

"We'll tell you what prompted him to strip for a good cause," she continued.

I let out a long sigh. The story ended up being about him raising money for Figure Skating in the Bronx, a local charity that benefited young girls with an interest in figure skating.

Mayor Wilcox skated with some of the girls in his shorts and a T-shirt in the 38-degree Sky Rink at Chelsea Piers.

Wait a minute. Who is that?

Something, more like someone, had caught my eye. I hit the rewind on the DVR and replayed the video in slow motion. As the camera panned the bleachers, there she was. Lucy! She was sitting with Comptroller Brownstein and together they looked like the perfect couple. To the average viewer, she looked like Richard's wife. Jimmy was also standing off to the side by the exit door. It all made sense now. Lucy wasn't just Richard's beard. He had been made to look like he and Lucy were an item all along so that she could be out with Walter without anyone getting suspicious. Meanwhile, Richard really had a thing going on with Jimmy.

This case is like an episode of The Young and the Restless.

"What are you doing up so early?" Liam's question startled me from my analytical state.

He was still naked as he walked across the living room and to the kitchen to get some water. His tight butt was turning me on.

"I couldn't sleep any longer. You looked passed out, so I didn't want to wake you."

My knees were pulled up inside one of his Hurley surfing T-shirts that I had thrown on. He came over and kissed my tired eyes.

"I like your outfit," I joked and slapped his thigh as he plopped down next to me.

"The last thing I would be doing if I couldn't sleep is watch the news," he commented.

"Well, you know I'm a news junkie. I have to make sure the world didn't blow up while we were fucking," I sarcastically explained.

He laughed at my quick tongue and I maneuvered his limbs so I was perfectly curled up under his arms.

"Baby...baby...your phone."

Whaaa?

Liam was shaking me. I had gotten too comfortable in his embrace and passed out momentarily. He dangled the phone in front of me like a hypnotist.

"Your girl Taylor has been blowing up your phone the past ten minutes. You fell asleep and I didn't want to wake you but she won't stop!"

I grabbed the phone from him and answered. I couldn't even get a complete "good morning" out because she sounded so hyped up, like she had too much coffee.

"Paige, *The Gotham Post* has been UP MY ASS. They need to see photos. They haven't had an update from you in days! They think you're dead or something," Taylor nagged.

Her demand was not typical Taylor. Liam was still sitting naked next to me and I didn't want him to overhear the conversation, so I excused myself into the bedroom.

"Taylor, I honestly have nothing new for them. Not until the actual interview!" I loudly whispered into the phone.

"I can only push back so much. I can't risk my reputation and my publicity business either. Just give me a couple generic pictures and notes to appease them, okay?" she begged.

I hated having to succumb to their demands especially knowing what they were really getting out of this deal.

After agreeing to Taylor's wishes, I now had to get back home stat. I figured I'd send them a bland rundown and some pictures to keep them out of my hair.

I could see Liam's anticipating disappointment on his face when I came back into the room. I sat on his bare lap, put my arms around his neck, and looked solemnly into his hazel eyes.

"Let me guess. You have to leave," he said with a sigh.

I could either leave like I usually do or I could take the risk and invite him back.

Maybe this would be a good time to tell him what I do and who I really am.

"I do. Do you want to come back to my place with me? My editor is just giving me a hard time."

My stomach knotted with the invite. After constantly using the excuse that it was easier for the both of us if we kept using his place to meet, I couldn't avoid it any longer. It took no convincing at all to get him to come with me. In fact, I noticed a sharp change in his demeanor after asking him. It was as if he felt excited and happier that I was opening up more.

We quickly changed and hailed an Uber to take us to Hoboken.

Crap, I think I left my spy equipment out. I hope Adam isn't there working. Oh man. I think I'm going to pass out.

It may have been a good idea to give him a disclaimer or confidentiality agreement explaining that what he was about to see was off the record. But I had waited too long. As the car pulled in front of my apartment building, I could feel my Rosacea flaring up.

Liam held my hand as we walked through the lobby and into the elevator. I hit the PH17 button with my shaky finger.

"Wow...penthouse, huh? I had no idea reporters made that kind of money," he commented.

"New Jersey is a lot cheaper. Plus, it's not really a penthouse. By the way, my place is a mess. I haven't had much time to clean lately," I warned.

"Babe, stop worry!"

We walked slowly down the dimly lit and quiet hallway.

"Here we are," I said and proceeded to open the door slowly as if it were booby-trapped.

Thankfully, it wasn't as disoriented as I feared. Stacks of papers and files sat out on the coffee table. Liam walked in without a hesitation and made his way over to the windows that looked out over the Hudson. That seemed to be a draw for anyone who entered. Then, I let him roam around as if inspecting for signs that I was cheating or hiding drugs. He did that while I coolly went over to the kitchen to get some water. I patrolled his movements like a warden. He walked back over to the leather couches, stopping to check out my night vision goggles on the floor by the end table.

Crap...

"Are those night vision goggles?" he asked, pointing down at them.

"Umm. Oh, yes, actually. They were a gift from my old law enforcement friend. I just keep them out for decoration...or inspiration...something," I fibbed. "Can I get you something to eat or drink? I just have to take care of some emails quickly in my office," I offered wanting to keep this visit short.

"Go for it. I am fine. I will just sit here and wait for you."

"Okay. Here. You can watch Netflix."

The recently watched list came up revealing nothing but crime and murder mysteries as if to say to him, "You're dating a psychopath." I handed him the controller, kissed him on the lips, and continued to my office. The door was slightly ajar so I could keep an eye on his movements through the reflection in the computer monitor.

I quickly scanned through all 103 photos, deciding on three random ones to send to Connie and Juliet. Then, I typed up some bullets for them so they knew about my progress. Cc-ing Taylor, I hit "send." Connie must have been waiting with her phone in her hand and eyes glued on the screen because within 15 seconds, she responded with a "thanks."

"Jesus Christ...your office..."

I turned my head sharply to see Liam standing in the doorway. His eyes wide and fixated on the three computer monitors displaying top-secret information, two TVs with frozen images of Mayor Wilcox, stacks of file boxes, and my glass lockbox containing my Glock, lucky pocketknife, and assortment of spy cameras.

"It looks like the Pentagon in here."

I was frozen in my seat. Making any sudden movements to push him out would only make this worse.

"Vixen Investigator?" he questioned, pointing to the badge on the desk.

I quickly hit the "Abort All" tab on my computer. It was a feature I had specifically designed for situations like this where all the computer screens and monitors would instantly turn off. It was now clear to him that I was hiding something. In an effort to try to explain things, I stood, trying to block everything that I was hiding from him these past months.

"Why did you have pictures of the mayor on those TVs? I thought you wrote about travel and lifestyle? Are you a CIA operative?! Who are you?!"

He got louder. Before I could muster up a response, Liam turned and hastily made his way to the door. I chased after him, nearly tripping over my own feet.

"Liam, wait. No, I am not in the CIA. Just stop for a minute!" I urged.

He stopped with his one hand on the doorknob and looked at me. I could see the disappointment in his eyes.

"I knew something was up with you. Those quick cancellations, jaunts to Texas, and who knows what else. You could've been honest. I probably would've thought it was cool!" he scolded.

"Just calm down. It's not easy to explain. I'm not like most women," I defended.

"I know you aren't. That's why I fell in love with you. But, you lied to me. You're a spy, not a reporter. Have you been spying on me?"

His accusations were hurtful and by nature, all I wanted to do was fight back. But he was right. I shouldn't have lied. I reached for his arm but he just pushed me away.

"Liam, I've never done anything behind your back. I've always respected you and the relationship. It's just something I can't get into before I really know someone. I run an infidelity...," I began to explain, but he didn't want to hear it.

He opened the door and went straight to the stairwell.

"Liam!" I said loudly while trying not to alarm my neighbors.

He was already gone.

MONDAY

"He didn't even let me explain."

I was trying to justify what happened with Taylor and April over Shake Shack burgers and milkshakes. The air was thick and heavy. It felt like it could downpour any minute. We were sitting at a wobbly table in Madison Square Park.

"What if he says something?"

"He's not. He's not that type of guy. He probably felt betrayed. I mean, you weren't honest with him," Taylor lectured, then paused. "If anyone should know about being honest with your partner, it's you."

"I was waiting for the right time. If I were just honest from the start, he wouldn't have even cared. It was the fact that I hid the truth from him for so long that really bothered him," I finally admitted.

I couldn't help but feel like a hypocrite. I demanded transparency from the men in my life and yet, I kept so much a secret.

Following the therapy session with April and Taylor, I decided to walk alone to the ferry terminal on the West Side. The clouds from the west were dark. Storms were rolling in. I could faintly hear thunder in the distance. While I risked getting caught in the rain, I thought the walk might make me feel a little better.

I shoved the earbuds into my ears and put on "The Eagles" channel on my Pandora app. "Lyin' Eyes" was the first song to play.

Very funny, Pandora!

Irritated, I turned the music off and decided it'd be best to just listen to the sounds of the city streets.

On the ferry home and with the city slowly getting farther away, I closed my eyes and let the wind smack my face. The boat rocked side to side. Big rain drops started to fall on the deck. We were in for a big storm. I was prepping to run for cover as the boat docked. Then, a text.

Walter Mobile:
Free for dinner this week?

WEDNESDAY

It took three days to finally get a response from Liam. I had so desperately wanted to explain myself to him for the sake of us and my business. Since he had to travel for work and I didn't want any distractions right before the interview, we settled on a date to talk a few days after. While he still weighed heavy on my thoughts, I turned my focus solely on Mayor Wilcox. *The Gotham Post* was more excited about the piece than a porn star on Viagra. I had teased the paper of the "juicy information" I had on the mayor. They knew they were in for a good story.

Walter seemed to also be hungry for me. I agreed to dinner with him. He wanted to see me away from the distraction of his subordinates and his family. Sleazy, yet a crucial opportunity for me.

We were meeting tonight at the hard-to-get-into restaurant Devin's, on the Upper West Side. It was a hyped-up, no-frills restaurant where, unless you were an A-lister or knew the family, it was impossible to get in. Wednesdays were apparently the best nights there because they only opened for the really special clients. One of which was Walter.

Walter had ordered me a car service, which had me at the restaurant promptly at 8 p.m.

Using taxpayer dollars to cart your date around, Mayor?

Walter was already sitting inside when I walked in. The place smelled like Sundays at my childhood home when my mom would spend all day cooking a roast and potatoes.

"Hello, Mayor," I said, bending over to kiss him on the cheek. He motioned for me to sit down.

"You look delightful," he commented about the tightest black dress I owned. "I'm glad you agreed to meet with me. I haven't been able to stop thinking about you."

"I tend to have that effect on people...especially men," I replied with a seductive gaze. "Tell me, why did you want to meet with me so bad? You know this goes against all journalistic ethics," I teased.

"You excite me, Paige Turner. There's something about you."

It was obvious he wasn't here to talk business. His desire of me had him just where I wanted him. He already seemed so much more powerless.

"I want you to be my new press secretary," he confessed.

Seriously? What about Jimmy? He's been so loyal to you all these years!

"Wow, sir. That is quite an offer." I played along.

Almost two hours of what seemed like nothing but flirting and bribery, we were finally ready to leave. The restaurant didn't even bring over a bill. We just left and there was a car waiting for him. He insisted I come home with him because "he didn't want to be alone."

"You know, this interview with you means a lot to me. More than an Emmy or Pulitzer or a big fat check," I confessed as we sat in the back of the town car.

I was tired and just wanted to go home, but kept my game face on. I ran my fingers down his shirt stopping just short of his waistband. I'd tantalize his sexual appetite by going in for a kiss and then pull away. His hand rested on my thigh.

"You give me what I want. I'll give you what you want," I whispered in his ear just before giving it a little nibble.

That simple move sent him over the top. He pulled my face to his and he kissed me hard. When I felt his attempt to shove his tongue deep down my throat, I playfully pushed him off of me but really wanted to slam his head against the window.

"Mayor! Please. Not this...not now!" I ordered. "I said...you give me what I want and I'll give you what you want."

Walter was breathing hard. I could tell he wanted me. A man in his power wasn't used to being turned away; that's why he was so turned on.

"I'm sorry. I don't know what got into me," he admitted.

I could still taste the stale wine from his mouth on my lips.

"John, please take Miss Turner back to New Jersey," he ordered the driver.

No amount of soap and water could wash the stench of Walter off of me. I wasn't even home for thirty minutes and already he was inundating me with texts about how much fun he had. As water from my wet hair dripped onto the phone, I didn't even bother texting him back. I knew not responding to him would drive him nuts.

I got under the silk covers with a big smile on my face that night.

Yes, Walter, there is something about me. I'm the Vixen Investigator.

With July 4th just a few days away, lots of people had taken the week off and the city was a lot quieter. It was a good time for me to hunker down and plan out my questions and attack-plan the big day. Victoria had entered an almost zombie-like state knowing that the end was near. There was still a lot she didn't know, but knew it wasn't good. I was honest but vague with her. Soon, I would be disclosing all. She had been spending most of her time in the Hamptons away from photographers and reporters. When she returned to town for her annual doctor's appointment next week—a few days before the interview—we had plans to reconnect to go over some final details.

Today, however, I had back-to-back meetings with Jimmy at City Hall and another with *The Gotham Post*. I decided to drive myself into the city to avoid that wretched smell of the city in the summertime and, not to mention, the heat of being underground.

"Miss Turner. Nice to see you again," greeted Stan, the City Hall security guard.

I was now on a first-name basis with all of them, which was rare and an accomplishment in itself. Their tough-guy attitudes were no match for my tight outfits and captivating charm.

As usual, I sat in the waiting area until the portly secretary came out to bring me in. She'd call me in and I followed her down the echoing hallways and into Jimmy's office, where he was sitting at his desk. I took a seat as he held up his pointer finger to silently tell me "one minute," like always.

"Just one more second...and...okay...finished," he spoke into his computer screen. "Sorry about that. I just get so stressed out, but I guess that's normal."

He was very jittery, like he had just done a line of cocaine or had too many cups of coffee. Even without prying, Jimmy would voluntarily spill all his anxieties to me. I got the sense he really hated his job after telling me how hard it was to keep tabs on Walter all the time. It was understandable, especially with the secrets he kept. Twenty minutes into what was turning out to be a therapy session for him, Jimmy finally got into the real reason he had called me in. There were apparently some concerns that my questions would drift to attacks and take a more political feel. My blood raced with such an assumption.

He concluded with a warning that if I got too hard with him, Leon would pull the plug on the interview, even if mid-taping. Jimmy's advice was more out of caution for me than an order from his boss. I appreciated the heads-up from him.

I gave Jimmy my word that I'd keep the interview strictly about his family and love life. We shook on it, but just as I was about to begin gathering up my belongings, Jimmy dropped his head into his hands and started sobbing. I was caught so off guard, I didn't know if I should call for help. Instead, I went around to the back of his desk and put my hands on his shoulders. It was then that he spilled the details about him and Richard. I let him talk without interruption as he explained their first encounter and how much he was in love with him. Like I already surmised, Jimmy didn't know how much longer he could go on keeping their relationship a secret. He wanted to quit, but said it just "wasn't an option."

On to meeting number two at *The Gotham Post*. I was a woman on a mission with no time to waste.

"Paige?" I had just sat down in the waiting room when Connie and Juliet both came out to greet me.

They were smiling and looked eager to chat. Down the hallway, past the giant conference room where I first got to know them, and into Connie's office, which looked out towards the Statue of Liberty, I followed. Juliet offered me the larger, leather chair while she stood to my side. It was like they were buttering me up for something.

"So," Connie started, leaning over her desk that reminded me of a garage sale: junk everywhere. "How's it going with the exposé? You ready for the interview? What are you going to wear?" Questions left her mouth faster than a tennis ball launcher.

"All going as planned. I am just waiting for the big day," I calmly said.

"Great. I know you're prepping for the interview and everything, but we just wanted to run some...ideas by you," Connie offered while my first thought went to how much I hated outside influence on my uncompleted work. "I know we've discussed this before...*The Gotham Post* is not a soft newspaper. Sure, it's fun and readers like our quirky writing style..."

"What Connie is trying to say is that, we need dirt," Juliet interrupted. "We need some dirty shit. Our readers aren't fans of the mayor. See if you could play up his lavish lifestyle in a way that would insult New Yorkers."

I appreciated how Juliet got right to the point, even if they were belaboring on the same one. We were all in agreement but they didn't even realize it. I took a deep breath, stood up, and turned to them both.

"Don't worry ladies. I know exactly what you want...and you will get exactly that. I said it was going to be a juicy story. And I mean, it will be juicy," I guaranteed.

JULY

The Fourth of July has always been one of my favorite holidays. It was the only day I felt that eating two hot dogs and a hamburger in one sitting was acceptable because it showed my devotion to the United States of America. With the holiday on a Saturday this year, the entire coastline surrounding the Tri-State area was sure to be packed. That's why I opted to stay put in Hoboken. The spectacular Macy's fireworks would be set off just feet away from me on the Hudson River so I decided to rent out the roof of the apartment building and invite my dearest friends over to watch the show. Theresa was in town and I was thrilled to have her back. She was coming over along with Taylor, Adam, April, and Jordan. Also on the attendance list: the now divorced and world traveling Leslie Schneider (formerly Benson) and her new boy-toy, actor and former clerk at The Hotel Versailles, Claude. I honestly couldn't wait to gossip about Steve. All I knew was that after I shocked his world, he was fired for using company funds to pay for his infidelities.

I was looking forward to seeing everyone outside of the work setting, although I was missing Liam. I asked him to come over, but he told me he "already had plans." He was still upset and it was understandable. I was just happy to be communicating again, whether or not he really had plans.

With the sun setting behind the western cliffs of northern New Jersey, hordes of people began making their way to the west side of Manhattan. My party was going through hamburgers, wieners, and tofu dogs (for Taylor) faster than Joey Chesnut at the Nathan's Hot Dog Eating Contest. It was nice to see everyone looking genuinely happy. I wondered how Victoria was doing. She, Walter, and Piper were together this holiday weekend, again, for press reasons only. With about twenty minutes to spare before the fireworks started I summoned my Vixen Investigations crew for a quick chat away from the rest of the group.

We all had our drinks and whatever remaining food in our hands as I started the conversation.

"I think you need to go full-out Vixen Investigator on the mayor, Paige," Theresa advised. "You obviously have so much on him, you can just present him with all the evidence and he wouldn't be able to do anything. That guy needs a good kick in the balls."

As much as I appreciated Theresa's two cents, her perspective was unrealistic. I couldn't throw it down like she instructed. I had to go about it smoothly and get him to confess. He'll just deny, deny, deny.

"I'm serious! That motherfucker shouldn't be in office. He's the reason I moved out of New York City, and I love New York City. Get him out and I'll move back," she continued.

"I can't just come out like a caged bull. There's a technique to getting him to tell me what I want. It has to be done subtly," I said.

Since we were literally counting down the days, I advised everyone to maintain their low profiles and keep doing their assigned tasks. Even though April was drained and we had plenty of information on Piper's tumultuous relationship with her father, we couldn't break character.

"April! Get over here, the fireworks start in one minute!" Jordan yelled over to us.

We made our way back to the other guests just before the first rocket shot from the barge. For 45 minutes, the space that separated New York and New Jersey was emblazoned with red, white, and blue balls of fire. I went and stood with my dad and Zelda. She seemed to be enjoying the fireworks herself, jumping up and barking every time a new one was propelled into the air. The fireworks were grand and beautiful, but they were nothing compared to the explosions about to come out of this investigation.

The Monday before the big day and I was in full crime-fighting mode. Today was the final meeting with Victoria, who already had lined up a lawyer. It was time to reveal everything to her from Lucy, *Rags and Riches*, Dallas, to the Hamptons party and the administration's cover-up. When she disclosed that she hired the city's most successful divorce attorney, that's when it really hit me. As strong of a woman as she was, I felt bad for her. She had spent the majority of her life with a man who was sneaking around behind her back. She didn't enter marriage thinking that her spouse might cheat. She planned on growing old with Walter.

Adam arrived at my place right at 10 a.m. to help me prepare for Victoria's arrival. I had already been up for a few hours and was ready for a drink. Adam looked worn out, too. We were both ready to close this case.

The PowerPoint presentation I'd detail to Victoria was a timeline of Walter's philandering events. I had collected more dirt on him than anyone would've ever imagined. From photos, phone records and bank statements, and audio recordings from the suspect and his cohorts, there was no way he could possibly argue his way out of this one. There was still one thing I desperately needed to find out: what was in those files stashed in Walter's desk?

Victoria arrived just after 11 a.m. To my surprise, she was rather chipper for someone who was about to go through an epic divorce. Maybe she was just excited to finally hear that everything she suspected of her husband, was true. Or, maybe it was the idea that she was about to start a new life without him. I gave her a welcome hug and escorted her to the couch. Adam brought us both a bottle of water. I positioned myself in front of the television screen.

"Victoria, before we start, I just want to let you know that you can tell me to stop whenever you need to. Some of what you're about to see and hear may be very upsetting."

She nodded and motioned to me to begin with the evidence.

I started with slide one, which detailed my efforts since she first came to me in January. Slide after slide revealed a new fact. I elaborated on the various press conferences I attended as a freelance reporter and pointed out Lucy, who was always in the crowd standing with Comptroller Brownstein. She instantly recognized her as the family's old babysitter. I explained to her that Brownstein was actually gay, but always appeared to be a straight and taken man in front of the press.

Next were some pictures of my trips to Dallas, where Walter was with the Roche brothers, the Roche wives, and Lucy. When I got into explaining how the three sorority sisters used the website *Rags to Riches* to find their sugar daddies, Victoria sank back into the couch and put her hand over her head in shame and embarrassment.

It's okay, Victoria. No logical wife would suspect their husband of doing these sorts of things.

I continued moving on to the pictures of the Lord Max's party and some additional snaps taken of Lucy and Walter out on the streets of New York.

"This was all my fault," I heard her mumble. "This..." Victoria pointed to the TV screen almost trancelike, "THIS is all my fault. I drove my own husband to seek sex elsewhere! And then he brings her back into our home and pretends to hire her as our nanny!" She lashed out.

"Victoria. This isn't your fault. You're the strong one, remember," I encouraged before continuing. "There is more. Walter had help hiding her. All his friends are in on this," I said and flipped to the next slide. "You couldn't figure out why he needed three phones, right? Well, one is the one you talk to him on, one is for his staff, and then the third...that's to communicate with Lucy."

Victoria closed her eyes and covered them with her hands.

"The money transfers...all going to an account set up for..."

"Lucy...of course," Victoria finished, as if now knowing where all the clues pointed.

I explained how Walter kept Lucy hidden in the Hamptons most of the time, but he'd occasionally bring her into the city and on trips to Texas.

"Is the entire administration in on this?" she asked.

I wanted to answer "yes," but it was too soon and I had no hard evidence of that just yet. I told her that I still needed to figure that out. If so, it takes this scandal to a whole other level.

I wouldn't let Victoria leave until I knew she was settled down. It didn't take much convincing to have her also agree to help me break into Walter's desk after explaining that I needed to see what was inside of it. She knew where he kept the key to the file cabinets. So, without a hint of hesitation, the three of us hopped into the Jeep and made our way to her home in record time. Victoria led us through the building's back entrance to avoid the lobby security.

Walter was still at City Hall, which gave us under and hour to complete "Operation: Seize Files." Adam followed behind me as I followed Victoria into Walter's office. The key to the filing cabinet was taped to the inside of the old circuit breaker box that was disguised to look like part of the wall behind the oak bookshelves. The rage Victoria was hiding inside had given her Wonder Woman strength, as she didn't even need my help moving the heavy shelves. She handed me the key and with a shaky hand, I excitedly opened the file drawer.

"PING...PING..." I heard the noise but ignored what it was or whose phone it might be.

"Oh, shit. Walter's on his way home," Victoria voiced.

"What? Shit! I thought you said he'd be home at five?! Try and delay him," I ordered loudly. "Adam, go downstairs and make sure to alert us if you see him. Try to stop him."

He did as told. I continued to pull out the individual files, each one containing pages of invoices. For "services rendered" all it said was, "Operation: Kryptonite Tiger."

It's a code name for something. Why does that sound so familiar?

"This is some sort of project. It's an undercover project," I realized and said aloud.

Wait a minute; the first text I ever received from that mystery caller was "Kryptonite Tiger"!

"Vic! What is kryptonite tiger? Does that ring any bells to you?" The urgency in my voice made her dart right back over to the office.

"Kryptonite Tiger? Oh my God. I haven't heard that in decades. It was the pet name Walter gave me back in college. He used to call me his kryptonite tiger. Why?"

It looked like all the staffers apparently involved in this operation were paid the same amount every month: $6,500. I snapped as many pictures as I could of the documents.

He was paying them for something. What was this operation all about?

Adam began blowing up my phone with texts to alert me that Walter was entering the building. My body shook in anticipation as I could feel the blood pumping even harder. I needed to get out of here. I dropped the files back in the drawer. But, before handing the key back to Victoria, I noticed one more file shoved in the back. The folder was rather thick. Thick like the file I saw being handed to Walter on the street!

It was the same file. It had to be!

The tab read, "Steve Benson."

Steve Benson?

With no time to spare and without even a hesitation, I grabbed the file and shoved it in my bag.

"Play dumb if he asks where this file went...and act normal," I ordered Victoria before slipping out the back.

Operation: Kryptonite Tiger?

"What do you think that it means?" Adam asked, as I uploaded the photos to my laptop. I had him drive us downtown to Battery Park, where it was generally quiet at this time of the day. There were some vacant tables and chairs near the marina where we could sit and regroup.

How clever of him to mask his secrets under such an innocent and unassuming name.

"The way the mayor spends his money, you'd think he were a billionaire," Adam observed.

He was right, between the transfers and what he was paying his cronies, in addition to funding his real family.

"I'm going to find a bathroom. B-R-B," Adam said and hurried off.

I Googled "Kryptonite Tiger." Nothing relevant came up. The breeze coming off the Hudson River felt good in the summer sun. My phone rang in my bag just as I was about to run to the bodega nearby for something to quench my thirst. It was April.

"What's up?" I asked and walked closer to the water for a better signal.

"Here's an interesting factoid," April began. "Last night, me, Piper, and two of her other girlfriends were out for drinks at The Jimmy. They started talking about a girl named Lucy..."

"What about her?" I snapped.

"Piper's friend said she heard that Lucy had a 4-year-old and she wanted to visit her to see the child, but Lucy just ignores Piper now. It sounded like the two had still been in touch after she was fired, but not so much lately...you there?"

A child? A 4-year-old?

"Oh my God," I blurted. "I've got to go."

Where the hell is Adam?

I hurried to gather my things. Again, my phone started ringing. "Unavailable," the caller ID said. I picked up without saying a word.

"Paige..." *That voice. That insane, robotic voice.* "Nice day, isn't it?"

I didn't know how to respond. All I could get out was, "Who is this?"

"Don't worry about who this is. Just worry about finishing the job," the voice said.

Finishing the job?

"How do you know about MY JOB?" I demanded.

"No need to get all defensive. I'm helping YOU out... remember? I know you were with Mrs. Mayor today. Hopefully she knows what is going on with her husband. The dumb woman couldn't figure it out after all this time?"

"What's your point?" I challenged.

"I know you're getting close to solving this puzzle. Don't forget to ask him about his new boat in your interview."

New boat? Interview? How did they know about that?

Before I could follow up, the mystery caller hung up. It was the longest conversation I had to date with the unknown caller. My breathing got heavier and that eerie feeling that I was being watched revisited me.

"You okay?" Adam calmly asked, yet making me jump. "Geez, Paige, you look like you saw a ghost."

"Where did you go? You startled me," I snapped. "I need to go see something. Do me a favor and go through the photos filed under "press conference" and pull any pictures that have a child with the group, specifically around the age of four."

I left Adam at the bench with my purse and the computer and went over to the marina.

Ask about his new boat?

The boats knocked into each other with every gust of wind. I took a walk around the dock. On the opposite side from where Adam and I were stationed was a sailboat that caught my attention. At first, I thought I was seeing things. There was nothing very special or elaborate about this boat, but something was pulling me to it. As I got closer, the wording on the starboard side became clearer. *Kryptonite Tiger*, it said. The boat's name was *Kryptonite Tiger*! I took out my phone to grab a picture of the registration sticker on the bow. It didn't look like anyone was in or on it.

I briefly mulled over whether I could make the leap from deck to the stern without falling into the mucky Hudson. I had no choice but to try. I pepped myself up, took off my shoes and waited until the next wake brought the boat close to the deck. Then, I jumped, making it, but nearly losing my balance and my phone on the way. I ducked so nobody would see me and climbed down into the spotless cabin. My phone rang again.

"Hello," I whispered.

"Paige, where the hell did you go? I'm walking around the pier." Adam sounded panicky. "You need to take a look at this Steve Benson file, F-Y-I."

"I'm on the boat named *Kryptonite Tiger*. Would you believe there is a boat here named that?"

I was obviously excited...and a little bit anxious. I didn't know what I was getting myself into; I rarely did.

"What? Where is the boat?"

"The opposite side from where we were sitting. You'll see my flats by the dock. You stand guard."

I hung up and continued to rummage. Nothing seemed out of the ordinary until I opened the drawers below the bunk beds. My heart raced at the sight. The drawer was strewn with a variety of items. There were sandwich bags, bed sheets, stuffed animals, and some sex toys. One vibrator looked like it hadn't been cleaned in months. It nearly made me vomit. I took some pictures of the suspected infidelity scene. There was nothing yet that indicated whom the boat belonged to. My phone vibrated signaling another incoming call.

"Yeah, what?" I sharply asked.

"Looks like a large group of people coming this way," Adam warned.

"Crap! Does it look like anyone we know?"

"I can't tell. They look like Spanish or Middle Eastern. There's like ten of them."

"Okay, text me if it looks like they're coming onboard."

I hung up, grabbed one of the folded washcloths to pick up the crusty vibrator and put it in a plastic zip-lock bag. As disgusting as it was, I figured if I had to, I could use the serial number to trace it back to the place and time of purchase. There was a stack of folders, a stuffed animal, and a DVD of *Teenage Mutant Ninja Turtles*. I grabbed everything and shoved the items in a garbage bag.

At this point, I didn't care what went missing. I want it all!

Adam Mobile (6:03 p.m.):
GET OFF THE BOAT NOW!

Climbing back up the stairs, I could see the group of people standing on the pier. They were just a few feet away looking like they were about to board the neighboring yacht named, *Grande Bolas*.

Who names their boat that?

I tossed Adam the garbage bag. The wealthy-looking family turned to look at me. I gave them a casual wave. Then, I launched myself off *Kryptonite Tiger* and back onto the pier, making it with only three inches to spare.

"What's in this bag?" Adam asked, observing its contents from the outside.

I grabbed my shoes and his arm and dragged him back to the car.

"A used dildo and a stuffed animal," I said casually.

"You know, you could've warned me."

"Oh, calm down. I think it may give us some more answers. Now, what about that folder?"

Utter disbelief. That's how I felt when we got back to the apartment. As I studied the file folder with Steve Benson written on the tab, things started piecing together even more. It appeared that Walter paid Steve one million dollars to carry out a hit on the former attorney general. It was all in the file. Walter was stupid enough to keep such documentation around. Steve didn't actually perform the brutal act, but oversaw the operation that took Henry Parker out. But why? What did the former AG know about Walter? Did he know about Operation: Kryptonite Tiger?

In my state of shock, I continued on. It was the excitement that kept me moving. Putting the file aside, I immediately started studying some of the items I had collected while Adam worked to track down the license number of the boat and whom it was registered to. I was neck-deep in scanning documents and carefully analyzing the pictures Adam pulled for me when he alerted me to his findings.

"Guess who the boat belongs to?" I took off my latex gloves and turned towards him sitting at his desk.

"Let me guess, Walter Wilcox," I answered.

"Nope. Richard "Dick" Brownstein."

"The comptroller? Where did "Dick" come from?"

Adam pointed to the screen of his laptop. Apparently "Dick" was his nickname or middle name.

Dick Brownstein? Richard Brownstein? RB? DB? DB?!

"That makes so much sense!" I blurted. "DB! Remember when Victoria first came to us? She kept saying Walter was texting with a DB about owing him money? Walter owed him $14,000!"

It must have been for Operation Kryptonite Tiger!

I started going through some of the files from the boat and assigned Adam another task: come up with a portrait of what a Walter and Lucy lovechild would look like.

In one of the files there were several Excel spreadsheets that detailed dates and payments. The second file contained paperwork that looked like a schedule of sorts with JD getting Mondays, TM getting Tuesdays, DB getting Wednesdays and Fridays, LO getting Thursdays, and WW getting Saturdays and Sundays. Those had to be the initials of the staffers, the only conclusion I could make.

When I got to the thickest file and saw the letterhead being from the NYC Department of Treasury, the hairs on my neck stood up. Carefully flipping through the pages, what I had in my hand was a copy of last years fiscal budget. Page after page listed the planned spending for the year for such things as roads, schools, and numerous pork projects. Then, deep within the text of page 189, was fiscal spending for "Operation: Kryptonite Tiger," with $980,000 being allotted to fund the project. What I had just unearthed warranted a full-scale FBI investigation. At some point soon, I'd have to alert government officials.

"Here he is," Adam said.

He brought over his laptop with the rendering.

"That's him," I blurted.

I immediately pulled out the pictures I had taken on my first trip to Dallas. There, standing next to Walter and holding onto Lucy's hand, was a little boy whose face nearly matched the rendering.

"Same bone structure, same eyes and nose..." Adam listed.

"It might explain that swing set and trampoline in the backyard of the house in the Hamptons. Maybe even this matted stuffed animal," I concluded while lightly squeezing its aged fur and cotton stuffing.

The wealth of information we suddenly seemed to have in our hands had left us in a state of silent excitement and anticipation. There was no longer a concept of time as the moon was now high in the sky. Monday was slowly turning into Tuesday, but neither of us was tired. Going through all the data, I had almost forgotten about the *Teenage Mutant Ninja Turtles* DVD.

"I have this sinking feeling that it isn't going to be Michelangelo, Donatello, Rafael, and Leonardo on that tape, Paige," Adam said while popping the tape into the DVD player.

The grainy video started to play.

"That's a naked man!" I declared.

This was no children's video; it was a raunchy sex tape starring Leon Olson and Todd Mitchell and each were banging each other's wives. Why they would have a wife-swapping orgy on the small sailboat rather than in their homes was beyond me. And, to mask it in a child's video case was just as disturbing.

"Just when I thought this case couldn't get more sordid," Adam announced. "Are the people running this city really this dumb and corrupt?"

19

New York City has had its share of good and bad mayors. And, despite the bad ones, it still hasn't stopped it from being the greatest city in the world. It's the place dreamers flock to for a reason. If you sow your seeds just right, who knows what will grow in between the cracked sidewalks and dilapidated brownstones.

I had reached a new height with my business all because the city gave me a wonderful gift: an asinine mayor. With the swath of evidence I now had against him and his staff, I could just turn everything over to the feds and the media. However, I am the Vixen Investigator and I always see things through until the very end.

Two days until the big interview. I had my questions ready and had rehearsed several times with Taylor. She was thrilled when I allowed her to select my wardrobe for the interview, under one guideline: the attire must consist of tight black pants, a tight blazer, and heels. I decided I'd wear my hair in a bun in an effort to mask my appearance a little since the interview was being videotaped. I also found a trendy pair of wide-framed glasses in my night table that I thought would complete the ensemble.

I figured tonight was my last night to "live it up" before the interview and I hadn't had a real night out in a long time. Adam's band was having its first city performance at Terminal

5, so I agreed to go and watch. Theresa, April, and Taylor also agreed to come to show their support. I wanted to invite Liam, but decided to just wait until our "talk."

The four of us were getting ready at Taylor's place. I glammed myself up in a black, low-cut, silk romper, nude pumps, gold bangles, and large hoop earrings.

"When does he have time to even rehearse? The way you work him, I'm surprised he even sleeps," Theresa commented on Adam.

We were both doing our makeup in Taylor's half-bathroom.

"What do you mean? He works hard by choice. He loves what he does," I defended, not knowing what Theresa was getting at.

"I mean he's in his early twenties. It's supposed to be the best years of his life...doing drugs and fucking girls. He's like a workhorse."

I put down my NARS blush and turned to her. She was still focused on teasing her hair.

"Adam's not that type of guy. He's the best assistant I could ask for. Plus, who else can I turn to on a whim?"

I never suspected that Adam felt overworked. Sure, he would often have to drop everything to come with me on a stakeout or fly to Dallas or wherever, but I took care of him. He never had to worry about finances like other guys his age.

"Well...what about me?" she coyly suggested. "This acting thing is for the fucking birds. Hollywood is filled with fake bastards who don't understand the concept of a clock. I haven't made one friend there," Theresa confessed.

And here she was making it look like a glamorous life on her Instagram and Facebook.

"Really? You, having trouble making friends in Hollywood?" Theresa nudged me with her hip, knowing I was sarcastically stating the obvious.

She had to have been the most conservative female in Los Angeles. I mean, her dad worked for Reagan and she was head of the College Republicans club at Yale. I now knew where her observations were coming from: she wanted a greater role in my business.

"I'd be open to that," I said, resuming my position in the mirror.

I brushed on the blush and applied my Vixen Red lipstick.

"There's just one thing," I started. She looked over at me. "I get to have the 'Theresa Swear Jar.'"

We both laughed.

"Fuck you," she replied.

Four hours of blasting music and I was pretty sure I had temporarily lost my hearing. It was 2 a.m. and I couldn't get the ringing in my head to stop. It was worth it, though. Adam's band was awesome and his solo drum riffs were out of this world. I never knew he had such talent. As I watched him perform on that stage and saw all the cute girls screaming for him, I felt so proud, just as a big sister would. Then, I thought about what Theresa told me as I tried to fall asleep. He did all he was asked and expected to do for Vixen Investigations and at the same time, managed to be an incredible drummer.

The countdown was officially on. Twenty-four hours away and sleep was off the table. All I wanted to do was run. Adrenaline surged nonstop as I anticipated what would go down tomorrow. I arranged for a special dinner with Adam later today as a way to say "thank you for your hard work." I thought it would be nice for us to go out and enjoy a nice early dinner to relax and discuss any last-minute concerns he had. Adam liked Cuban food, so I took us to Son Cubano, just a few neighborhoods north of us in New Jersey. I ordered us a pitcher of sangria and an order of their out-of-this-world sweet plantains, to start.

"So, you ready for tomorrow?" Adam asked while taking a bite of his food.

I confidently replied with an, "Of course." It would be the biggest exposure for both of us and it was good he'd see all his hard work pay off.

"What about you? Ready to be my transcriber and protector should things get physical?" I joked.

"I'm used to it by now, Paige," he replied.

We talked a bit more about work, then about his band and the dreams he had for it. I was his boss, but I was also his friend and I wanted him to know that. Right before the check came, I surprised Adam with two tickets to the Jay Z concert at Barclays Center. It was the one artist he always wanted to see. When I found out he was performing in two weeks, I hit up one of my security contacts who owns a suite there. I made sure Adam would get the VIP treatment he deserved, and he couldn't have been more thankful.

JULY 9th

Thanks for everything and your help with this. What happens next will be one for the Vixen Investigations' books," I said to Adam.

I could tell he was nervous as we sat in the Jeep waiting to go into City Hall. He took a long breath, but didn't say anything.

It was a cooler, crisp day for early July. The city seemed a little too quiet, I noticed as we walked shoulder to shoulder into the building. The guard let us through after checking our bags and we took a seat in the sterile waiting room. Adam couldn't seem to stop shaking his foot. The cameraman was allegedly already here and had set up in Walter's office. I continued to go over my notes and the questions I had scribbled on my reporter's notepad. Adam's ceaseless foot shaking was really starting to irk me. I looked over at him as if to say, "Knock it off." I was feeling extra irritable.

Where is Taylor? I told her to meet me at 9:40 a.m.

I caught Adam looking intensely at my face, then down at my feet. I was the one who was now fiercely and unknowingly shaking their foot. I closed my eyes and tried to clear my thoughts. I could hear the clacking of high heels getting closer. I thought it was an illusion, at first.

"Hey, guys!" Taylor bubbly announced her arrival.

"You're five minutes late!" I nagged and stood to give her a strong hug.

Even though I had been in the business of nabbing cheaters for several years, I still got nervous and anxious before a bust. The wall clock ticked closer and closer to 10 a.m. The more it neared the hour, the louder I could hear the ticking.

"Doesn't look like we're going to start on time. Maybe you should e-mail Jimmy," Taylor suggested.

She, too, had noticed we were seconds away from our scheduled interview time, and I still needed to set myself up. I wondered how the cameraman was allowed in so early.

"I don't care if they start the damn interview at eleven as long as they give me my full hour," I replied. "I'll give them five more minutes and then I'll just bust through the door," I joked.

But I wouldn't have to. The portly secretary emerged right on time.

"I almost didn't recognize you with your hair up and those glasses," she observed and led us down the hall.

Good. That's the whole point.

Straight ahead, I could see a small video camera on a tripod with a spotlight illuminating Walter's desk. It looked like the camera would shoot right over the back of my left shoulder, which was perfect as it completely hid my face. My heart thumped harder and faster.

Walter was sitting down, but stood in excitement when I entered the room. He didn't seem at all keen on Taylor and Adam being in my presence. The way he locked eyes with me, and just me, was all too familiar.

"There she is! The woman of the hour," he boasted, coming from behind his desk to give me a hug.

The cameraman, who looked nonthreatening and like he had been in the business for decades, observed our exchange.

"Hello, Mayor. Nice to see you again," I replied with a kiss on the cheek in return. "Feels like I've been waiting forever to get this done..."

Walter seemed too at ease; as if he took a relaxant or he just trusted that the interview would be a cakewalk for him. He was wrong if that's where his head was. I took a seat in the chair placed in front of his desk. There were three seats in the back behind the cameraman. However, Jimmy and Leon already occupied two of them.

"I think we need one more seat," I said to Leon.

Adam and Taylor stood in the doorway as if already knowing that one of them would have to leave.

"Oh, I forgot to tell you. Taylor can't stay," Leon composedly replied.

"Wait," I blurted while feeling oncoming rage. "We agreed that Adam and Taylor would stay for this weeks ago."

"We decided it would be best if she didn't stay," Leon reiterated.

He gave me a sly smile. I just wanted to knock his over bleached teeth out. However, I felt I had two options yet again: argue and have them nix the interview altogether, or oblige for the sake of the case.

I turned to Taylor and her somber face and mouthed, "Sorry." The secretary escorted her back out to the waiting area while Adam took a seat. His mission was to take notes and pretty much just watch my back.

I could now feel the sweat building on the bridge of my nose and under my lips from the combination of heat from the spotlight and the anxiousness to get started. Turning my attention back to Walter, who was leaning over his desk with his hands in a lazy prayer pose, I was ready to begin. He looked like he wanted to tell me something very important. I brought my face closer to his to let him whisper in my ear.

"You look so sexy," he commented.

I looked at him in the eye and half-smiled. I couldn't wait to be done with this act.

"Fire when ready," he ordered, louder this time.

I indicated "one minute" to the cameraman and pretended to fumble around in my oversized tote bag. I hit the record button on my backup audio recorder hidden inside. Then, I took the main tape recorder and placed it on the desk in front of him. I knew these guys could easily snatch and destroy whatever I got on tape with him. Having a backup device was essential. I sat straight back in the uncomfortable wooden chair, took a few breaths, and signaled to start rolling tape.

I began with several softball questions to really get Walter comfortable and puff up his ego a bit more. He knew how to work the camera. Every so often he'd look at the lens to make sure it was capturing the emotions displayed on his perfectly powdered face. Our mini audience in the back listened as he dished about his upbringing in Queens, being an extreme introvert in grammar school due to his lisp, and getting teased about it. Like me, he was obsessed with the news as a child and enjoyed watching the nightly news with his parents on Friday nights instead of going out with friends. Politics and current events were typically the topic of discussion at dinners every night, he said. His dad worked for the Army doing financial tasks and his mom was a history teacher. I saw a change in his tone when he got more into his parents. It was somber, yet a little too much, like he was putting on an act. I felt he was just bullshitting us all.

10:10 a.m.

Walter still looked cool and collected. I shifted slightly in the chair, trying to find any comfortable position. It was hopeless. It was like they purposely kept these hard wooden chairs like this to prevent people from overstaying their welcome.

"What propelled you into actually studying public policy in high school and college?" I asked next.

"Vindication..." he began. "I wanted to get back at all those people who made fun of me, belittled me, and silenced me for all those years," he confessed.

His statement sounded more devilish than that of pride. In other words, his desire to seek office came from a place of hate and revenge. I looked back over my shoulder briefly. The cameraman was standing with his hands in his pockets and looking rather bored.

I got Walter to open up even more. It was like he had no control over what was coming out of his mouth. He just kept going on with the timeline of his life. He regaled me in how he had his eyes set on running New York City when he entered Columbia University. He was a different person at Columbia than he was in his youth. In college, he became popular and liked, and that eventually put him in prime position to represent all students at the university by making him class president.

"Did you govern Columbia like you do New York City...like in that 'Robin Hood meets Pablo Escabaresque' way?" I sarcastically, yet seriously, wanted to know.

Now that Walter got the sense that the interview was going just as he wanted, I felt it was time to throw him a few hard-balls. He shifted for the first time in his chair as if not expecting that kind of question.

"Ha, sure. Minus the cocaine of course," he replied with a grin and leaned back in his chair. "Seriously, Miss Turner, I have always been for the struggling civilians. Some have it so easy and some have it so much harder," he said, bringing his tone back down.

I heard some shuffling around and some light talking behind me. I turned my head sharply to give whoever was chatting a look to keep it down. It was Leon and Jimmy. They weren't even paying attention to the interview or me. Adam was looking down at his pad of paper and vigorously took notes; although, I don't know what he could've been writing so much about.

"But Mayor, with all due respect, your way of running the city and being a hero to the lower class seems contradictory to the lavish and luxurious lifestyle you live. Wouldn't you agree?" I let the question slip as a way to test the waters to see how Walter would respond.

While fidgeting with his pen, Walter continued to reiterate that he works hard for the people who need him the most. Knowing what I knew about him, his family life, his affair and alleged second family that he was paying his staff to keep their mouths shut about, it made hearing him boast about himself rather enraging.

Walter took a big sip of water from a Poland Spring bottle he pulled from his desk drawer.

10:20 a.m.

"Let's talk a little more about your family life, Victoria and Piper..." I proceeded to lead.

Mayor Wilcox relaxed his face and shoulders now that we were moving off politics. His recount of his marriage was on par with Victoria's. However, I had no idea about the story of their daughter. Piper was a "blessing" as Victoria was told she would

242

never be able to have children when she and Walter started trying. That put a strain on the marriage, until the day Victoria actually did get pregnant. In speaking of Piper, I noticed Walter changing his tone from cocky and authoritative to sensitive and humble. He came across as genuinely sincere speaking about how he would take Piper to skating practices and soccer games on the weekends.

"And, you didn't want a second child? Perhaps, try for a son?" I sneakily asked.

"No, no...it would've been too much for Victoria. I'm happy as a clam with Pipes. She is quite a handful anyways!"

"Yes, Piper is quite the outgoing one. I follow her on Instagram," I said with a smile.

To hear him talking about his daughter the way he did, the viewer would think Piper was the apple of his eye, or "daddy's little girl." The reality was, she hated him. I wonder if he even picked up on that.

I took a quick glance at the clock to gauge my time and noticed that Leon had stepped out.

10:30 a.m.
"I would now like to delve a little deeper into your lifestyle, social circle...all the fluffy stuff as we discussed," I began.

Walter sat up straight again and folded his hands in front of him on the desk. He glared at me as if to remind me of what we discussed when it came to this part of the interview. I returned a reassuring smile that must have made him feel like he was in complete control. Again, he changed positions. His constant movements were beginning to make me uneasy.

He rubbed his hands together as if warming them and leaned back in his chair. He then placed his hands behind his head as if lounging back.

The camera kept rolling and was streaming back to the control room at Channel 6 News. Connie and Juliet also had access to watch the feed from their computers. They were probably on the edge of their seat, hoping and praying for something big.

I reached into my tote and pulled out the first file of "innocent"-looking pictures I had taken of the home and spread them on his desk like a tarot card reader. One was a shot of the living room, one of the office, and another of the photos on the wall. He looked down at them with his eyes only, never leaving his reclined pose.

"I would love for you to explain your interior choosing for the living room and the office. I feel like one screams Victoria and the office screams, you."

In a calm manner, Walter went on to describe Victoria's taste in interior.

"Sometimes you just got to let the woman have her way to distract them and keep 'em busy," he cockily replied. "It lets us men focus on our own thing."

10:35 a.m.

I could tell Walter was now starting to get antsy the way he kept touching his ear, then his temple, then his chin and lips.

Never trust a man who touches his mouth when talking to you.

I pulled out the picture of the family, specifically the one with Lucy in the photo. He didn't seem to flinch.

"Can you tell me about this picture?" I pushed.

He picked it up and brought it closer to his eyes. Then, he let out a deep sigh.

"I remember this day. This was when we took Piper and our former babysitter sailing in Martha's Vineyard."

His eyebrows went up as if thoughts of that day were making him sentimental.

"Whatever happened to that babysitter? Is she still close to the family?" I interrogated.

Walter put the picture down.

"No," he quickly said and cleared his throat. "That was just a temporary situation. Can we continue?"

"Fine. Let's go back to you and Victoria. She mentioned the cute little pet name you gave her back in the day, *Kryptonite Tiger*."

Walter leaned forward again and placed his hands palm down on the desk. He looked seriously at the camera and then back to me. Then, he forced out a fake smile.

"Where did you get that pet name from?" I asked.

He refused to answer and just looked down at his watch as if this were a basketball or soccer game and he was running the clock.

10:40 a.m.

Ask about the boat.

I took a quick glimpse behind me to see that Leon had returned and him and Jimmy were quietly chatting with each other. The cameraman was looking down at his phone and Adam had his eyes on me. Anxious yet collected, I continued.

"When it comes to activities, what are some things you like to do with the family?"

Walter rattled off some random answers like movies and walks in Central Park. He sounded even more eager to wrap up the interview. His answers had become curter.

"What about sailing? Ever do any of that?"

"Sometimes," he blurted and rubbed his hand over this chin and mouth again.

I proceeded to pull out a picture of the boat with the name *Kryptonite Tiger* on it and presented it to him.

"I have to laugh because the other day I saw a boat docked in the marina with that same name on it," I pointed out while Walter studied it. "Do you share that boat with Comptroller Brownstein, Mr. Mayor?"

"How did you know it belongs to him?" he suspiciously asked but I ignored him.

"Now, there has to be more to this name because when going through your, umm, records and proposed projects, I found one called Operation: Kryptonite Tiger, as well. I just find it almost too coincidental that there would be a boat and a city-funded projected named after the nickname you gave Victoria."

I had now switched to complete interrogation mode, getting firmer and slightly louder. Even the cameraman seemed to be showing greater interest as he readjusted the lens and the light. Tiny beads of sweat were starting to rise above Walter's upper lip. Meanwhile, Jimmy and Leon had stepped out, leaving a defenseless mayor and two empty seats.

"I have no idea what you're talking about. I thought we were talking about my family and nonpolitical stuff," Walter sternly stated with minor hysteria.

He was trying to avoid launching into a fit of rage while the camera kept rolling. I pulled out another file containing a photocopy of the section of the budget that briefly detailed project "Operation: Kryptonite Tiger."

10:45 a.m.

"Can you explain this part of last year's budget? Nearly $1 million allotted for this. What exactly is this money funding, sir?"

I pushed the documents towards him. By now he had to have an idea of what was going on. The questions about his babysitter, about Victoria's pet name, and wanting another child; Walter knew he had been conned. New York City's favorite mayor was about to be taken out by the Vixen Investigator.

"No. I can't explain it," he nearly shouted.

Fear and anger radiated from his hard posture. He was now at his most vulnerable self. Any sudden move would all be caught on camera.

"Why is your former babysitter at all your press conferences?" I asked while pulling out the most valuable photo: the one of Lucy, the comptroller, and the 4-year-old boy standing with the three of them. "And, why is Lucy partying with you all in the Hamptons?"

I handed him another picture and then another until he had been inundated with snaps of him, Lucy, and the little boy. He studied each of them as fast as he could but didn't say anything.

"Where did you get these? What is going on here?! Turn that camera off!" he yelled, knocking his "New York's Best Mayor" mug on the ground.

He ripped off his microphone. Adam ran to the door, locking Leon and Jimmy out.

"Keep rolling, keep rolling!" I ordered.

The cameraman looked startled but likely knew the video he was getting was Pulitzer-worthy. I rose sharply off my seat and met Walter's gaze. We were face to face as if we were about to engage in a cage match.

"I know about everything! I know about your affair and secret family with the ex-babysitter. I know how you met her on *Rags and Riches* and what goes on, on that sex-infused sailboat of yours and Brownstein's..." I shouted.

Walter stared back into my eyes with such force. He had been betrayed by someone he let himself trust: me. His chest rose up and down with every deep breath of outrage. The security guard was now charging at the door. After three loud thumps, it flew open along with a big chunk of the doorframe. The big guard started reaching for my arm.

"You need to leave now. Turn that camera off and give me the tape. Do as told and nobody gets hurt," the guard ordered.

Leon and Jimmy came running in and pulled Walter aside. I watched the cameraman pop out the cartridge, but when he went to hand it to the guard, he faked him out and threw it to Adam instead. Adam ran out of the office.

"You're paying your buddies to keep their mouths shut. You're swindling the residents of New York City to fund your secret affairs. You and your entire cabinet should be in jail!" I yelled towards the three men.

None of them said anything. They were fucked and they knew it. While the cameraman distracted the guard, I grabbed my tape recorder and bag, but before bolting out, I informed them all that the evidence I had uncovered was already in the hands of the FBI and the State Attorney's office. The three administration officials huddled together as if trying to figure out what to do. I darted out of the office before the beastly guard could grab me. He tried to chase after me, but tripped over one of the knocked over chairs.

As I ran down the hallway, I looked back to see Walter's eyes on me. No doubt he was in full panic mode.

I was breathing heavily as I pushed past the small crowd that had gathered outside in the hallway. At the same time, I couldn't help but smile.

21

With a full-scale investigation currently underway, by tomorrow morning the entire city and nation would be aware of the scandal. After nearly getting chased out of City Hall, I went directly to *The Gotham Post*, where Taylor and Adam were already waiting for me outside. Adam handed me the tape and I kissed it as if kissing an Oscar. He, like me, was still panting with excitement. We gave each other a big success and relief hug before heading up to Connie and Juliet's office.

"Why didn't you tell us about all this from the beginning? This is unbelievable," Connie asked while rewatching the videotape. "I see a huge, weeklong exposé on this. The whole administration is involved. What a soap opera!" she raved.

"So, you think the administration had something to do with Henry Parker's murder?" Connie asked me.

"Yes, honestly. But that's out of my wheelhouse. That's for the FBI to figure out. I'm just a...reporter," I coolly answered.

Now that the scandal was out, protecting Victoria and Vixen Investigations was priority number one. Connie and Juliet had no idea that Walter's wife had hired me to investigate her husband, and it had to remain that way. My role as a reporter was done, but not as the Vixen Investigator.

The next morning, I didn't even bother to change out of my pajamas before running to the corner deli for *The Gotham Post*. As I hustled by the bus stop, people waiting in line had their heads buried in a copy, as well.

There was only one more copy of the paper in the bodega and in big, can't-miss letters, the headline read, MAYORAL AFFAIRS. I grabbed the paper and slammed the $1.75 on the counter. I didn't even bother to find a place to sit outside; I immediately flipped to page three.

EXPOSED COX: NYC's Favorite Mayor Hides Secret Family With Daughter's Ex-Babysitter; Staffers Paid To Keep Silent.

The four-page spread, by *Gotham Post* staff, was a complete breakdown of the events. The article was written like a script of sorts. I was about to turn on to page five when I saw an incoming text from Taylor. She had already read the article and was ecstatic about the press. The whole scenario was obviously insane, but I didn't feel as thrilled about the report as she was. I thought about Victoria. I hadn't spoken with her yet.

What followed was an influx of texts from friends, colleagues, and contacts I didn't even have stored in my phone.

Was this you?
Did you read about the Mayor?
Yo, did you bust Wil-cocks???
What a scandal!
What's happening in your city?

It was so overwhelming I had to turn off my phone. When I got back to my apartment, after absorbing everything that had been revealed so far, I flipped on the news to see how the story was playing out on the air. As expected, every local and national news channel was on it and all were attributing Channel 6 and

The Gotham Post. There was not a mention of Paige Turner anywhere.

I clicked the TV back off. I needed to make a phone call.

"How are you doing?"

"Honestly...relieved." Victoria sounded a lot more relaxed than I thought she would, given the circumstances. "Piper is a wreck. I'm taking her to a therapist in a few hours. The whole thing about Lucy is very traumatic for her."

"What's been the exchange with Walter?"

"Well, he warned me last night, after your interview and after he met with his lawyer, that something big was going to be coming out about him. He prepared me, but I already knew. He was probably surprised at how calm I was, honestly," Victoria debriefed.

I apologized to her for having the scandal go public as fast as it did. The fact that Walter's staff was being paid to hide it all took the case to a different level; a level that was out of my control. As more revealed itself, feds came to discover that there were even more people involved in the cover-up than first thought. The portly secretary, several security personnel, and even the cleaning lady and doorman were all getting a cut to stay silent.

When I hung up with Victoria, I bravely put the TV back on. Every channel seemed to have the same LIVE video of Walter, Jimmy, and Leon being escorted by three attorneys and several security guards through a sea of cameras, reporters, and civilians. One resident held up a sign that said, *My Money Funds Your Affair.*

As I watched and listened to the reporters talk about it being the "biggest sex and fraud scandal" in the city's history, I was jolted again by the sound of my ringing phone. The caller ID said "Unavailable."

"Good work, detective," the robotic voice said.

"Who is this? You may as well reveal yourself now," I responded.

There was a brief bout of silence.

"I'll be waiting for you on the second bench to the right of the BP gas station on the East River Bikeway at noon today," they said and hung up.

The heat of the summer sun seemed to match the intensity of the city right now. The traffic leaving Manhattan was already bumper-to-bumper and it wasn't even noon yet.

I had an Uber drop me off at the corner of 1st Avenue and 20th street, not far from Taylor's apartment. I walked across the remaining East Side and up a few blocks to where the gas station and my mystery informant were.

Momentum built the closer I got to what looked like a person in a baseball cap.

It was a woman. A young woman.

I don't believe this.

She kept her face looking out across the river as I approached.

"Lucy?" I smoothly asked.

"Hello, detective," she flatly replied.

"It was you, wasn't it?"

I took a seat next to her and stared across to Long Island City. She was wearing a yellow cotton Jersey dress and a lime green Titleist cap.

"So, spill it, why were you helping me?"

I didn't push her, but let her respond at her own pace. I was eager to hear her response. It took her a few minutes to gather her thoughts.

"He's been hiding me and Devin..."

Devin? Your son?

"...for way too long and the thought of it continuing even after child number two comes along..."

Child two? I thought she looked a little round in the belly.

"...I just couldn't accept it. If he weren't going to man up, I'd do it for him. He can be such a pussy sometimes," she said, gently rubbing her stomach. "He has spent enough time with Victoria and Piper. The little brat is so ungrateful anyway. She'd always tell me how much she hated her dad. She probably still says it. It is my...our turn now," she argued, if actually believing everything that just happened was fair. "I love him. I don't want him to be the mayor anymore. I want to get out of this city and live on a ranch in Texas, like he promised me years ago. Instead, he keeps me caged up in the Hamptons like Rapunzel. I have to pretend to be with Richard, who is so gay, by the way, and in love with Jimmy. My life's been hell."

She sounded delusional and almost psychotic.

"Does anyone else know about you calling me? How did you get my number...and Adam's?"

Lucy turned to me, finally revealing her face. She looked me straight in the eyes. Though she was still cute with the big brown eyes, olive skin, and plump lips, up close, I could see the stress in her face.

"I had some help," she confessed and turned back out to look at the water. "Jimmy gave me your number and fed me the clues. He wanted Walter found out just as bad as me so he could carry on his relationship with Richard."

"Yeah, but now he's facing jail time," I stated.

Lucy divulged that Jimmy hated his job so much, he contemplated running away. He feared ending up like Henry Parker if he quit. Jimmy knew too much; there was no way the administration would let him leave knowing what he knew. It was like the mayoral mafia.

"Tell me," I started. "How do you know about...what I do for a living?" I hesitantly asked, as I was worried it had gotten out that Victoria had hired me.

"Please, Paige. Everyone knows about you."

What?! Who is EVERYONE?

I swallowed hard.

"You don't have to be so modest. You're like the best reporter in New York City. Jimmy had followed your reporting career more than me. He knew you'd be the only one who could sniff out what was going on. That's why he sent you that "kryptonite tiger" text. It was almost fate that soon after, you were showing up at Walter's press conferences. Why do you think Jimmy got so lenient with you?" she explained.

Her recount made perfect sense. And, little did they know that the whole time, I was really working for Victoria. I was relieved, most of all. I didn't even realize that my name was still floating around as being one of the best reporters in the city.

Lucy and I sat for another ten minutes. As the sun beat down on my shoulders, Lucy continued to fill me in on why she joined the sleazy website and her love for Walter. She felt he "saved" her by helping her and her father avoid student loan debt. I cringed when she mentioned feeling like Walter's daughter at times. When her town car pulled up, she rapidly stood to not make the driver wait. She bent down to give me a hug.

"Thank you, Paige Turner. Now I can live the life I always wanted and deserve," she softly said into my ear.

I hugged her back with deep concern. Concern for the welfare of her two children. She cocked the lid of the hat down more over her eyes and hurried to the car that pulled up alongside the bike path. She hopped in and that was that. I stayed sitting on the bench to think.

The heat on my face felt good. I could feel my nose getting burned. The humming of the cars speeding by was therapeutic. It's been a while since I really listened to my surroundings. At that moment, for the first time in a long time, my head cleared and I entered a perfect meditative state. I enjoyed it until my cell phone started buzzing. With a smile, I answered.

"Nice job on the mayor story," Liam said.

It was the first time I had heard his voice, and not to mention, the first nice thing he's said to me, since finding out about my private eye business.

"I'll kill you if you tell anybody," I joked. "It just kind of exploded into this massive mayoral scandal. I had no idea what was going on until I started peeling back the layers."

"Ha. His administration does stink...I'm sorry I got so heated. I shouldn't have flipped out like that," Liam confessed.

"It's understandable. I wasn't honest with you and you were nothing but open to me. I'm sorry, too," I admitted.

A moment of silence.

"I don't want to keep pushing, but why couldn't you just tell me? Why the secrets?" Liam asked.

"Liam...my investigations aren't your typical 'Nancy Drew mysteries.' How would you have felt if I told you I sought out cheaters and investigated white-collar infidelity? You would've run without even hearing what I am all about. It's not something I put out there right away. When I realized I really liked you, I guess I got concerned that you would...well...act the way you did when you found out," I tried to explain.

My words still felt like they were coming out wrong.

"You've been surrounding yourself with the wrong men for a long time," was all Liam said.

I smiled on the other end of the phone. I hoped he could sense my content.

Following the explanations of our actions, we caught up more on other life events like his work, the heat, and the new boardwalk going up in Asbury Park.

"Maybe we can hit up McLoone's before the end of the summer," Liam suggested.

My heart fluttered like it did those first days of us exchanging texts and phone calls. He mentioned actually wanting to hear more about the investigation process, too. We set up a real date when he got back from his family vacation in the Adirondacks. I was hopeful that things would return to how they used to be, minus the secrecy.

AUGUST

"HAPPY BIRTHDAY!" August 15th. My birthday rolling around always indicated three things for me: I am another year older, who my real friends are, and that the summer is nearing an end.

I tried to keep a low profile for the last month following the news of Walter. Besides helping the authorities where I could, I didn't take on any new business, nor was I trying to. There was now a federal case against Walter and his staff. It seemed like every day, local news was reporting on something new. The interim mayor seemed overwhelmed by the entire cleanup he was in store for as Walter was expected to step down soon. His former staff members were all fired and had quickly been replaced.

Meanwhile, Victoria was already out in Santa Barbara with Piper. She decided to move there, indefinitely, while her daughter was about to start her second year of college. They felt it was better to both stay out of Manhattan and away from all the press. Their lavish penthouse apartment was still occupied by Walter, but Victoria was likely to get ownership once the divorce settlement is finalized. She still checks in with me every few days to let me know how she is doing. She is currently considering becoming a hiking guide at a resort in southern Utah once Piper is more mentally stable. She always had a love for hiking and the outdoors. She even thought about starting her own charity that takes underprivileged children on hiking trips.

Lucy and her lovechild, Devin, were still being kept under wraps in the Hamptons, as they awaited more on Walter's punishment. I haven't spoken to her since the day we met by the river. I hoped she was being advised on what to do when Walter likely ends up in jail. I didn't know how much loving and genuine support she really had, especially with another child on the way.

"Make a wish, Miss Vixen Investigator!"

I watched as the hunky waiter decked in white came out with a huge slice of Godiva Chocolate Cheesecake with two candles in it. The girls and Adam insisted on taking me out for my birthday at the restaurant of my choice.

"Out of all the amazing restaurants in New York City and we have to come to The Cheesecake Factory in fucking Jersey. You're so fucking strange, Paige," Theresa complained while taking a sip of her Johnnie Walker on the rocks.

"That's $50 in the swear jar," I teased.

"Fuck you," Theresa responded.

We all laughed as the eyes of every parent in the establishment focused on us.

"This place is my favorite. Plus, it's my birthday."

I sucked in, blew hard, and made my wish.

"Well, I have some beaucoup news for you, Paige, dear," Theresa started.

Uh-oh. The last time she started a conversation like this, I found out she was starring in some film about symphony players who moonlighted as escorts.

"I might have another case for you already. I can't tell you everything, because a lot is rumored. But, it involves a famous Hollywood couple," she hinted.

"I just told you, I'm laying low until the end of the summer!" I reiterated. "Let's talk in a few weeks," I said, raising my glass to initiate a cheers.

Adam proceeded to push a gift my way. He smiled as I looked at him questionably. It was small and wrapped in gold paper with a perfectly tied bow. I carefully unwrapped the box. Inside rested a long gold chain with a mini magnifying glass dangling from it.

"I love it!" I proclaimed and put it around my neck.

He remembered my obsession with antique magnifying glasses and found a matching necklace for me.

"It was undoubtedly my favorite case. You kicked ass," he commended.

"*We* kicked ass...we all did."

After three gorging hours at my favorite chain restaurant, the five of us stood for a minute in the parking lot before breaking off for the night. The moon was out in full force, creating enough light where I could see all of their faces.

"So, what's next for the Vixen Investigator?" April inquired.

"Going to relax a little bit more. But, I'm needed. You should see my inbox," I replied.

"Geez, doesn't anyone stay faithful these days?" Taylor's question sounded more like a rhetorical one.

"Fuck guys," Theresa blurted.

"Theresa?!" I shook my head at her. "Taylor, please get her home safely," I urged.

We all hugged goodbye and parted to our cars. In that moment, I was feeling extra thankful. With their help, I was able to turn that administration upside down. As I drove home, I wondered what my life would've been like if I had gone into teaching, nursing, or another job that would allow me to live a normal life. If we're all put on this earth for a reason, is there even a point in worrying about what could've been? I knew I was made to investigate infidelity and I am pretty damn good at it.

ACKNOWLEDGMENTS

Ever since I could remember, I always wanted to be an author. The satisfaction of seeing Paige Turner come to life is unexplainable. All the time, energy, and emotion spent on *Vixen Investigations* and I'd still do it all over again. Keep up the good fight, vow enforcer and betrayer slayer, Vixen Investigator.

A very special thank you to my mentors and friends, Lis Wiehl, Robi Ludwig, Cooper Lawrence, Lori Bizzoco, Brian Claypool, Leslie Marshall, Kevin McCullough, Lyss Stern, Brad Thor, Jenna McCarthy, Paul Hokemeyer, Annie Scranton, Stephanie, Genevieve, Dee, and always, Marcy. I do not go a day without appreciating the support you've given me throughout my writing career.

Another huge thanks to *all* my friends and family who love and support me no matter what challenges I take on...even if it is competitive skydiving or log throwing. I love you all so much.

How can I not thank my amazing agent—Maura, you've been the most encouraging of all. Throughout all the edits and planning you've always been right with me. I really couldn't have achieved this goal without you.

And, of course, my publishing team. A big thank you to them for making this dream a reality and taking their chances on me and Paige Turner.

My German Shepherd children, Bruno and Hazel. Thank you for keeping me sane at times.

Jay, who stood by me throughout this long and often steep road. I love you so much.